THE DAN BRADY MYSTERIES

CONTAGION OF THE NIGHT

A NOVEL BY

EDWARD J. LEAHY

Black Rose Writing | Texas

ISBN: 978-1-68513-487-7
PUBLISHED BY BLACK ROSE WRITING
www.blackrosewriting.com

Printed in the United States of America
Suggested Retail Price (SRP) $23.95

Contagion of the Night is printed in Baskerville

*As a planet-friendly publisher, Black Rose Writing does its best to eliminate unnecessary waste to reduce paper usage and energy costs, while never compromising the reading experience. As a result, the final word count vs. page count may not meet common expectations.

ALSO BY
EDWARD J. LEAHY

THE KIM BRADY MYSTERY SERIES

Past Grief

Deceived By Ornament

Proving a Villain

THE DAN BRADY MYSTERY SERIES

Enemies of All

And will he steal out of his wholesome bed,
To dare the vile contagion of the night…
–Portia in
Julius Caesar, Act II, Scene 1

CONTAGION
OF
THE NIGHT

ONE

Friday, May 14, 1943

"Forty-Fourth Precinct, Detective Brady speaking." But as soon as Danny heard who the caller was, he knew it had been a mistake to pick up the lieutenant's ringing phone.

"Detective, I'm the desk sergeant at the Fortieth Precinct. Our captain asked me to give you boys a call. We've had what looks like a homicide and we have no detectives available. The captain says your squad is on call to cover."

Danny's partner of six years, Detective Frank Larkin, appeared in the doorway. "Told you not to answer it." Larkin, two years older than Danny and married eleven years longer, delighted in dispensing fatherly advice.

As if Danny needed to be reminded. He sighed and grabbed a pencil and notepad from the lieutenant's desk. "Where?"

"St. Ann's Protestant Episcopal Church, St. Ann's Avenue…"

"…and East 141st Street. Yes, Sergeant, I'm familiar with the neighborhood. Any details?"

"A patrolman walking past the church saw something suspicious, investigated, and found a woman lying dead in the graveyard. That's all I've got."

"Is he still on the scene?"

"Yeah."

"Tell your captain we're on it." He dropped the receiver into the cradle. "Bollocks." He repeated the news to Larkin.

"You want to charge over there now? For the love of Mary, it's fifteen minutes until our tour is up."

"It's a homicide, Frankie. You know, the sooner we jump on it, the better."

"My wife expects me home on time these days, what with the crime rate so low. Your wife could pop at any moment."

Larkin had a point. It was now eight months and two weeks since he and Meg had married. They'd spent a week at the Larkins' summer bungalow at Breezy Point, Queens, and Meg was now "great with child", as Larkin liked to say, usually as a prelude to snickering speculations about how premature the baby's birth might be.

Danny glanced at the clock. It was close to midnight, and they were scheduled to have the next two days off, followed by a shift change back to days. Meg was having difficulty sleeping, and a ringing phone jolting her awake was the last thing she needed. "She'll be fine. By the time she wakes up, I'll already be home. You go home, Frankie. The crime scene lads will be there, as well as someone from the coroner's office. I'll just get the information on the case."

***

Danny found Patrolman William Kelly waiting at the entrance to the churchyard. The victim, an attractive woman with dark eyes, was lying on her back dressed in a light tan skirt suit, a white scarf still tied in a tight knot around her neck. He judged her to be in her mid-to-late thirties, about five-five, with curly brunette hair, not quite shoulder length. A box of buns from a bakery was on the ground nearby, and a local crime scene unit had already set up a perimeter.

"Any identification?" Danny's boyhood experiences in Dublin running messages for Michael Collins and the Sinn Fein, combined with his work as a homicide detective, had hardened him to these situations.

"Nope," Kelly replied. "Didn't find a handbag anywhere in the area. Looks like a mugging."

Danny knelt, moving the scarf slightly lower for a better view, but careful not to pull it off. There were several cuts to the woman's throat. "These appear to be made with a blunt knife."

"You think that's what killed her?"

Danny gestured for Kelly's flashlight and studied the woman's throat. "I'll leave that call to the coroner, but my guess is no. See those? They're ligature marks. She was strangled. And the scarf is still white, meaning either those cuts weren't deep enough to bleed, or she was already dead. Tell me what happened, from the top."

"I was just walking my beat, passing by along St. Ann's Avenue, when I thought I saw a flicker of light from inside the churchyard. But it went dark so fast, I couldn't be sure, so I waited. Then I saw another flicker, like something small flaring…"

"A match?"

"Yeah, that's what it looked like. I immediately pulled my flashlight out and probed the yard to investigate. As soon as I did, I heard footsteps, like someone running on gravel. As I reached the opposite side of the church, I heard a plopping noise from the street…"

"Which street?"

Kelly pointed to East 141st Street. "The land slopes down to the street level, and there's a fence. I figured the sound was him dropping from the fence."

"You're sure about the sequence?" Danny asked. "The two flares of light, then you entered the graveyard, then you heard the steps and the drop to the street?" When the patrolman nodded,

Danny asked, "About how much time elapsed between the second flare and the sound of the footsteps?"

"Only a minute. Why?"

"If those flares were from striking matches, he was looking for something. You probably interrupted his search, which means whatever he was looking for might very well still be here. I'll talk to the crime scene guys and have them do a careful search."

Kelly glanced down at the dead woman. "Some dish."

"Not anymore."

After speaking to the head of the unit, Danny waved Kelly back to St. Ann's Avenue. As they walked to the corner, he spotted Officer Sean McHugh approaching from the street. At six-two with curly red hair that his cap kept only partially contained, he was hard to miss.

McHugh had been assigned to Danny's unit temporarily a year earlier while Danny was investigating a ring of saboteurs with the FBI's cooperation. He'd been returned to the precinct's patrol team, but they all had hopes he would soon make detective. "Hi, Danny. I signed in for the graveyard shift and saw a note from Frank Larkin to come join you here."

Knowing Frankie had his back was comforting. Danny checked his watch. It was 1:05, already later than he'd intended to stay. "Thanks for coming." He filled McHugh in on what they had, then led Kelly and McHugh to the corner and pointed west on 141st. "The killer landed on the sidewalk below. Which direction do you think he would have taken?"

Kelly scowled. "I never saw him; I only heard the footsteps."

"He'd run away from the church," McHugh said. "He'd have gone toward the west."

"How do you know that?" Kelly asked. "You're just guessing."

Danny let McHugh finish the thought.

"True," McHugh said, "but it's a reasonable one. At that point, you had two options if you were going to give chase: hop the fence after him or run back to St. Ann's Avenue and go around. He wouldn't have taken the chance of going east and running into you, ergo…"

"I agree," Danny said. "Where he would have gone next is a mystery. Her handbag isn't here, so he must have been carrying it. But he also wouldn't have carried it too far, fearing being seen. I want you both to search the neighborhood. Start by going west on 141st to Alexander Avenue. Then, Sean, you go north on Alexander to 144th street, and Kelly, south to 139th, then search each block in turn until you come back here."

"You're gambling on him only carrying the bag a couple of blocks?" McHugh asked.

"Yes. If you find nothing, we'll get more manpower in and extend the search come daylight."

"What about the buns, Danny?" McHugh asked.

"Don't forget to bring them in."

TWO

Saturday, May 15, 1943

"American bombers, flying out in record numbers, devastated key targets in four Nazi-held cities, including an important U-boat base in Kiel, Germany, and factory targets in Germany, Belgium, and the Netherlands. In the Pacific, American troops landed on Attu, the westernmost island in the Aleutian chain, first taken by the Japanese last June as part of the Battle of Midway."

***

Someone from the coroner's office confirmed that the woman had likely died a short while before Kelly saw the flares of light. "And you're right, Detective. She was strangled."

Danny knelt to examine her throat again. "The cuts look fresh, very recent."

"Correct, Detective."

"Are you certain they never bled? Is there any chance she could have cut herself earlier and wore the scarf to hide them?"

"Fresh is fresh, Detective. There's no sign of coagulation. Making a similar cut now would result in an identical appearance. They were almost certainly made after she was dead. And even if she'd still been alive, they wouldn't have done any serious damage. They're not deep, and the blade that made them was likely not very sharp."

Danny was still kneeling next to her, looking for any sign of a struggle, but he found none. Her skirt suit looked new, and her shoes weren't even scuffed. Most telling, there were no defensive wounds.

He only nodded.

It was almost four when McHugh and Kelly returned. McHugh was holding a light tan leather handbag with a shoulder strap. Danny was pleased to see he was wearing gloves. Sean McHugh was going to make an excellent detective.

"Found it tossed behind the driveway gate of a semi-attached house on 141st Street near Alexander Avenue," McHugh said. "It's the only handbag we found in the entire area of the search."

Danny studied the bag and the dead woman's skirt suit. "They match."

"Thought so. No money in it, but there's a driver's license. Carla Maxwell, home address is in Yonkers. There's also a New York Central commutation ticket between the Glenwood, Yonkers station and the Mott Haven Station on East 138th Street."

"No money," Kelly said. "Like I said, a mugging."

Danny said nothing.

"What?" McHugh asked.

"Muggers don't attack their victims with scarves. They usually grab their forearms or knock them off balance. They don't often kill their victims unless they figure they have no choice, but when they do, they don't make cuts with a knife afterward. No, this wasn't mugging."

"So, what was it?" McHugh asked.

Danny thought back to what he'd seen. "She had no defensive wounds of any kind. So, either he took her by complete surprise, or she knew him. Either way, the attacker likely planned his actions in advance.

"What about the knife cuts?" McHugh asked.

Another concern of his. "There's no logical reason for them. The reason must be emotional or illogical. Perhaps he was enraged."

"But he grabbed her money," Kelly said.

"If she had any, yes. It seems like it was meant to look like a mugging. That's probably why he left the driver's license. A mugger wouldn't care about that. When we catch him, he'll no doubt be pleased to know he fooled at least somebody."

"If we catch him," McHugh said.

"We'll catch him," Danny said, "but first, let's find out if Carla Maxwell is our girl. I'll see you at the precinct in the morning and we can get started. Deliver the bag to the fingerprint unit in the meantime.

Danny glanced at his watch. 4:10, and he still had to return the car to the precinct before heading home on the subway.

Shit.

***

As Danny approached the building on 45th Street in Sunnyside Gardens, where Meg had joined him once they were married, he glanced with trepidation at the second-floor window.

Sure enough, there was a light on.

And it was nearly dawn.

I should have called.

He climbed the stairs as quietly as possible on the off chance that she might have dozed off, desperate for a way to smooth this over, knowing it was no use.

All she did was glare, sitting on the couch, her long, dark red hair tousled and hazel eyes burning with fury.

"I'm sorry, Meg, but…"

She held up a hand. "Stop right there. I don't want to hear it. We've talked about this. We agreed if you were going to get stuck late, you would call me no matter what time it was."

"I know, but…"

"There is no 'but'. You promised. I called the precinct three times, and no one knew where you were. Three times! When I don't hear from you, and you're not at the precinct, I have no way of knowing what's going on, so I need you to call me to let me know where you are and what you're doing. No one else will do it. I worry about you every time you walk out that door, and I don't stop until you come home." A tear spilled down her cheek. "Do you have any idea what I've been through tonight?"

"I know, but…" He tried to sit next to her, but she dragged herself off the couch and moved away.

"No, you don't know. You can't know because you haven't lived through it like I have." She stormed into the bedroom and slammed the door shut.

Meg had brewed coffee and there was some left. He heated it and gulped down a cup. Next, he needed a shower. The challenge was explaining to Meg about working on his day off.

They had first met eighteen months earlier while he was investigating the murder, robbery, and attempted rape of a Bronx Sunday School teacher. Meg, then twenty-one, ten years Danny's junior, had come to his attention because she'd been raped by someone using the same *modus operandi*. When he'd first interviewed the willowy redhead and her husband, who made no secret of blaming her for the rape, Danny was instantly sympathetic. When she'd later confronted her attacker, he'd been thoroughly smitten.

Four months later, Meg had divorced her husband, but Danny made no move until he could deliver the news that her attacker had been executed. Afterward, he never looked back.

He still had no plan as he dried himself off. He hadn't even brought clean clothes into the bathroom with him, so he wrapped the towel around his waist and held his breath as he entered the bedroom.

She was in bed, lying on her side, turned away from him. "You're going in today, aren't you?"

No way around it. "Yes, Meg. Right before my tour ended last night, we got a call, a murder in Mott Haven. I honestly thought I'd only be an hour late. I didn't expect it to drag on like it did. That's why I didn't call. I didn't want to wake you for nothing."

"It would have been worth it. We agreed."

"I know. I'm very sorry."

"And why you, Danny? Why could Frankie go home while you couldn't?

He was too stunned to answer.

She turned to stare at him. "When I couldn't find out anything from the precinct, I called Helen to ask if Frankie had come home. She said he had, right on time."

Meg and Frank Larkin's wife had become fast friends almost as soon as they'd met. So, now he'd hear it from Larkin as well.

He sat on the edge of the bed.

She turned away from him. "I know. You need to go in. The case won't wait. So, go."

"I'm very sorry, Meg."

"Yeah."

He got dressed in silence. When he was ready to leave, he said, "Meg, I don't want to leave it like this…"

"Sorry, I can't help you with that. I guess it's a good thing I gave up my job at the library. Imagine working all day with no sleep."

Their fights were rare, and neither had ever left after one without a reconciliation.

A first time for everything.

THREE

The bacon sandwich he'd picked up at the place on University Avenue had no flavor, nor did the coffee he'd gotten with it. His black mood persisted as he made his way over to the station house on Sedgwick Avenue.

"Here he is, now," Larkin called out as Danny entered the squad room.

Their unit commander, Lieutenant Greco, was standing with him. "What's this all about?" Greco's family hailed from Calabria, Italy, and his black hair, olive skin, bulbous nose, and stocky build telegraphed that he brooked no nonsense.

Danny recapped everything he'd learned about the murder. Larkin said nothing.

"Okay, Danny, you've got the ball. Now run with it." Greco retreated to his office.

Larkin waited until the lieutenant was out of earshot. "What the hell happened? Meg called Helen at four this morning asking if she knew where you were."

"Yeah, I heard."

"We should've begged off last night…"

"Leave it alone, Frankie. To begin, we…"

"Not 'we', boyo. First, fix things with your wife."

Danny's rebuke died in his throat. Larkin was right. He should have walked out and let the damned phone ring. He turned and headed to Greco's office. "I did you a favor last night by taking that call from the Fortieth precinct. Now, I need one from you. It's not our case, it's theirs. I need you to kick it back to them."

Greco crushed his smoldering cigarette butt in the overflowing ash tray on his desk and leaned forward. "Sorry, Danny, but that's impossible. Military service has caused a drastic shortage in the number of available men. Crime rates are way down, so Mayor La Guardia is content to let things sit the way they are. You and Larkin are probably the only detectives qualified for homicide work in the Bronx."

"Can you help me get rid of some of this other crap?"

"No can do. You're still on the hook for that work with the FBI on anti-American activities, and…"

"That's been quiet since we stopped that sabotage ring last year."

Greco picked up a coffee-stained file. "It's gotten louder."

"You just said we were the only homicide detectives in the Bronx," Danny said.

"True. I'm afraid you're stuck with both. Look, Danny, I know it's none of my business, but if things are a little rough at home…"

Danny grabbed the file and stormed out, making a bee line for Larkin's desk. "Jesus, Mary, and Joseph, you're worse than an old washerwoman."

Larkin pushed his wavy brown hair off his forehead and held up both hands. "He asked me what happened last night, because he heard about Meg calling the desk three times." When stressed, Larkin's voice occasionally rose to what Danny called, "John McCormack with a head cold" and his normally sleepy eyes flew wide open.

"I don't care. I don't gossip about you and Helen, so keep your gob shut about Meg and me."

McHugh had been on his way over, but he froze when Danny yelled. Danny caught it out of the corner of his eye. "What the hell do you want?"

"Yonkers police say there's been no Missing Persons report filed on Carla Maxwell. I called the house and spoke to her husband. He said she hasn't been home since she left for work yesterday morning. I figured you'd want to head up there to interview him."

"Or," Larkin said, his voice back to its normal range, "to interrogate him."

Danny dropped the file folder from Greco on Larkin's desk. "You can plow through this and summarize it when I get back." He turned to McHugh. "You're with me."

***

Meg had been dozing when the door buzzer sounded. Somewhat disoriented, it wasn't until the buzzer sounded a second time that she remembered the conversation with Helen Larkin that ended with, "I'm on my way."

Meg hadn't wanted her to come—it was an arduous drive from their home on Lincoln Road in Brooklyn's Lefferts Manor with no direct route—but Helen had hung up before she could argue. She dragged herself out of the easy chair and caught a glimpse of herself in the mirror. "Good Lord, I look like who-did-it-and-ran." She reached up to do something—anything—with her hair, an unruly mass of dark red curls, but it was no use. She pulled her bathrobe tighter around her bulging middle and waddled to the door.

"A portrait of loveliness," Helen said with a grin. "Another Maureen O'Hara."

"Like hell." But she held her friend in a tight embrace.

"I may have forgotten to mention," Helen said as she stepped inside the apartment, "all-nighters are hell when you're this pregnant."

Meg tried to laugh but couldn't. "All he had to do was call. He'd promised. And if that wasn't bad enough…"

"He ran out again this morning. Yes, I know. Frankie ran out, too. I just hope he comes back alive."

"Danny?" It was a muted cry.

But Helen laughed. "No, Frankie. He loves slagging people, especially Danny, but he never knows when to stop. Might be dangerous today." When Meg said nothing, Helen sat on the couch, patting the seat next to her, and Meg joined her. "I never tell this story. Frankie always does, and I usually become annoyed when he does. But it happened, and it might help you to know about it."

"What?"

"I was in your shoes, feeling as moody as you do, expecting Dorothy."

"I am not moody."

Helen patted her hand. "Certainly not. My mistake. Anyway, Frankie came home from work, and I was at the stove, making a light dinner. Ham and eggs. He hung up his hat, slipped off his jacket and his holster, and asked me what was for dinner. As if he couldn't see what it was. I got so angry I picked up the spatula and flung it across the kitchen at him. Of course, I missed, and bits of egg flew all over. According to Frankie, I stormed out and sat in an Adirondack chair in the back yard for a few minutes. Then, I came back to the kitchen and finished making dinner, and, Frankie swears, acted as if nothing had happened."

Meg stared at her. "I don't get it."

Again, Helen patted her hand. "I don't remember any of that. I only know it because Frankie used to tell the story every chance he got. And he's only ever laughed at it."

"I can't laugh at this. He promised me."

"And he loves you like Rick loved Ilsa, and even more because, unlike Rick, he won the woman he loves. That's it, pep talk over. Now, go shower, get dressed, look pretty, and I'll take you to lunch."

Meg glanced downward. "I'm afraid pretty is out for me these days."

"Nonsense. A glass of wine will put roses back in your cheeks."

"Put me to sleep, more likely." She cast an involuntary glance at the phone as she passed it.

FOUR

Danny's first thought as they entered the semi-attached two-family house where Carla Maxwell's family lived was that Robert Maxwell made for an unlikely murder suspect. Slight of build, balding, and only about five-foot-seven, standing in the front parlor that served as his office, he was soft-spoken and mild-mannered. Danny wouldn't dismiss him based on looks alone.

When Danny showed him Carla's driver's license, he said, "Yes, that's hers." Next, he showed him her commutation ticket, and he asked, "What's this about?"

"Why did she have a ticket to Mott Haven?" Danny asked.

"That's where she works. St. Francis Hospital on East 142nd Street. Has something happened to her?"

"Does she have a tan shoulder bag that matches a tan skirt suit?" McHugh asked.

"Yes, now…"

Danny described the appearance of the woman in the churchyard,

"Yes, that's my wife. Now, please tell me what has happened."

"I'm sorry to tell you she was found dead on the grounds of St. Ann's Church in Mott Haven just before midnight last night," Danny said.

Maxwell gasped and staggered back before regaining his balance. "What happened? How?"

"A patrolling officer spotted something suspicious and discovered her. Did you know she wasn't coming home last night?"

"I… she often stays out late… with friends… and works late…" Maxwell said.

"Has she ever stayed out all night?"

"Sometimes she misses the last train."

Danny was making notes. "You didn't find it unusual? Didn't feel a need to call the police?"

Maxwell's melancholy deepened. "No, I figured it was another missed train. Besides, I had already put the kids to bed. How did she… I mean, was she…"

"She was strangled. Her clothing was otherwise undisturbed. Would you like to sit down, Mr. Maxwell?" The man looked like he might faint.

"Yes, thank you." He staggered to an easy chair.

Danny sat across from him on the sofa, gesturing to McHugh to follow. "How many kids do you have?"

"Two. Well, they're not mine, they're Carla's from a prior marriage. Mary is ten, and Ken is seven."

"Do you know who their father is, where he lives?" Danny asked.

"His name is Anthony LaMarca. He lives in Queens. Woodhaven, I believe." Maxwell turned thoughtful. "I suppose he'll get custody of the children now. He doesn't see them very often."

Danny exchanged a brief glance with McHugh. This guy's reactions weren't adding up. "You stayed home with the kids last night?" Danny's manner remained soft. "All evening?"

"Yes." Maxwell grew horrified. "Why? You don't think that I…"

"We just need answers to these questions for a complete picture. You said your wife often stayed out late with… friends. What friends?"

"People she worked with. She wasn't one to run around, though. I have no doubt about that."

"Can you think of anyone with a possible motive to kill her?"

"No. No one."

"Anyone who had a beef with you and maybe took it out on her?" Danny asked.

Maxwell stared back, dumbfounded. "I don't have any known enemies."

"And you're sure she never ran around?" McHugh asked.

"Well, I… that is… as certain as anyone can be."

Danny took over again. "What do you do for a living, Mr. Maxwell?"

"I'm an accountant. I work out of my home."

"No business matters gone bad?" McHugh asked.

"No."

Danny stood, and the others followed. "I think that's all for now, Mr. Maxwell. We'll let you know if we need anything else. The Bronx Coroner's Office will need you to come in and identify your wife for the record." He gave the widower his card. "Please call me if you think of anything else. Very sorry for your loss."

Maxwell took the card and nodded. Halfway to the door, Danny stopped and turned. "Did she ever mention where she liked to go with her friends from work?"

He stared back at them with a blank expression. "I don't believe so, no."

"Thanks, Mr. Maxwell," Danny said. "If anything else occurs to you…" He gestured to the card in Maxwell's hand.

Once back outside, Danny said to McHugh, "You drive."

"Where to?"

"Woodhaven. I'll give you directions."

"Your neck of the woods?"

"Not too far. We'll stop someplace along the way to check the Queens phone book, then we'll pay Mr. LaMarca a visit. After that, you can drop me at home."

As McHugh drove, Danny thought back over the interview. After the initial shock at hearing the news that his wife had been murdered, Maxwell's biggest concern had been who would get the kids, and his deepest outrage had been at being questioned about his whereabouts at the time of the murder.

And he hadn't shed a tear.

Not a single, "God, no!"

But he had appeared nervous.

"What did you think about that?" he asked McHugh.

"Guy seemed like a pretty cold fish to me."

So McHugh had caught the same scent.

FIVE

Detective Frank Larkin lit a Lucky Strike cigarette before turning back to the file Danny had left with him and heaved a deep sigh. Lt. Greco had gotten it from an FBI agent Danny had worked with on two cases the year before. One had been a series of anti-Semitic assaults and burglaries connected to a pro-Nazi sabotage ring, all the members of which were now dead.

But the assaults had recently begun again.

"Where's the rest of the Emerald Society, Frankie?" Detective Vince Rossi gestured to bum a cigarette.

Frankie shook one out of his pack. "I take it you need a light, too?"

Rossi nodded toward the pack. "I only own the habit, kind sir."

Frankie fished a Zippo lighter from his pocket and flicked it until it produced a flame.

Rossi took a deep drag and blew out a stream of smoke. "Thanks. May I assume the Sinn Fein is out on a case?" Danny's history in Ireland had become common knowledge.

"Yeah. The broad found strangled last night in Mott Haven."

"And you weren't invited?"

No, he would not tell Vinnie. Danny was already in a foul mood. He gestured to the file. "Other demands. The G thinks our sauerkraut-loving friends may be back."

Vinnie laughed. "From the dead?"

"Reinforcements."

"What does His Eminence think?"

"Father Brady has not yet expressed an opinion. Yes, I know, unusual for him."

Vinnie shrugged and said, "Not surprising, what with Meg due any time. Anything new on your junior member's situation?"

"Personal or professional?"

"Either."

"Professionally, the lieu is beating the drums to get McHugh the gold badge and having him permanently assigned to us. Personally, he and the Jewish girl have finally broken the news to their families about each other. My understanding is that her father took the news better than his family."

"I knew something was up when he brought her to Danny's wedding." Vinnie took another long drag, this time blowing smoke rings. He pointed to the file. "What do you make of it?"

"Not much." He'd been wrestling with it all morning. Danny was the expert in analyzing patterns in shit like this because he had the patience of a saint. Frankie had none. And, as Helen liked to point out, his habit of saying the wrong thing at the wrong time was growing worse.

He stared at the file: a Jewish boy beaten by a gang in Morrisania; an elderly Jewish lady whose purse had been snatched in Morris Park; a lone man mugged outside of a synagogue on the Grand Concourse; a few small Jewish businesses burglarized in various locations around the city. "If there's a pattern here, I can't see it."

Vinnie crushed his cigarette butt in the ash tray on Frankie's desk. "Thanks for the smoke."

No sooner had Vinnie ambled away than the phone on Frankie's desk rang.

It was Helen. "Get Danny. Meg's gone into labor."

***

It was just after eleven in the morning when Danny and McHugh rang the bell of Anthony LaMarca's basement apartment in a house on Park Lane South in Woodhaven. After several rings, LaMarca opened the door in a stained bathrobe, barefoot, hair tousled, unshaven, and bleary-eyed. "Yeah?" The odor of alcohol wafted across the doorway.

Danny flashed his badge, taking the lead. "Detective Brady, Officer McHugh, police. Do you know a woman named Carla Maxwell?"

LaMarca snorted. "Yeah. We were married once but got divorced five years ago. Why? She complaining she didn't get enough money?"

Danny gestured to the door. "May we come in?"

LaMarca waved them both inside.

The apartment looked like it had been ransacked. "Rough divorce?"

"Yeah. She cleaned me out. Left me with these lovely surroundings. What's this about, anyway?"

"Had she been in touch with you lately?"

"No, why?"

"When was the last time you had contact with her?"

LaMarca shook himself, as if to clear his head. "I dunno. Four years ago, I guess. Got a letter saying she'd changed her name and had a new address up in Yonkers. Got me off the hook paying alimony, so it was fine with me."

"And you haven't seen her since?" Danny kept his tone conversational.

"No, never."

"What about when you see your children?"

"I never see the little brats. She convinced them I'm evil." LaMarca's eyes narrowed. "Why are you asking me all this?"

"Just checking up. Someone murdered her last night in the Bronx."

LaMarca chuckled. "Huh. I'll bet she was playing the field, again."

Not the response Danny had expected. "What do you mean?"

"That's what led to our divorce. No one was ever gonna tie her down, certainly not some weasel accountant from Yonkers."

"You mean she was running around on you?" McHugh asked.

"Damned straight."

"Can you explain how you ended up with nothing in the divorce?" Danny asked.

"I was stupid. When I realized she was two-timing me, I went out and got some of my own, and I didn't make any secret of it, either. So, she hired a private detective and had evidence, while all I had was some overheard conversations and her getting home late from her job."

"Sounds like you have a lot of resentment," McHugh said.

"Not anymore." But when he saw the look on Danny's face, he grew serious. "Wait, don't get me wrong. I won't deny I think she got what she deserved, but I never would have killed anyone. Not even Carla."

"Could you tell us where you were last night?" Danny asked.

"What time?"

Danny dropped the friendly manner. "The whole evening."

"Okay, I got off work at five. Carter's Plumbing, over on Woodhaven Boulevard. My boss and I grabbed dinner at the Chinese place on Jamaica Avenue and 91st Street. Afterward, I walked to the Victory Tavern for a few beers and shot some games of pool. Then I walked home."

"What time did you leave the bar?" Danny asked.

"Don't recall. Maybe ten, maybe a little later. Somebody kept playing 'I'll Never Smile Again' on the jukebox. By the sixth or seventh time, I couldn't stand it anymore and asked the bartender to tell whoever it was to knock it off, and he just shrugged. So, I left. Went home, listened to the radio, and went to bed."

Danny closed his notepad. "I guess that will do for now. If we have other questions, we'll return."

LaMarca relaxed. "Sure. Anytime."

At the door, Danny turned back. "And the kids, who gets custody?"

"The weasel accountant can have 'em."

SIX

The radio squawked as Danny and McHugh got back to the car. It was the dispatcher calling them. When Danny answered, the dispatcher said. "Detective Larkin reports Mrs. Brady was taken to Horace Harding Hospital in Elmhurst."

Danny pressed the microphone button. "How long ago? Over."

"Detective Larkin didn't say."

That figured. "Roger that. Over."

He drove to the Victory Tavern. "Sean, talk to the bartender. See if he was on duty last night, and if he remembers Mr. LaMarca. Get whatever information you can on him." He strode to the phone booth, closed the door, and dialed Larkin's number.

"Detective squad, Forty…"

"It's Danny. What happened?"

"Jesus, Mary, and Joseph, boyo, where the hell have you been?"

"You know where I've been because you had the dispatcher contact me."

"Yeah, okay. Meg went into labor while she was out with Helen, who drove her to the hospital. Helen called me just as they were leaving your place. About thirty minutes after you left. Greco got sick and went home, so it took time to get the dispatcher to radio you and figure out which car you took…"

"Have you heard anything further from Helen?"

"Yeah, just a few minutes ago. It was false labor. The doctor explained it might happen again before she gives birth. He told Meg how she could tell the difference."

"Is she still at the hospital?"

"No, Helen brought her home to the apartment and is keeping her company."

"Okay. I'll have McHugh drop me off and bring the car back. Sign me out for today." He hung up, then dropped another nickel into the phone and called his home number.

Helen Larkin answered.

"Hi, Helen. It's Danny. I just heard. I'm in Woodhaven and I'm on my way, now."

"Great, Danny. I'll tell her."

"Is Meg okay?"

"Sure." But she didn't sound reassuring at all.

He waited until Sean was driving north on Woodhaven Boulevard to ask what he'd learned.

"The bartender worked until closing last night," McHugh replied. "He knows LaMarca and remembers him coming in around seven with his boss. They had a couple of beers, then the boss left. LaMarca started shooting pool with another customer. A third guy joined them, and they started playing loser sits. LaMarca had several more beers."

"What about the jukebox business?"

"Bartender confirms it. LaMarca complained a few times, but when the song came on yet again just as he was getting ready to shoot, he got aggravated and missed his shot. That's when he got belligerent. He left shortly after ten, looking none too steady on his feet."

"Turn left on Queens Boulevard. Funny that LaMarca didn't mention that. You'd think he'd want to tell us anything to show he didn't do it."

McHugh made the turn. "Maybe he figured if we knew he was loaded, we'd suspect him more. Less self-control."

Danny considered it. "Perhaps. But he was specific about where he'd gone and what had happened. He had to know we'd check his story."

"You think he did it?"

"I keep coming back to those cuts on her throat. This wasn't a mugging and there's no evidence of rape. I'm betting she knew her killer, and those knife cuts suggest he was enraged. Maxwell is no fool, he probably suspected she was running around, regardless of what he told us. LaMarca knew she had for certain." Danny lapsed into silence.

"That gives us two guys with a motive. Where do I turn?"

"You'll make a right on Forty-Fifth Street, three blocks after the el turns onto Queens Boulevard from Roosevelt Avenue, the beginning of the viaduct." Danny thought about motives. "LaMarca lost his motive—immediate financial relief—once she married Maxwell. Unless there had been something recently to fuel new anger, I don't see him in the picture. Maxwell is another story."

"But he has an alibi," McHugh said.

"We'll need to check it out. See what the neighbors say. This is Forty-Fifth coming up." Right now, he needed to shift his attention to Meg.

SEVEN

When Danny got to the apartment, Helen was already gone. Meg was sitting on the couch, her eyes puffy and red, a library book lying open on the coffee table, face down.

"I'm sorry, Meg. I rushed home as soon as I knew. Are you okay?"

"Fine." Her voice was like ice. Before he could respond, she added, "Helen said you were in Woodhaven. What were you doing there?"

"Interviewing the ex-husband of the murdered woman."

"Did he confess?"

"No, and I don't think he did it. What did the doctor say?"

"That it was false labor. It can happen anytime during the last two months. He said it might happen again."

"Helen told Frankie there are ways to tell the difference between false labor and the real thing."

For the first time, she met his gaze and nodded. "False labor contractions are felt in the abdomen. With the real thing, they usually start in the lower back. Helen called the precinct before we left for the hospital. What took you so long?"

"Lt. Greco had gone home, so Frankie had to convince the dispatcher to call our radio car on his own, and he didn't know the procedure or have the authority. He also didn't know the number of our car, so all that took time to resolve. Until the baby is born, I'll make sure that whenever I leave the precinct, it's in a radio car and the desk sergeant on duty has the number. I'll also make sure whoever is on the desk knows if you call for any emergency and I'm not at the precinct, he's to have the dispatcher radio me immediately. I'll clear all of this with Greco."

A hint of a smile. "Sounds complicated."

He met her smile with one of his own. "Can't help that. It would be easier if we had two-way wrist radios, like Dick Tracy, but that's a comic strip and this is real life, so it's the best I can do. I'll try to keep the overtime to a minimum until the baby comes, but that'll be hard with this murder case."

"Does that mean you're going back to work today and tomorrow?"

"Not today. Can't promise about tomorrow, but I'll do my best."

She broke into a genuine smile. "You're best is usually pretty good."

The phone rang. It was Larkin. "Yes, Frankie, what is it?"

Meg burst out laughing.

"Just checking to make sure you're still alive. McHugh just got back."

Danny could picture Larkin's sleepy eyes brimming with humor. "Thanks. I trust he's filled you in."

"He has. Sounds like there's plenty of chasing left to do. The lieutenant checked in a short while ago. He thinks it's something he ate and plans on coming in tomorrow."

"Good. I'm taking the rest of today and tomorrow as well. In the meantime, I'd appreciate it if you and McHugh would head back to Yonkers and check out the husband's alibi."

"Yes, Father Brady."

"If I was Father Brady, I wouldn't have a beautiful wife great with child." He grinned at Meg, and she stifled a giggle. "And thanks, Frankie, for doing what you could to let me know." He hung up.

Meg walked over and nestled against him. "We both had a lousy night. Let's rest for a while."

***

Frank Larkin cast a wary eye toward McHugh as he pulled up outside the Maxwells' house, skeptical about being partnered with someone so green. McHugh had been assigned to their unit a year earlier, and he made no secret about his ambition to secure a gold detective's badge, an effort Danny supported.

But McHugh had stopped trying to keep his romance with a Jewish girl a secret, and that made for some derisive whispers around the precinct. Rebecca Stoneman was a nice kid, the daughter of a jeweler who'd been burglarized during an anti-Semitic crime spree a year earlier.

"Think Maxwell will notice us?" McHugh's question broke Frank's train of thought.

It was hard not to like McHugh—he was bright, hard-working, and conscientious. But this was the first time Frank and McHugh had worked together without Danny around. Even though he had less seniority than Frank, Danny had been top dog in the unit ever since he'd gotten the FBI and a score of police departments up and down the East coast to cooperate on that serial rapist case that had gotten McHugh assigned in the first place. McHugh was Danny's boy, at least until now.

"I doubt it, since we're in an unmarked radio car." And today, in this car, Frank was top dog as they tried to determine who had killed the woman they were now calling the Bun Lady. "If he does, it might mean he's our guy."

"What makes you think that?"

Maybe he wasn't as sharp as Danny thought. Or maybe he was just testing. "A guilty person checks for observers. A caring father's priority is his kids."

"Is Mrs. Brady okay?"

"She's fine. False alarm. Why?"

"I just figured since he took the rest of the day off…"

"All-nighters are tougher when you're married." Frank lit a cigarette. As he inhaled, he thought about the victim, Carla Maxwell. Dark hair, smoldering eyes… loose…

"There he is now," McHugh said. "And the kids."

Frank shook himself. Shouldn't have such thoughts. He watched the kids. The girl was ten but appeared a little older. The boy was seven. Neither spoke as they got into the car.

Robert Maxwell walked around to the driver's side, not giving even a cursory glance around before getting into the car.

"Guess he's not our guy, after all," McHugh said as the car pulled away.

Frank took another drag rather than bite the lad's head off. "I didn't say it was a definitive test."

McHugh stared at him. "Frankie, I was joking."

One last drag to calm himself. He crushed the butt in the car's ash tray. "Not a problem. Let's go."

They rang the bell for the apartment above Maxwell's, and a woman about fifty answered wearing a faded floral print housecoat.

Frank showed her his badge.

"Are you here about the murder?" she asked.

So, word was already out. "Yes, ma'am. May we come in?"

She led them upstairs and into a small living room and gestured to a heavy couch with ornate scrolling and faded beige velvet upholstery with a tufted button back and a slightly musty odor. "I'm not sure if I can help you."

"Did you know Mrs. Maxwell well?" Frank asked.

"No, just to say hello. She worked long hours. I know her husband better, poor man."

"Did they get along?"

Her eyes narrowed with suspicion. "You don't think he…"

Frank grinned. "We haven't concluded anything, yet, ma'am. We're just trying to get the complete picture. You said she worked long hours. Was that a problem for him?"

"Sure, it was. The burden of the children fell on him, not that he minded. He dotes on them."

"What kind of work did she do?" McHugh asked.

The woman snorted. "She was an office worker at a hospital in the Bronx. What hospital office worker needs to work late hours?"

"Did she work late often?" Frank avoided thoughts of her doing something other than working.

"Often enough. I'd hear her come in, sometimes as late as two or three in the morning. I'm a light sleeper."

Frank shot McHugh a glance. "Did you ever hear them argue about it?"

"No. He seemed like a devoted and attentive husband. I imagine he waited on her hand and foot."

"But you think she was running around?"

"Not for me to say. It certainly didn't look good. Plus, the way she dressed and carried herself—like she thought she was a model or something."

"How do you mean?" An interesting comment deserving further explanation.

"She wore stockings all the time. What woman can afford stockings nowadays? Most wear that leg makeup that just came out, or draw lines on the back of their legs, or else just wear socks, like I do. She seemed to have an endless supply."

"Where did she get them?" McHugh asked.

"That's my question." She shook her head. "That poor man. He has such a good heart."

Time to switch gears. "Was Mr. Maxwell home all Friday evening?"

"Definitely."

Too fast. "How is it you're so sure?"

"I… never heard them go out. I always hear when they do."

Frank studied her. "Did you hear activity…"

"Yes."

"…downstairs?"

Interesting that she'd answered the question before he'd finished asking it.

She blushed. "Sorry. Yes, I did. Sounded like the radio. I heard music and voices."

"Mr. Maxwell's or the children's?" Frank asked.

"Both, but I couldn't hear what they were saying. I mean, it's not as if I was eavesdropping. I'm no busybody, and I wasn't trying to hear."

Frank flashed a reassuring grin. "Of course not."

"Around what time was this?" McHugh asked.

"I don't know because I didn't check the time. I'm sorry I can't be of more help."

Frank patted her arm. "You've been just fine. Thanks for your time."

The other neighbors they interviewed spoke equally well of Robert Maxwell, and less so of his departed wife.

EIGHT

Monday, May 17, 1943

"The War Food Administration and the Price Administration Office jointly announced yesterday the establishment of a War Meat Board to crack down on black markets. The announcement stated the Board would take steps to allocate and distribute the nation's meat supply more effectively, considering the total meat available from day to day and week to week.

"Here in the city, Mayor La Guardia announced that the Department of Markets might allow food dealers to reduce the ration point values of cheddar cheese in danger of spoiling if the OPA did not act. Appealing to the federal government to break the black market, the mayor reported that the latest scheme of illegal food operators was to corner the new crop of onions."

***

Larkin checked Danny over after signing in. "No visible wounds, so that's good. I take it you're out on good behavior?"

Danny could only laugh. "Don't push it, Frankie, or I might forget to thank you for Saturday."

"Least I could do." He gave Danny the latest from Maxwell's neighbors in Yonkers. "How's Meg?"

"All right, now that she knows what false labor feels like. I've left instructions for them to contact me if I'm out and she calls in."

Greco emerged from his office. "Morning, Gents. Join me inside and let's evaluate where we are."

Once in his office, Greco picked up the still-smoldering cigarette butt in his ashtray and used it to light another. "From what Frankie tells me, you have two possible suspects. Are we certain this wasn't a mugging? The guys on the scene recovered the knife from the churchyard on Saturday. About as dull as a senator's speech."

Danny shook his head and restated his reasons, adding, "Besides, muggers sure as hell don't stand around lighting matches trying to find a cheap pocketknife."

"They might if it had prints," Greco replied. "And this one did."

"Sorry, Lieu," Danny said, "no sale. Whoever did this was hopping mad. She was already dead, and the knife cuts wouldn't have had an effect if she'd still been alive. And he dropped the knife, so I doubt he was thinking straight."

Greco nodded. "And we have two fellas who qualify, the hubby she may have been running around on and the ex-hubby she soaked in a divorce. Do we prefer one suspect for the murder?"

Danny exchanged glances with Larkin, who spoke up. "The hubby claims he was home all night, and that he didn't think she was canoodling. The neighbors can't confirm he was at home, but two were certain she was two-timing him. I can't believe he didn't see it."

"Willful blindness on his part?" Danny wished he and Larkin had been able to talk this through, first.

"Could be. If we could prove he knew, that would give us a motive. The neighbors claim he's a definite homebody, devoted to the kids."

"Even though they ain't his?" Greco gave a humorless laugh. "I'd say we don't have enough to rule him out. Danny?"

"Agreed. The ex-hubby admits he's glad to see she finally got what she had coming, but he left the bar after ten, and he was fluthered, which…"

"He was what?" Greco asked.

Larkin laughed. "Fluthered. Loaded. Three sheets to the wind."

"Jesus, Danny," Greco said, "speak plain English, will ya?"

"Fine. Call it what you want, but it means he would have needed to get on the Jamaica Avenue line, take it into lower Manhattan, switch to the Lexington Avenue line, and make his way up to Mott Haven and know where to meet her, lead her to the churchyard, and kill her, all in ninety minutes."

Larkin acted like he was thinking it over. "So, I take it you don't think he did it."

"I do not."

"Agreed," Greco said. "I think the hubby makes a better suspect."

"Not too much better," Danny replied. "If he's so devoted to the kids, I don't see him leaving them alone while he goes out and kills their mother." He turned to Larkin. "And if he did, do you think he'd strangle her?"

"Nope. He struck me as more of an arsenic-in-her-tea type. He'd also have to have known where to find her."

Greco held up a hand. "Hold on. Wasn't she killed a short walk from where she works?"

"Yeah," Larkin replied. "About seven hours after she'd have gotten off from work. The only thing that bothers me is that one neighbor gave a strong hint Carla was running around."

"What kind of hint?" Greco asked.

"Late hours, mostly. And apparently Carla had a large supply of stockings."

That caught Danny's attention. "Stockings? You mean nylons?"

"Yeah. The neighbor said she wore them almost every day."

"Where the hell would she get them?" Greco asked.

"Good point." Danny added. "Meg says they're impossible to get at any price. The black market comes to mind. What else did this neighbor say, Frankie?"

"She was quick to claim Maxwell was home all evening. That bothered me."

Danny agreed. "Also, Maxwell claimed LaMarca saw his children infrequently. LaMarca said he never sees him and doesn't care who gets custody."

"What difference does that make?" Greco asked.

"I'm curious to find out. Frankie, let's pay another visit to Mr. Maxwell and ask him if he knew any places she liked to go with her… friends… after work."

"I already did. He said he didn't."

"Let's ask him again. We can also ask him for a recent photo. Then, we can ask her coworkers and find out who she socialized with. Maybe we'll even find a boyfriend."

"If there is a boyfriend," Greco said.

"There is," Danny replied. "I'd bet on it."

***

The false labor incident had made Meg wary of venturing out on her own. She barely fit behind the wheel of their car, and the mere thought of climbing the stairs to the Flushing Line made her legs ache. But Helen Larkin had once again come through, taking her to the library where she had recently stopped working and then out to lunch at the Garden Grill Restaurant on the corner of Queens Boulevard and 48th Street.

They had just sat at a table when Meg glanced down and said, "I can't believe I'm this big."

"Must be a boy."

"Danny says the same thing. I just hope it's not twins, although the doctor says it isn't."

"Danny's probably hoping for a boy. Men always do."

Meg grinned. "True. Although I'd love to see him with a little girl. She'd wrap him around her little finger."

"It's obvious they miss you at the library."

"I miss them, too, and the job. The director, Miss Soloway, promised me I could come back whenever I wanted." She patted her stomach. "Perhaps when he's in school."

"Unless you have three more."

They both laughed.

And then Meg spied a familiar face, and her laughter died as the familiar face approached.

It was her ex-husband, Hal Corwyn. "Hello, Meg. I see you're expecting."

"Yes, I am. Any day, now."

"I never thought I'd see the day when you'd bring a bastard into the world."

Meg pushed up out of her seat. "Not that it's any business of yours, but Danny and I were married last summer. And I've never been happier in my life."

A shocked expression flashed across his face. "Happy as an adulteress?"

"I divorced you sixteen months ago, Hal, after you deserted me. Accept it." She looked him up and down. "Still a second lieutenant?"

He stiffened. "Still serving my country, if that's what you mean."

"In the Quartermaster Corps. I told you the day you walked out on me that putting on a uniform wouldn't change the fact that you're a coward, and it hasn't. It appears the army doesn't hold a much higher opinion of you than I do. Now, leave me alone."

He pivoted and stormed out without another word.

Helen watched him go. "Wow! Remind me never to cross you, Mrs. Brady!"

***

Danny and Larkin settled back into the radio car. Maxwell had admitted he hadn't been truthful about LaMarca seeing the kids, and he wasn't surprised that the man had no interest in custody of his children, but he hadn't wanted to speak ill of anyone.

"Including his cheating wife," Larkin said now as he held a three-year-old photo of Carla Maxwell. "I can't believe he's sticking to his story that he didn't know where she went or who with, and that, as far as he knew, she had worked late Friday night and missed the last train home."

Danny agreed. "Even more incredible, he admitted it wasn't the first time it had happened, but he knew nothing about where she stayed when it did." He drove a little further before making the left turn onto Gun Hill Road. "He had to know, even if he didn't want to, so he's lying."

"Which gives him a motive, besides acting guilty now." Larkin paused to light a cigarette, cupping his hand around the flame of the lighter to shield it from the breeze from the open window. "But I still have a hard time seeing him doing the deed that way. The coroner confirmed she was strangled with the scarf, so the killer didn't take her by surprise—no sudden blow to the head."

Danny made the half-right from Mosholu Parkway onto the Grand Concourse. "The coroner's report says her blood alcohol level was 0.14, just below the legal limit. Which means she would have had four or five beers or glasses of wine." He drove several blocks in silence.

Larkin broke the silence. "Enough to be tipsy. So, he could have possibly caught her off guard and off balance You said, yourself, the knife cuts suggested whoever killed her was hopping mad at the time. And we still can't verify his alibi."

"I give you motive, Frankie, but let's not get ahead of ourselves. He doesn't need to prove he was home with the kids; we must prove he wasn't. And if she was a regular party girl, a 0.14 blood alcohol level might mean she was only feeling happy." It was a quick trip the rest of the way to St. Francis Hospital.

***

Meg recalled that terrible day from two years earlier.

Lying face down on the bed, her wrists tied behind her back.

A handkerchief stuffed in her mouth.

Helpless as the hem of her dress was yanked up… and afterward, feeling utterly violated, filthy…

She shook the memory away and opened the door to the balcony, looking over the garden that gave these apartments their name. The little magnolia tree had lost its blooms just before Mother's Day, and the azaleas were just about done. But the dogwood was still lovely, the tiger lilies were ready to burst forth as were the roses. The soft spring breeze that brushed her face bore a lovely mixed fragrance.

She loved this place almost as much as she loved Danny, the tough cop with a heart as soft as down who'd hunted down the beast who'd raped her while Hal blamed her for it.

She shook her head and took another deep breath of the fragrant air.

But the memory of the attack and its aftermath refused to fade.

Hal was back.

NINE

Danny's inner siren was wailing.

None of Carla's coworkers wanted to talk about her. None of them ever socialized with her. Her post-work activities and companions were a mystery. Her supervisor said only that she never worked late.

"Frankie, the whole thing smells like week-old fish." Danny stopped on their way out to speak with the security guard. "What time does your shift end?"

"I go off at six. Why?"

"Were you on duty Friday?"

The guard's expression clouded over. "Yeah, why?"

"Just give us straight answers and you'll be fine." Danny showed him the photo of Carla. "Did you know her?"

"Yeah, just to say hi. She worked in the office."

"Did you see her leave Friday night?" The guard nodded. "What time?"

"About twenty to six."

Danny made a note. "Was that unusual for her? She finished work at five, right?"

"Yeah, she usually left with the crowd."

"Did you notice anything else unusual about her as she was leaving? Was anything she said unusual?"

"She didn't say nothin', and she usually said, 'goodnight'. Looked like she had something on her mind."

Another note. "Did anyone meet her? Was anyone waiting for her?"

"Didn't see nobody."

This was like pulling teeth. "Did you see which way she went?"

"No, sorry."

"Did you ever see anyone meet her after work?"

"Not as I can think of."

Danny put his little notepad away. "Thanks."

***

It was ten to six when the phone rang. The phone ringing at that time of day meant Danny would be getting home late, something Meg hated. Maybe it was Helen checking in.

But, no, it was Danny. "Everything okay?"

She forced a cheery note into her voice. "Fine, Honey. Helen took me to the library today and then out to lunch. I take it you're going to be late."

"Any other pains?"

He was such a dear. "No, I'm fine. How late? Where are you?"

"At the victim's place of employment, St. Francis Hospital, trying to get some answers. The night cleaners start at six. I'll be home before eight if I get what I need, otherwise I'll call. Okay?"

"Swell." As soon as she said it, she was sorry. It came out sour.

"What's wrong?"

She couldn't tell him. Not now. She had no desire to tell him, ever. She was usually stronger than that. But she couldn't lie, either. "Nothing major. Please don't worry, I'm fine. We can talk when you get home. I love you."

***

"Everything okay?" Larkin's partner radar was strong.

"I don't know. Meg's okay, but it sounds like something's bothering her. She had lunch with Helen today, so she should be in good spirits."

"Want me to call Helen for some intelligence?"

That made Danny laugh. "I do not. She'll call Meg, and the last thing I need is for Meg to think I'm checking up on her. No, I'll just see her tonight."

"I think this is our guy." Larkin gestured toward a tall, thin black man in stained coveralls approaching with a mop and a large pail on wheels. The hallway instantly reeked of industrial disinfectant.

Danny flashed his badge and introduced himself and Larkin. Then he showed the janitor the photo of Carla. "Did you know this woman?"

The janitor's manner became guarded. "Not really. She worked days."

"In this office, correct?" Larkin pointed to an office door with "Billing Department" stenciled on the window.

"That's right." The janitor opened the door, switching on the lights.

Danny stepped inside, where desks were arrayed in three rows of three, with a supervisor's office in far right the corner of the room. "Which was her desk?"

The janitor pointed to the desk in the left front corner. "That one there."

Danny led him over to the desk. A comptometer and telephone sat on the right side of the desk, an in-out box with papers on the left, along with a cup holding pencils. In the middle stood a framed photograph of her husband and the two children. "You ever see her working here when you came to clean up?"

"Sometimes."

Danny flashed a reassuring grin. "Relax, sir. We just need some information. Did she often work late?"

"Now and then. Maybe once a week, sometimes twice."

"What nights?" Larkin asked.

"It varied."

Danny took over. "How late did she usually stay? What was she doing?"

"Never looked like she was doing anything. When I'd see her, she just be sittin' there, maybe lookin' at the newspaper. Didn't keep track o' what time she left, but it was usually around the time I finished with this office."

"You always clean this office first?"

"Yes sir. I start here and move to other offices and floors."

"How long does that take you?"

"About a half hour."

"So, she'd have left around 6:30 on those nights you saw her?"

"I'd say between 6:30 and 7:00."

Danny was making notes. "Did you see her Friday night?"

"Yes sir."

"And did she leave between 6:30 and 7:00?"

"Now that you mention it, she was still here when I finished upstairs. That was about eight o'clock. I came down to refill the bucket and noticed the light still on. I checked back again an hour later, and the office was dark."

"Anything unusual about her when you saw her, like a different coat?

"Only thing I saw was one of them boxes bakeries have, tied with string. Thought that was kinda strange. Usually, folks buy stuff at the bakery before they come to work, so they can bring it with them."

Danny exchanged looks with Larkin. "Are there any bakeries near here?"

"Yes sir, there is. Right over on 141st Street, just past Beekman. Good one, too."

Danny thanked him and they left. On the way out, he checked with the woman at the front desk, but she didn't recall seeing Carla leave Friday night.

"All we know," Larkin said, getting back in the car, "is that she left the hospital between eight and nine that night."

But they knew more than that. "We know she went out before six and returned, she didn't spend any part of the evening with coworkers, and she waited longer to leave than usual." The fishy odor was growing stronger.

"So, what next, Danny boy?"

"She left the hospital and was killed close by, suggesting she might have remained in the neighborhood. Tomorrow afternoon, we scout around to see what bars and restaurants are nearby, and we interview bartenders. We'll also stop in that bakery on the off chance she bought the buns there."

"Why not tonight?"

"Can't. Meg seems troubled, and I need to know what's wrong. This can wait one day."

"Oh, and Danny, the buns were excellent." When Danny shot him a glare, he shrugged and added, "Hey, I kept the box as evidence."

***

Frank pulled into his driveway and glanced at his watch. Almost 9:00. Helen wouldn't be pleased, but if he told her a few things about the case, that would likely calm her down.

He thought about the photo Robert Maxwell had given them of Carla, with her seductive eyes and pouty smile.

And an endless supply of stockings.

As he walked up to the house, he tried not to speculate on her extra-marital activities.

***

Danny entered the apartment, and Meg struggled to get to her feet wearing a maternity dress, saddle shoes and bobby socks, her usual garb these days. A few weeks earlier, Danny had said she looked like a knocked-up teenager. Although he'd meant it as a joke, she'd blown up at him. She'd later apologized, but he'd never repeated it. Nevertheless, he still thought it was true.

"Sorry I'm late."

"It's okay. I'll heat your dinner, lamb stew. How's the case?" She'd decided it was foolish to be spooked about Hal's sudden appearance. Better to just forget it.

He retrieved a bottle of Burke's Stout from the ice box. "We're making a little progress, but in baby steps."

"So, was it the husband or the ex-husband?"

"Probably neither. I think she was cheating on him, and it might have been the boyfriend, whoever he is."

"An adulteress." There was no missing her bitter tone.

He'd poured the dark beer into a glass but halted and set the bottle on the table. "What's the matter, Meg? You sounded funny on the phone today and you seem upset now. Please don't make me interrogate you."

When he questioned her about her pregnancy, she sometimes said, "Stop with the interrogation." It had become their little joke, and it made her smile, now. "There's nothing wrong, Honey."

He didn't say a word, but only gave her The Look.

"Honestly, there's nothing." But The Look remained. No choice but to tell him. "I saw Hal today at the Garden Grill while Helen and I were having lunch." She recounted the conversation.

"Sounds like you sent him away with a flea in his ear. Good for you." But his grin soon faded. "What the hell was he doing around here in the first place?"

"That's what's been bothering me. I've been trying to convince myself all day that it's nothing, he just happened to run into me."

"Like the night we saw him at Roseland last year."

"Yes." They'd been out for a night on the town with the Larkins, Sean McHugh, and Rebecca Stoneman, when Hal had appeared out of nowhere. "Is it possible that neither was a coincidence?"

He stood and embraced her. "Possible but not likely. Do you still have any photos of him?"

TEN

Tuesday, May 18, 1943

Danny left for work an hour early and got off the Flushing Line at the Vernon-Jackson stop in Hunters Point. The 108th Precinct was a stone's throw from the subway entrance. Detective Morris Klein was waiting for him. "Good to see you, Danny. I hear you're going to be a papa, soon."

"Any day. Meg can't wait. She's getting awfully tired of being an expectant mother."

Klein laughed. "Hey, I still remember the day you met her. You were so nice to her she dumped her loser of a husband and married you."

"It wasn't quite that simple, but he's the reason I wanted to see you. Do you remember him?"

"Sure. Puny, whiney, and it was all her fault. What a loser. What's this all about?"

"He's an army officer, now…"

"Shit, they made that jerk an officer? So much for the war effort."

"I doubt he'll hurt us too badly. The thing is, he's made himself a nuisance on a couple of occasions, most recently yesterday. Meg's worried, and I can't rule out the possibility it could become a problem. Any chance you and your boys could keep an eye out for him?" He handed Klein the photo Meg had found.

"Sure. It's too quiet around here lately. Not everyone has the opportunity to hunt Nazis. If we see him, what's the plan?"

"Convince him loitering around the Sunnyside area is not in his best interests. If you see him more than once, let me know."

"Consider it done. And have Meg call me if she sees him again."

***

As soon as he saw the bar and grill on the corner of St. Ann's Avenue and East 142nd Street, just a block from the churchyard where Carla Maxwell had been found, Danny suspected it might have been the place she'd been before she was killed. That, combined with the news he'd gotten the moment he'd arrived at the precinct that the lab had found a set of prints on the handbag, and they matched those on the recovered knife, gave him reason to grin as he parked the car.

"You still haven't told me what the fingerprint guys found," Larkin said.

"They found a handprint that wasn't Carla's wrapped around the top of the bag, a left hand. They're checking the files. But there was one oddity. Four fingerprints on one side, no thumb print on the other."

"How would you hold a bag from the top and not use your thumb?"

Danny picked up a notebook, holding it with the palm of his hand, thumb extended so as not to touch it. "It's possible but uncomfortable, especially when holding tight, which you'd do if it was a handbag." Then, he added, "Frankie, call me daft, but I think our killer is missing his left thumb."

There were only a handful of drinkers at 2 PM. When Danny and Larkin showed their badges, the bartender shrugged. "What can I do for you fellas?"

Danny returned his badge to his pocket. "Were you working Friday night?"

"This past Friday? Yeah."

He showed Carla's photo. "Did you see her here?"

"That's the dame who bought it over by the church, ain't it?"

"It is."

He gave the photo back to Danny. "She came in around 8."

"Was she with anyone?"

"Not when she first got here. She sat at a table, crossed her legs, and ordered a glass of white wine. Nice pair of gams. Shortly after, a guy met her, and she left with him."

"What did he look like?"

The bartender hesitated. "I was getting ready to leave. The night bartender was supposed to arrive at seven, and he was late, so I didn't get a good look. About six feet, dark hair. I really didn't notice much more, except his nose was bent, like he'd stuck it someplace it didn't belong and paid the price."

"Did you recognize the woman?"

"Not as I can recall. Like I said, I don't work nights. Freddie does."

This was leading nowhere. "Did you hear anything they said? Did they mention if they were staying or going?"

"No, I can't... wait." He closed his eyes. "Now, I remember. She stood up when he came in and said, 'I hope we're not having dinner here.' And he said, 'Are you kidding? I'm taking you to the Criterion.' That's all I heard."

"I guess their menu's better than yours," Larkin said.

"Shit, yeah. Rationing sure has taken the 'grill' out of 'bar and grill'. Spaghetti is our best-selling item. And it ain't bad."

"And Freddie comes on at seven?" Danny asked.

"If I'm lucky."

"One other thing," Danny said. "Did you notice if she had anything with her when she walked in?"

"Yeah, she was carrying one of those white boxes you get at a bakery, tied up with string. Took it with her when she left."

"Thanks." Danny turned to Larkin. "Let's stop at the bakery, then we'll check out the Criterion."

"You buyin'?"

***

Meg had taken a book down to the garden, but it was such a lovely spring day that she couldn't concentrate. The baby kicking made her think that he, too, was restless. Or she.

A kick so powerful she had to wrap her arms around her abdomen underlined her assumption that it was a boy.

She closed her book. They were low on coffee, and it was a short walk to Hudson Dairies on Skillman and 46th Street. She took her time climbing the stairs, fetched her purse with her ration books, and set off.

The owner of Hudson Dairies chuckled when he saw her. "My goodness, Mrs. Brady, that's quite a load you're carrying. Would you like me to have my boy deliver your purchases when he comes in after school?"

"No, thanks. I just need coffee and sugar if you have it."

He frowned. "Sugar is scarce these days, even with rationing. How much can you get by with?"

"Two cups? It's just for coffee right now. I'm afraid I'm not up to doing any baking these days. Coffee isn't a problem, I hope."

"No, Mrs. Brady. In fact, there's talk that coffee rationing might end by the summer. Perhaps our brave boys are switching to tea."

She laughed at that as he ground the coffee and measured out the sugar.

"Are you sure you wouldn't like me to send this over later today?"

"Thank you, but I'll be…" She gasped with a contraction.

"Are you alright? Is the baby coming? Here, sit down."

The contraction eased even as she was sitting. "Sorry about that. No, it's just false labor. I panicked the first time it happened, but I'm getting used to it. Danny says I'm a real trooper."

"He's right. I think you'll make a world-class mom, and a beautiful one."

"Thanks." She picked up the bag of items and left.

She was crossing Skillman at 45th Street when she saw him, more than a block away, watching her.

Hal.

She hurried as fast as she could. It was less than a block to the apartment, but it felt like miles.

***

The woman behind the counter at the bakery remembered Carla Maxwell. "Yes, she came in Friday just before closing. We were out of turnovers, which is what she wanted, so she settled for the buns even though I told her they might be a bit stale."

Danny shot Larkin a look. "What time was she here?"

"Just about closing time, six o'clock. She said she wanted to bring something sweet home to her husband. I thought perhaps they'd quarreled."

"Had she ever talked about how she got along with her husband?" Larkin asked.

"Not at all. It was the first time she'd ever mentioned she was married."

He'd gotten another piece of information he'd needed: her arrival at the bakery fit with the time the day guard at the hospital said he saw her leave. Now, he needed to learn what ensued after she left the bar.

Located in the stately American Real Estate Company building, the Criterion Restaurant exuded refined dining, providing live music along with quality meals. The headwaiter frowned when he learned Danny and Larkin were detectives, but he cooperated. "Yes, that woman was here Friday night. She arrived with a man between eight-thirty and nine o'clock."

"Had he made a reservation?" Danny asked.

"Yes, under the name of Sam Jones."

Larkin laughed. "Original."

Danny remained serious. "Could you describe him?"

"About six feet tall, thin, dark hair, heavy dark eyebrows, brown eyes. In my opinion, he bore a remarkable resemblance to Boris Karloff."

"How did they get on during the meal?" Perhaps the headwaiter had caught something.

"I'm sorry, but neither I nor my staff make a habit of eavesdropping on our patrons' conversations."

Danny didn't snap at him. "I didn't mean to imply that you might. I'm interested in their general manner. Were they friendly? Cold?"

"I would say his manner was sincere, and hers was reserved when they first arrived, but she warmed up as they talked more. They were holding hands when they left."

"Did you see what time that was?"

"Shortly before ten, would be my guess."

Danny thanked him and they returned to the car.

"I think I prefer Gallagher's," Larkin said, referring to the famous steakhouse in Manhattan. "Even with the meat shortage."

"It couldn't have been their only stop, they left too early. How the hell did they get from here to St. Ann's?"

"The subway's right there," Larkin pointed to the corner kiosk.

"That would take them back toward the Grand Concourse." Danny started the engine.

"Well, St. Ann's Avenue is only a few blocks from here. They could've taken the L trolley back down to East 142nd and the bar."

That made sense. "Then we'll head for the barn and return to the bar this evening."

"Fine by me. In the meantime, you can look over that file on the anti-Jewish attacks. I couldn't find anything suggesting another sinister plot."

***

Meg walked as quickly as she could manage, glancing back every few steps. Hal's pace picked up as she made her way up 45th Street. As she approached the front door, he was only a half block behind her.

She fumbled with the key to the vestibule door, took a deep breath, and tried again, but dropped her keys. Squatting to pick them up, anxiety mounting, she took one last deep breath and willed her hand to remain steady.

This time she slid the key into the lock.

She locked the door behind her, resting against it, panting. After a moment, she trudged up the stairs to their apartment. She waited until her breathing returned to normal, then she picked up the phone and dialed. "Hello, this is Mrs. Brady. May I speak with Lieutenant Greco, please?"

ELEVEN

"What did Klein have to say?" Larkin asked as Danny hung up the phone. "Everything okay with Meg?"

Danny had alerted Klein as soon as Greco had told him about Meg's call. "Meg's fine, other than being shaken. She told me I should get back to work because she didn't want me working on her problem on the city's dime." He gave a rueful laugh. "It's really Klein and his guys doing the legwork. They scoured Sunnyside and half of Woodside but found no sign of the little bollocks. I suspect he took off at the first sign of a patrol car, and we've likely heard the last of him."

Larkin gestured toward the file Danny had been studying. "See anything interesting?"

"Oh, yeah. Delinquents with too much idle time. Joining the sea scouts or participating in scrap and rubber drives would be good for them." When Greco approached, Danny slipped all the papers back in the file and held it up. "Sorry, Lieutenant, but there's no evidence of any gang of Nazis here. Let's check what the barkeep has to say, Frankie."

***

The bar was crowded when they walked in shortly before seven-thirty. Danny flagged down the bartender who appeared as though he had a beer barrel concealed under his apron. "You Freddie?"

"Yeah, what's it to ya?"

Danny flashed his badge, and Freddie dropped the tough guy act and grew serious. "How can I help you, Detective?"

Danny displayed the picture of Carla. "Ever see this bird in here?"

Freddie gave the photo a desultory glance. "Nah."

"Do you believe him?" Larkin asked Danny.

"I do not." He reached across the bar, grabbed the bartender by the shirt, and yanked him hard enough against the other side to rattle some glasses, causing heads to turn along the length of the bar. "I think you've seen her here before, and even knew her name. So, cut the shite and answer me straight. Has this bird been here? When?"

Freddie cast nervous glances left and right. "Okay, okay. Yeah, she's a regular. Name's Carla. Don't know her last name. She was here last Friday. She's the one got killed, ain't she?"

Danny released his grip. "She is. When did she arrive and leave?"

"They walked in a few minutes after ten, maybe ten-fifteen."

"They?" Larkin asked.

"Uh, yeah. She came in with a guy. I seen him with her a few times before."

"What time did they leave?" Danny asked.

"They stayed maybe an hour. I didn't check the clock, but they only had two drinks. She left first, I remember that. They'd been talkin' in low voices, so I didn't hear what they said, but when she got up to go, I heard her say, 'Nobody tells me what to do.' Then she left, and he followed her out."

Danny pulled out his notepad and started writing. "How was her mood when they came in?"

"Happy and hanging all over him. He had some smudges on his face, so I figured they'd been necking. She grabbed a table in the corner, and he ordered drinks, a shot of Vat 69 with a beer chaser for him and wine for her."

Danny kept writing. "And what was his manner when he followed her out?"

"He didn't say nothin'. Just left a buck on the bar and chased after her."

"Did you catch which way they went?"

"She turned right, so I'd say she was headed down St. Ann's Avenue toward 138th Street."

Danny nodded as he wrote. "And the guy, could you describe him?"

Freddie's description matched that of the other bartender, and of the maître d' at the Criterion but added nothing.

"Did you notice anything unusual about his appearance?" Danny asked. "Any unusual marks?"

"Anything missing?" Larkin asked.

Danny shot him a glare. He disliked prompting witnesses. Larkin gave a sheepish grin.

"Nothing I could see," Freddie replied.

"Did he do anything unusual at all?"

"He didn't carry both drinks to the table like a guy usually would. Instead, he handed the woman hers and then picked up his."

An opening. Danny stared as he reread the notes he'd just made. "You said he stopped at the bar and left a buck. Did he already have it out, or did he take it from his wallet?"

"What difference…" Freddie jumped back as Danny grabbed for his shirt again. "Okay, okay. Sorry. I don't…"

Danny reached again. "Think."

Freddie closed his eyes. "Yeah. He pulled out his wallet. Had some trouble pulling the bill out."

"What kind of trouble?"

"He held the wallet in his left hand and pulled the bill out with his right. But he was in a hurry, and his grip on the wallet slipped and…" He hesitated.

"What?" Danny nearly exploded.

"You know what? That guy had no left thumb."

TWELVE

Wednesday, May 19, 1943

"The Royal Air Force hammered German airfields in Northern France yesterday while the deadly new American P-47 Thunderbolts battled enemy fighters over Belgium, carrying the furious allied air offensive through its sixth successive day. In the Pacific, US Army B-24 Liberator bombers hammered Wake Island with special blockbuster bombs, while American troops closed in a pincer movement against Japanese forces on the island of Attu."

***

Danny and Larkin waited outside Robert Maxwell's house in Yonkers until the children left for school before ringing his bell.

When he answered the door, he was wearing a shirt and tie. "Oh, good morning, Detectives. I was expecting a client."

"We won't keep you long, Mr. Maxwell," Danny replied. "We just wanted to update you on the investigation."

Maxwell brightened. "You know who did it?"

"Not yet, but we've learned more about him." Danny gestured to the interior. "May we come in?"

"Oh. Sorry, yes, of course."

They followed him into the parlor-office.

"We know that Mrs. Maxwell left the office shortly after eight Friday night, although she had no work reason to be there so late. She met a man at a bar down the street and then accompanied him to the Criterion Restaurant on 149th Street, where they had dinner. After dinner, they returned to the bar until they left shortly after eleven o'clock following a disagreement of some kind."

Maxwell stared at the floor.

"You don't look surprised, Mr. Maxwell," Larkin said.

"You lied to us about LaMarca's relationship with your children," Danny added. "In my experience, people who lie about one thing often lie about other things. Your reaction to what I just said about Mrs. Maxwell suggests you lied when you claimed you were certain she didn't see other men."

Maxwell met Danny's gaze. "She promised me. She promised."

"What did she promise? That's she'd stop running around on you?" Larkin added a derisive laugh. "They never stop."

Danny cut in. "When did she promise, Mr. Maxwell? And please, the whole truth this time."

"About a year ago, Carla came home late from work very upset. She'd been seeing someone, and he'd started pushing her around. Carla said she was sorry and promised she would never do it again."

"Did she report him to the police?"

"Of course not. They'd have said she'd gotten what she deserved, and they'd have done nothing."

"And when the late nights at the office resumed," Larkin said, "you suspected nothing?"

"She said a coworker of hers quit, so everyone had to work extra. It seemed reasonable."

"The guy who'd hit her," Danny said. "Did she tell you his name?"

"Steve. She didn't mention his last name."

"How long ago did the late nights at the office start back up?" Danny assumed they had been a regular thing in her prior affair.

"Right after the new year."

Interesting that Mr. Maxwell didn't bother to correct his assumption.

"What did you folks do for New Year's Eve?" Larkin asked.

"I did nothing. I was down with the flu. Carla celebrated with her friends from work."

"Where?"

"The Joe and Joe Restaurant, in Castle Hill. The building used to be the Bailer Hotel. Why?"

Danny ignored the question. "What time did she get in?"

Maxwell grew defensive. "I don't know. I was asleep."

"What did she mention about the party the next morning?" Larkin asked.

"Hardly anything. She wasn't feeling well."

Danny worked hard to hide his smirk. "Not unusual, given the day. What about after she was feeling better?"

Maxwell looked helpless. "She never wanted to talk about it."

Larkin jumped back in. "And when she suddenly had to work late a lot, right after a whiz-bang New Year's Eve party, you suspected nothing?"

"I… She'd promised…"

"You didn't want to know." Danny shook his head. "Even knowing she had a prior history." When Maxwell protested, Danny added, "Yeah, I know, she promised."

Outside, a car door slammed.

Maxwell's attention jerked toward the front door. "That'll be my client."

"One more thing," Danny said, "and we'll be on our way. In all these late nights she worked, did you ever see anyone drop her off?"

"Never."

Danny exchanged glances with Larkin. "Okay, Mr. Maxwell, we won't take any more of your time. But if you remember any helpful details, please contact us."

"Thank you. I will."

As they got back in their car, Danny noticed a maroon 1937 DeSoto sedan, with its distinctive hood ornament, parked in front of the house next door, a man wearing a fedora and black-rimmed glasses in the driver's seat. Danny kept walking.

***

"Okay," Larkin said as Danny parked around the corner from the Joe and Joe Restaurant. "You ain't opened a mouth since we left Maxwell. What's bothering you?"

"Why would he lie about knowing Carla was two-timing him?"

Larkin laughed. "Hold the phone, Sherlock. He was obviously afraid even to admit it to himself."

"No, Frankie. He knew, and he was afraid we'd figure that out, which is why he was so emphatic when he denied ever seeing anyone drop Carla off."

"You think he was lying?"

"No, I think he was telling the truth about that, and relieved in the safety of it."

"Care to explain, oh, seer of seers?"

Danny opened the door but didn't move. "Learn to listen closely, not only to what people say but also how they say it. While we were there, Maxwell spent a lot of time fencing with us. But when I asked him if he ever saw anyone drop his wife off, you could hear the relief in his voice when he said, 'Never.' In my experience, people are almost always more tense when they're lying than when they tell the truth, unless they're pathological liars. And Maxwell doesn't strike me as one."

Larkin followed him out of the car. "Why is he afraid? We've checked out his alibi and we know he didn't do it."

"Exactly what's bothering me, Frankie. Well, it's one thing."

"What else?"

Danny stopped walking. "We all heard a car door slam."

"Yeah, and he was expecting a client. That was probably him."

"Correct. He was sitting in his car when we left. Why?"

Larkin considered it. "He may have seen a police car parked and decided not to interrupt."

"Yeah. That's probably it." Danny knocked on the restaurant's door, even though it had a "closed" sign.

"Danny boy, can't you read? They ain't open."

"Doesn't mean there's no one here." He pounded again.

A guy in his late twenties pulled aside the curtain behind the door window. "We don't open till noon."

Danny flashed his badge. "We're not hungry."

The man reluctantly opened the door. "We ain't had no problems here. We run an honest business."

Danny didn't mention rumors of mobsters patronizing the place. "I'm sure you do. Are you the owner?"

"No, his son."

Danny laid the photo of Carla on a nearby table. "Ever see this woman in here?"

"No."

"Did you have a group from St. Francis Hospital here for a New Year's Eve party?"

"We had a big New Year's Eve bash, but there weren't any specific groups. Hospital staff may have joined us, but we did not make a specific reservation for them."

"Did everyone need to book in advance?"

"Yeah."

"Can you provide us with a reservation list for that night?"

A deep sigh. "Yeah. It'll take a few minutes. Have a seat. Can I get you guys something on the house?"

"A cup of coffee would be nice," Danny replied.

"And a cannoli," Frankie added. "At least for me."

"If you give me the reservation book, I'll be glad to copy the information," Danny added.

A momentary hesitation. "Sure."

While Larkin enjoyed his cannoli, Danny flipped through the pages of the reservations book and copied all the entries for the evening of December 31st.

THIRTEEN

Robert Maxwell held the door open for the man in the fedora and glasses.

"I see you've had visitors." He was taller than Maxwell, with a dark complexion, bushy eyebrows, and a muscular build. His glare suggested disapproval.

Robert kept his hands at his sides, gripping his trousers to quell the shaking. "I told them I knew nothing. And I told them I was expecting a client in case they saw you."

A humorless grin. "That's fine."

"I still don't understand…"

"And you won't. You're a bright guy, a college guy. Bright enough to know how dangerous it would be to ask questions. So, just be glad you're in expert hands." He tipped his hat and left.

***

"So?" Larkin asked. "Whaddaya got?"

Danny had been staring at his list for twenty minutes without a word. Staring but not seeing.

"Danny? Hello?"

It snapped him back. "Sorry. Do you still have that list of people you interviewed at the hospital?" Larkin handed him a sheet of paper, which Danny laid next to his own list so he could check each name. Four names down, he stared off into space.

"Spill it, boyo," Larkin said at last. "Otherwise, neither of us will get anything done."

"That guy pulled up behind us. Our radio cars have no markings on the rear, only a small precinct number marking on the driver's side, and a tiny NYPD over the left front wheel. How did he know we were cops?"

"Maybe he didn't. Perhaps he pulled up and didn't want to intrude on another client."

"No, Frankie. He wouldn't have left the car in that case. But he got out. We heard the door slam. Once. He left his car, had second thoughts, and got back in. I'm guessing he probably checked the side of our radio car."

Larkin threw up his hands. "What's your point?"

"It suggests he knew cops had a reason to be there and didn't want to be seen close up by us, which makes me wonder what else we need to be considering." He resumed examining the two lists.

It didn't take long. "Here we go. Eileen Stanner, one of Carla's coworkers, made a reservation for ten people for New Year's Eve. Can you check your notes and see what you got from her about Carla?"

Larkin shuffled some papers. "I remember Miss Stanner, good looker, dark hair, shoulder length, nice legs. And here's my note on the interview. 'She was kind of quiet, nice girl, just did her job. Didn't see her socially.' That's all I've got."

Danny pulled out the photo of Carla. "Tell me, Frankie, does this woman strike you as a nice, quiet girl who just did her job?"

"She does not."

"And the comment about not seeing her socially sounds a lot like, 'Please don't ask me anything else.'" Danny picked up his hat. "Let's go have a chat with Miss Stanner."

***

It was nearly one o'clock, and the children would be home soon, it being Wednesday and their parochial school just having instituted release time to allow for religious instruction of Catholic children who attended public schools. Ken had been more affected by their mother's death than Mary, who was not only showing signs of growth but also of coming teen rebellion.

"No one will want us," she'd said when they heard the news.

"Not so," he'd assured her. "You'll always have a home here." But she hadn't been convinced.

The visit from the unknown fedora man was more unsettling than the detectives'. It was the second time he'd come around, and he still refused to give Maxwell his name. But worse, he made vague references to Carla's death and mentioned being in expert hands without explanation.

The detectives' questions suggested they thought Maxwell had been responsible for Carla's death, and his denials only appeared to strengthen their suspicions. For one wild moment while they were here, he'd considered telling them about the fedora man and his veiled threats. But the fedora man's warnings, again, mostly implied, terrified him.

He stared out the window. Every time a stranger walked by, or a car drove down the street, his stomach tightened.

What in God's name had Carla gotten herself mixed up in?

***

"Yes, I'm Miss Stanner," she said with a heavy accent. "My real name is Stanislavski, but my father changed it shortly after we arrived from Poland in 1922. Is something wrong?"

"Did you make a reservation for ten people at Joe and Joe Restaurant for New Year's Eve?" Danny asked.

"Yes, why?"

"Did you attend?"

"Yes. Has something…"

"Was Carla Maxwell one of the other nine?"

"Yes."

"When we spoke the other day," Larkin said, "you said you never saw her socially, that she kept to herself."

"That appears not to be true," Danny added.

"No, you don't understand. We got a group together to go. I invited everyone in the office, and Carla accepted. I was surprised. She'd never joined in anything before."

"How did you all get there?" Danny asked.

"We each got there on our own. My fiancé drove us. When anyone from our group got there, they needed to say they were with my party."

"So," Larkin said, "anyone could have come off the street and pretended they were part of your group?"

"No. I gave a list of names to the restaurant."

Danny didn't mention the list he had in his breast pocket. "Did you see Carla arrive?"

"Yes."

"Was she alone?"

No answer.

"Miss Stanner, it's a simple question." Danny's inner alarm was blaring again.

"Yes, she arrived alone."

"But someone picked her up there?" Larkin asked.

"I don't know about…"

Danny shot Larkin a glare. "My partner just means did she stay on her own while she was there or did she mingle with others?"

But Miss Stanner didn't relax. "I'm not sure."

A lie. Danny was certain of it. "I don't believe you. Miss Stanner, has someone threatened you in some way?"

"No!"

Where did that come from? "Then can you explain why you are so upset by these questions? I realize it's difficult to learn of a coworker's death, but we need to uncover the facts if we're to sort this out."

She swallowed hard. "Carla met someone there, yes. A tall, thin man. They seemed to hit it off well together. That's all I know."

Danny backed her into a corner. "No. Miss Stanner, I don't think it is. Did they arrive together?"

"No, she came alone."

"Did they leave together?"

"Yes."

"What time?" Larkin asked.

"I don't know. My fiancé and I left around one-thirty."

"So you don't know if they left together," Larkin said.

"I guess not."

"Unless she told you the following Monday," Danny said. "Did she?"

Miss Stanner was now near tears and could only nod.

"What time did she say they left?" Danny pressed.

"She didn't name a time, only that they left when it closed."

Larkin glanced at Danny. "Probably around three in the morning."

"What else did she tell you?" Danny asked.

"Nothing. She…"

"…told you how wonderful it was." Danny showed his impatience. "Where they went and a hint of what they did, and how much more exciting he was than her drab, accountant husband. Right?"

A tear tracked down her cheek and she nodded.

"Did his missing thumb bother her?" Frankie asked.

She shook her head as she dabbed at the tear with a handkerchief before freezing. "I mean…"

"You don't need to explain," Danny said. "What was his name?"

"I don't know."

Larkin closed in with Danny. "Sure, you do. She wouldn't have kept it a secret."

"Yes. She said she wasn't allowed to repeat it. Something about the work he did."

Danny leaned forward until his nose almost touched hers. "But she told you."

"She made me promise never to repeat it."

"She's dead," Larkin said. "You're free to tell us."

"Or," Danny added, "we'll wonder why you wouldn't."

"She said his name was Nick, but that night I heard others call him Tom."

Danny made a note of it. "You said she wasn't allowed to repeat his name because of the work he did. What kind of work?"

"She didn't say, and when I asked, she said she enjoyed living dangerously, but not that dangerously."

"Has anyone else approached you about this?" Danny asked.

"No."

Danny showed her the list of names from the restaurant's reservations book. "Please check all the names you gave the Joe and Joe Restaurant, with two checks for anyone who isn't a coworker."

She checked ten names, six coworkers and four guests. All the guests were spouses.

"One last question," Danny said. "Was there any mention of stopping at the bakery after work on the day she was murdered?"

"What an odd question. Yes, she did."

"Did she say why?"

She blushed. "It's rather delicate."

"We're not," Larkin said. "So, just tell us. We've already established she gave you some of the more salacious details."

Her blush deepened. "She said that Nick liked turnovers, and she wanted some for the following morning."

"Thank you, Miss Stanner."

Back outside, Larkin said, "Think he killed her because he didn't like buns as much as turnovers?"

"I think whatever Eileen Stanner thought this Nick character does for a living scared the daylights out of her."

***

Meg put down the library copy of *The Robe*. In recent weeks, coffee had upset her stomach and so she had switched to tea, much to Danny's amusement. She gathered herself for the effort to push herself up from the easy chair to put the kettle on, but the seat was slightly wet as she pushed up. She groaned, thinking she'd had an accident.

The first contraction hit, starting from the lower back.

FOURTEEN

Larkin was still shaking his head and chuckling when they returned to the precinct. "They called him Tom. Tom Thumb. Cute."

It was circumstantial, but likely accurate. "Not funny, Frankie. The deeper we dig, the more I…"

Greco was waiting for them. "I was about to contact you by radio. Helen called. Meg's gone into labor and Helen took her to Horace Harding Hospital. Use a radio car for the round-trip. And give Meg my best."

***

Helen, looking every bit the experienced mom, met him in the waiting area. "She's fine, Danny, but they say it will be awhile before the baby comes. Contractions are more frequent but still irregular. I told her you were on your way, and the nurse will tell her you're here."

"Thanks, Helen. You're a good friend."

She patted his arm. "So are you. I have a suggestion for you, though. Go get something to read during the long wait."

Something was still bothering him since their conversation with Miss Stanner. In fact, it had started before that. He spotted a phone booth near the door to the waiting room. "Thanks, but I need to call someone first."

Once he closed the door to the phone booth, he pulled out all the loose change in his pocket, a dollar forty-five. Perfect for a long phone call.

He dialed a number and waited.

"FBI, Agent Cogan."

Bill Cogan, whose family had emigrated from County Kerry after the Civil War, had become a good friend a year earlier, working with Danny on the first case involving inter-departmental cooperation, Meg's serial rapist who'd also committed murder. "Afternoon, Bill. Have a minute?"

"Sure. How's Meg?"

"At the moment, she's in labor and doing fine. Thanks for asking."

"Why are you talking to me on the phone?"

"Since I'm not going anywhere, can we discuss something?" He recapped what he'd learned in the Carla Maxwell case, but nothing about his suspicions.

"Sounds like she was canoodling with someone and one of them broke it off, but the other wasn't having it." When Danny said nothing, Cogan added, "But you don't think that."

"I do not."

"You think it's something larger, more sinister."

Danny waited for Cogan to say it first.

"You think it's connected to racketeers?"

A statement would have been more reassuring than a question, which suggested Cogan had doubts. But that he'd mentioned it at all convinced Danny he wasn't crazy. "Let's just say I'm allowing for the possibility. Someone was providing her with a constant supply of nylon stockings."

"No doubt purchased through the black market."

"To which racketeers would likely have the greatest access. Who are the major operators in the Bronx currently?"

"Have you asked anyone in your department about this?"

A good question. No doubt, now, that they were thinking along the same lines. "No. I didn't want to trigger any speculation."

"Or leaks. Because anyone who's operating rackets up there likely has cops on the pad. Let me look into it. You say this guy was missing a thumb?"

"Left hand."

"Okay. He might have been an enforcer type. It would help if you had a last name."

"I'm not sure about his first name. Tom is obviously a joke, but Nick might not be his real name, either."

"True, but I'll use it as a starting point. I guess you'll be taking the next few days off."

"Assuming Meg gives birth today or tonight, I'll be back to work tomorrow. I'll wait until she comes home from the hospital to take time off."

***

Frank Larkin knew a thing or two, perhaps some things his more illustrious partner didn't. It didn't take a genius to guess where Danny Brady's thinking was going on this case, and for once Frank was going to follow the trail rather than trying to prove it didn't exist. Carla Maxwell had to be getting her nylons from some place, and it wasn't Gold's Department Store up on Jerome Avenue. He struggled to avoid picturing how those nylons would have looked on her legs.

His first step was to meet his old friend, Detective Charlie Lavery, formerly of County Down in Northern Ireland, lately of the 46th Precinct, for coffee.

"Danny called me the other day," Lavery said as he took a seat in the coffee shop on Ogden Avenue. "Mentioned a resurgence of attacks on Jews."

"He wanted me to find patterns, but I couldn't. When I finally got him to look at the reports, he decided he didn't see any, either. Just as well. We have no time for that."

Lavery chuckled. "He's probably got the jumps. Meg must be getting close."

"She's there. Went into labor this morning. Danny dashed off to join her at the hospital."

"Typical. She'll have that dumb jackeen henpecked for sure." He took a sip of coffee. "So, if those attacks are nothing more than the usual schoolboy nonsense, what's eating you to where you needed to seek me out?"

"He and I are working a murder case…"

Lavery smirked. "The bun lady."

Word got around fast. "Yeah. There's evidence the killer was missing his left thumb. Word is his first name was Nick—and, no, we don't know his last name—but friends routinely call him Tom."

Lavery rolled his eyes.

Frank snorted. "Yeah, I know. But if I know Danny, he's thinking there could be mob involvement."

"Because the guy is minus a thumb?"

"There's something weird about this case, including the dame who got killed. It's like pulling teeth to get anyone to talk about her."

Lavery chuckled. "Nobody likes to speak ill of the dead."

"That's what I said. Still, this case reeks, so I'm digging while Danny is tied up in the maternity ward."

"Why call me?"

"As I recall, you were involved in busting up that numbers racket. Any suggestions on where to search?"

Lavery's brow furrowed at the memory. "That was in '38 when I worked the 51st. They ran it out of a grocery store a few blocks down Grand Avenue from the station house in Kingsbridge. The papers had a field day on it. We bagged the peons, figuring they'd blow the whistle on whoever the big shots were, but nobody talked."

Frank lost his flippant humor. "So, whoever the big shot was had these guys in his pocket and completely terrorized."

"Yeah." Lavery stared into his coffee. "Shit, I could really use a dram of Bushmill's right now."

"I could go for a Jameson's, myself." Mentioning the Dublin whiskey in opposition to the Belfast whiskey usually prompted a laugh from Lavery.

But Lavery remained serious. "It's not just the peons that are terrified."

"I don't know what that means."

A humorless laugh. "Sure, you do." Lavery checked for eavesdroppers. "What's the only plausible explanation for a criminal enterprise operating on the same street as a police precinct?"

"Cops on the pad."

Lavery snorted. "Give the man a cigar. That was one fucked up investigation. No one would look anyone else in the eye. I got the hell out of there as soon as I could, before it ended."

Frank's brain was telling him to go slow, but curiosity won out. "Who did you suspect of heading the operation?"

"I never got a name. But I'm certain that someone knew." He looked Frank in the eye. "I know what you're thinking, so I'll save you the trouble. Only cops on the pad know, and they're not just beat cops. It's got to be at least part way up the command structure. Do us all a favor: put Danny off this particular scent."

"If I do, it'll only make him more determined. You know that."

"He has a wife to consider now. And a kid."

Frank did, too, as Helen had been reminding him recently with increasing irritation.

FIFTEEN

Danny finally understood why everyone pictured expectant fathers pacing in the waiting room as he returned to his seat after his third trip to the water cooler.

Helen patted the seat next to her. "Relax. Women have been giving birth for years."

"I know. And next you'll tell me Frankie was as big a basket case when Dorothy was born."

"No, Frankie was Frankie, at least while he was with me." Her smile vanished. "Probably even more jovial when he wasn't. Meg is so lucky she has you. You're a rock, and you'll always be there for her."

"Thanks. Frankie is always there for you, I'm sure." When she said nothing, he added, "I hope there's nothing wrong between you two."

"No, no. Just… Never mind."

"Tell me, Helen." He tried to make a joke. "If you don't, Meg will."

"Meg doesn't know."

"I thought you shared everything with each other."

Helen crossed her legs at the ankles, and Danny noticed that she was wearing saddle shoes and bobby socks the same way Meg often did. But while they were cute on Meg, on Helen, a woman pushing forty, they looked slightly inappropriate. She sighed. "She's been focused on having the baby, so I didn't want to spoil it."

"You won't spoil anything for me. And I'm tough; I can take it."

She sat silent for several moments. "Can I ask you something? This case you're working on. Is there anything unusual about it? Anything special about the victim?"

"Divorced mother of two, remarried, cheating on her new husband, got killed, possibly by the guy she was seeing on the side. Why?"

"Frankie rarely tells me anything about a case, but he hasn't been able to shut up about this one. Was she good looking?"

"That's a matter of taste. To me, no. Definitely not my type."

"What type was she?"

Danny pulled the photo from his jacket pocket. "You tell me."

She studied the photo a long time. "Good looking. But cheap."

Danny snorted. "In a nutshell. But then, I already told you about her."

"No, she has that look about her." She handed the photo back to him. "Confirms my suspicion."

"Which is?"

"Frankie finds her attractive. He's excited by what she was doing outside the home and probably wishes it had been with him."

"Helen, I really don't think…"

"How has he been with the women you've been interviewing?"

"All business. Why?"

"When you tell Meg about the women you interview, do you describe them?"

Danny had to think about it. "Maybe by age—a girl in her twenties, an old lady. If she has a unique characteristic, such as missing an arm or walking with a limp, I might mention it. But mostly, if I describe them at all, it's about their manner—scared, angry, helpful, distraught. Why?"

"Frankie's been telling me about the women you've been interviewing, and always includes something about their hair, how they're dressed, and even if they've used that leg makeup Max Factor has put out, or if they've used an eyebrow pencil to draw a seam on the back of their legs so it looks like they're wearing stockings. He never says if they're attractive, but I can always tell by his descriptions when they are."

"Lots of guys look, Helen. What's the popular saying? Lookie, no touchie?"

"What about you, Danny? Do you look?" When he didn't answer, she said, "I didn't think so."

***

Greco was waiting when Frank returned to the precinct. "No word, yet, from Danny. Anything new on the Maxwell case?"

Frank gestured to Greco's office. They retreated there, and Frank closed the door. "No, nothing. Charlie Lavery and I discussed the anti-Semitic incidents, but he agreed it's unlikely there's anything to it."

"Let Danny know when he gets back, and he can close out the file." After a moment, he added, "Did he ask you to call Lavery?"

"No, I did that on my own."

"I'd have thought you had enough with the Maxwell case to keep you busy."

Decision time. It was wiser to say nothing. "We're marking time on that until Danny gets back. The fingerprint unit found nothing on file for the prints on the handbag and the knife."

"What did her coworkers have to say? Danny mentioned that the husband's story sounded fishy. Did her coworkers reveal anything else to you?"

"The husband's alibi checks out. Her coworkers said very little."

"I'm sure that got Danny's antenna up. What's he thinking?"

So much for decisions. "He doesn't like it." Frank recounted the bit about New Year's Eve.

Greco stared at him. "So, what are you telling me? What doesn't he like?"

"He thinks there could be a rackets angle."

"And what do you think?"

He wouldn't contradict his partner, but this wasn't a ball he wanted to run with. Greco wanted an answer. "I gotta admit, it's a possibility, although I can't see why a mobster would want a hospital worker dead."

"Maybe she knew more than your average hospital office worker should know."

So, Greco was buying this? "I think that's the idea. And Lavery didn't…" He froze.

"Lavery? You told him about this?"

Shit. That slipped out. "Well, yeah. I recall his involvement in that snafu in the 51st precinct years ago. I ran Danny's theory by him to see what he thought of it."

Greco sat back, staring off into space. Not the reaction Frank would have expected, so silence was the best option.

"And what did he think?" Greco asked at last.

In for a penny… "That it was plausible, but that we should step lightly."

"Why?"

"There's a reason he transferred out of the 51st, and it ain't because the gin joints are nicer in the 46th." He waited for a reaction, but there was none. "I guess he was right."

Greco snapped back to the present. "Yes, he was. Please don't discuss this investigation with anyone outside the precinct. Tell Danny to do your best with the leads you've already gotten and don't go looking for bigger fish."

"With all due respect, Lieutenant…"

Greco glared at him. "Something wrong with your hearing, Detective?"

"Not a thing." Danny was going to blow his stack.

SIXTEEN

Meg was groggy but happy. "Did you see him? Isn't he handsome?"

"He is that. Patrick Michael Brady." They had already agreed on the name. "He'll be a fine man."

"He'll go to college. I insist."

He bent over to kiss her again. "Absolutely. Notre Dame, to be sure."

"And he'll play football?" Despite the grogginess, there was a teasing lilt in her voice.

"American football, since Gaelic football isn't played in American colleges." She was having trouble keeping her eyes open, so he added, "You need your sleep. I'll be back tomorrow evening for visiting hours."

"Going home?"

"Not yet. I need to return the patrol car to the precinct." He kissed her one more time. Leaving the hospital, he said a silent prayer of thanks that she was okay, and she was his.

***

He arrived at the precinct after Larkin, McHugh, and Rossi had left. Greco was gone, too. He checked the car back in. Larkin had signed him out when he'd left. Danny stepped towards the door but turned back to his desk instead.

He called Bill Cogan at the FBI.

"I didn't think I'd hear from you tonight," Cogan said. "I understand congratulations are in order."

"Patrick Michael Brady weighed in at seven pounds, eight ounces, and Meg is doing fine." On his way to the Bronx, Danny had rehearsed the spiel. "I'll have a cigar for you when I see you next."

"So, what are you doing on the phone with me? Shouldn't you be out celebrating?"

"I'll wait until Meg can join me. I wondered if you've come up with anything since our chat earlier today."

Cogan recapped the facts Danny had provided. "It sounded to me like either Hubby Number One or Hubby Number Two had good motives."

"Yes, but they also have alibis that check out."

"You're thinking one of them might have hired a killer from the local mobster?"

"Number One couldn't afford it, and Number Two was too broken up about it. It smells to me like the boyfriend might be connected to a racket. Tomorrow morning I'll ask the Fingerprint Unit to send over the prints we got from the victim's handbag. Without some direction, I'll never get off the dime."

"Ooh, Danny Brady utters an Americanism."

"And Bill Cogan is bobbing and weaving rather than answering a direct question. Let's both revert to character, okay?"

"Sorry, I couldn't resist. Racketeering isn't my area of expertise, so I'm afraid I don't have a shortcut for you. But I'll make some inquiries with my contacts and make certain the prints get reviewed. I'll search for something worthwhile and update you within a couple of days. In the meantime, step lightly, Danny."

SEVENTEEN

Thursday, May 20, 1943

As Frank drained the last of his morning coffee and slipped his .38 into his holster, Helen cleared away the rest of the breakfast dishes with more than the usual clatter. Something was wrong.

He could tell because Dorothy hurried off to school, dashing out with hasty goodbyes. He knew he should ask, but if he asked now, he'd be late signing in, and he didn't want to miss Danny's arrival.

Helen slammed a plate onto the counter and broke it.

Uh oh.

"Helen, what's the matter? You seem upset."

"Really? What gave you that idea?"

"The smashed plate was a powerful indicator." As soon as he said it, he was sorry.

She turned on him. "Don't think you can dismiss me with a wisecrack. This is serious."

He sat at the table and gestured for her to join him. "I'm serious. What's the matter? It's obvious I've done something, but I have no idea what, so please tell me."

"You think you can fix this in thirty seconds?"

"I can't fix anything until I know what it is."

"You know what it is. You just won't face it."

This was getting ridiculous. "Helen, I'm sitting here asking you. Please tell me." Despite the late hour, he had to resolve this. He tried a furtive glance at the clock to see how late he was.

She caught it. "Oh, yes. You're late for your oh-so-important work. Go."

"Now, wait a minute…"

"Get out!"

***

"Frankie hasn't come in, yet," McHugh said as Danny walked in. "Congratulations. I heard it was a boy."

Greco's office was dark, so he had no choice but to keep it cheery until at least one of them arrived and he could turn his attention to the Maxwell case.

McHugh accepted a cigar and put it in his pocket for later. "When will the hospital discharge Meg and the baby?"

"Saturday morning, assuming no problems. They tell me she came through like a trooper. How are things on your home front?"

"Neither family is in a rush for the wedding. Rebecca wants to wait a while. She's afraid they'll repeal the exemption for law enforcement from the draft. She's superstitious that way." After a moment, he added, "Have you noticed anything strange about Frankie, lately? He seems distracted."

Danny remembered his talk with Helen. "I've been occupied with my own home front, so I'm not sure."

"Don't blame you for that."

Frankie entered the building, as jovial as ever. "And there's the proud poppa in all his glory."

Danny gave him a cigar, and soon most everyone at the precinct gathered around to offer congratulations and grab a cigar. When they finally dispersed, he pulled Larkin aside and told him about the previous day's conversations with Bill Cogan.

Larkin updated Danny on his conversations with Lavery and Greco. "So, we've still got nothing."

"Lavery and Greco are acting mysteriously and Cogan's playing for time, which is making my nose twitch." Danny caught sight of Rossi walking in and waved him into the empty conference room. "Just the man to see."

"Congratulations," Rossi said. "Am I too late for a cigar?"

"You are. I have one left but I'm saving it for my supervising officer."

"But he ain't in, yet, and I am. How's Meg?"

"Doing fine. Tell you what, Vinnie, if you can answer some questions we've got, I'll risk the anger and disappointment of my supervising officer and give you his cigar."

Rossi laughed. "Sure. Whaddaya need?"

Danny gestured toward the table, and they all sat. "Enlighten me about the Bronx rackets."

Rossi's grin vanished. "What, you think all us guineas hobnob with mobsters?"

"By all the saints in heaven, I do not. But I'll tell you, there I was this morning, shaving and whispering a Hail Mary in thanksgiving for my wife's safe delivery, when a sudden thought struck me like a revelation: Vincent Rossi, a fine detective with many years of dedicated service and encyclopedic knowledge, with numerous contacts, upstanding and otherwise, must surely know something about what goes on in the Bronx, possibly including its less-savory citizens. Why not ask him?"

Larkin shook his head. "You're an evil man, you are, Danny boy." But then he turned to Rossi. "Well, do you?"

Rossi tried not to laugh. "Like what?"

Danny turned serious. "For a start, who runs the show these days?"

"I'm not the one to ask. I haven't worked on a rackets case in years, thank God. There was one guy, Giuseppe Calvino—Gravedigger Joe, they called him—and he was rumored to be the big boss running the rackets in the Bronx, but he fled the country about five years ago, after his operation was taken down. After that, whatever they did, they kept it quiet."

"Wasn't that the racket in the 51st?" Larkin asked.

"Yeah, probably," Rossi replied. "I remember that. The papers made a big deal about it at first, then hushed it up. Charlie Lavery might have information about that since he was assigned there back then. Or maybe he transferred out before it happened, I'm not sure. Ask him and see."

McHugh knocked on the door. "Sorry, guys. Danny, we got a call from the 45th. They got a stiff, washed up on Goose Island."

Danny handed his last cigar to Rossi and grabbed his fedora. "See you later, Vinnie."

EIGHTEEN

"Just drive across the Bronx to the Hutchinson River Parkway," Danny said, "following it to the river."

Larkin lit a cigarette, "You can't get there from here." But there was no humor in it.

Danny cranked down his window. "Ah, but you can, Frankie. Just not in a straight line. Didn't the City Planning Commission announce a plan to build an expressway from the George Washington Bridge across the entire Bronx? A couple of years ago, I think."

Larkin's mood turned dark. "Before the war. We'll probably be long dead by the time it's done. If it ever gets done." He puffed away as Danny stopped for yet another traffic light. "What the hell are we supposed to do once we're there? To get to the island itself, we'd need to swim."

"Or go by boat."

"The land on both sides of the river is swampland. No roadways." Larkin's scowl grew deeper. "I should've worn the waders I use for trout fishing."

Danny cast a sidelong glance at him. "You've got a bit of a puss on this morning."

"It's nothing."

"It's something if you don't mind my saying so. You're usually the one for joking and wisecracks. Are you jaded?"

"Only from this interrogation. Oh, and your route won't work. The northbound Hutch has no exit at the river, and Bartow Avenue on the west side of the bay doesn't extend to the water's edge, so there won't be anyone on that side.

"Then I'll stay on the Hutch until we cross the bay."

Larkin got huffy. "Well, genius, save both time and trouble by turning on Southern Boulevard instead of Westchester Avenue and take it to Pelham Parkway, which you can take to the opposite side where all the police units will be."

"And you're certain of this?"

"Bet you a sawbuck." As Larkin finished his cigarette, he used the dying embers of it to light another.

Larkin's poor betting record against Danny was legendary. "You're on."

***

Robert Maxwell watched Mary and Ken leave for school while looking for the now familiar man in the fedora and glasses. But he was nowhere to be seen, and Robert breathed a little easier.

He had no client appointments, so he could work at his own pace and enjoy this lovely spring day. He relaxed a little more by spending an additional moment imbibing the scent of blossoms, a scent that reminded him of Carla.

She often wore perfume with a similar scent, including the day they'd met. He'd been to the hospital visiting a friend, and she'd plowed into him in the lobby, rushing back from lunch. Almost as tall as he was, she'd flattened him. She'd helped him up and begged his forgiveness.

She'd also taken his breath away. Never had any woman so beautiful spoken to him with such tenderness. "How can I ever make it up to you?"

In a rare bold moment, he'd replied, "Allow me to take you to dinner."

"I'd love to, but I have two young children. I've recently divorced. He beat me and was cruel to the children."

"Bring them along," he'd replied. "I'd love to meet them, too."

She had, and three months later, they'd been married.

A maroon sedan drove past the children as they turned the corner, snapping Robert's attention back to the present. He recognized the driver who passed his house, despite not making eye contact.

There would be no relaxing today.

***

"You forgot about the train tracks, Frankie." They were on Pelham Parkway, approaching the Hutchinson River crossing, when Danny glimpsed the top of the railroad bridge. "The line runs right through the park."

An officer waved them over near a parked radio car on the road shoulder. "You the homicide guys?"

"We are," Danny replied. "How do we cross to Goose Island?"

"There ain't no easy way. The Coroner's office is trying to get a boat to bring the body over. They got a couple of guys over there, now, with the crime scene guys. Hardly enough room for 'em on that pile of rocks." He turned toward the island. "Here comes a boat, now. Best bet is park here on the shoulder and cross the road to the shoreline."

Danny turned to Larkin while waiting for traffic to pass. "You were right concerning the route, wrong about the location. Shall we call it even?"

"Are you that tight for money?" But his face was hard, not a ray of humor in it. "The bet was about the route."

"Relax, Frankie, I was having you on, is all."

The small motorboat nudged up onto the rim of sand at the water's edge, and they both climbed in. As they pulled out and turned upriver, passing under the railroad bridge, Danny was tempted to ask Larkin again what was bothering him, but decided against it.

"Goose Island is nothing more than a collection of rocks with dirt and vegetation filled in," the officer manning the boat said. "There's no beach, and the water around the island is pretty deep. You'll need to step directly from the boat onto the rocks. I'd say your shoes, and possibly your trousers are in for a bad time."

"We'll live," Danny replied. At least he hadn't worn one of his suits. He preferred risking his shoes to jumping into the freezing water.

Someone from the Medical Examiner's office waved him over to where several men were clustered around a dead body, a male in his thirties, wearing a bright red jacket. "We found him laying just as he is now. Fatal gunshot to the back of the head."

"So, not self-administered." Larkin said.

"Unless he had an incredibly flexible neck."

Danny noticed another wound a few inches from the gunshot. "What's that?"

"Looks like he hit it pretty hard against a sharp corner of some kind."

Before he was shot, there was probably a struggle. "He's lying on his side."

"Yeah, he probably was killed elsewhere and dumped here. He's dead ten to twelve hours and was never in the water. A fisherman was headed upriver, saw him, and radioed the coast guard. They called us."

"Why would a fisherman sail upriver?" Larkin asked. "It's all industrial. Decent fishing is in the bay."

Danny glanced around. "Inconvenient place to leave a body. Did we get the name of the guy who called it in?"

"Yeah, they have it at the 45th." He made a vague gesture around. "There are easier ways to dispose of a body than sticking it on a boat and taking it to an island in the middle of the river."

There were, indeed. "Any ID on the guy?"

"Nothing. The fingerprint guys took a set. I told them to contact you if they got a match on anything. Oh, that reminds me, there is one very unusual detail about this guy."

"Let me guess," Danny said. "He's missing his left thumb. Does he also have a bent nose?"

***

He overheard a casual remark which took a moment to register before it rang a bell. Although Detective Charlie Lavery had learned during his time in the 51st Precinct to ignore certain potentially dangerous comments, this one remained.

Tom Thumb.

He'd heard it during a return visit to the 51st Precinct to check an old case file. But he recalled his conversation with Frankie Larkin, and his promise to listen for anything that would shed light on the murder of a floozy by a guy with a missing thumb. Dan Brady suspected mobster involvement.

Now, Charlie Lavery did, too.

When he'd transferred out of the 51st back in the summer of '38, he'd hoped to escape the clutches of the rackets. He'd known, just as everyone in the 51st knew, of the increasingly brazen exploits of Gravedigger Joe. Charlie had never taken a cent, but he'd known enough to avoid assignments where bribes might be offered. He'd even begged off a stakeout of Calvino's home, claiming he had the flu. Two days later, he'd filed for a transfer to the 46th.

Although he'd complained about being drafted to assist Dan Brady on the string of anti-Jewish crimes, he'd welcomed the chance to shine in the light of the commissioner's boy, as Danny was called in certain corners. Anything to wash away the stench of the 51st.

He hadn't counted on the commissioner's boy catching a case connected with mobsters, or Frankie Larkin recalling Charlie's past. Danny and Frankie needed help that Charlie could provide, and there was no avoiding it.

He needed to act without risking his own safety, or his wife's and children's.

One name occurred to him, someone much closer to the rackets than Charlie.

***

Danny gave Larkin a five-dollar bill as soon as they got back to the car.

Larkin took it with a sheepish grin. "Sorry I blew my stack."

"Apology accepted. Now, maybe you'll tell me what's bothering you. And don't say that nothing is."

Larkin lit a cigarette. "It's not something you can help resolve."

"Good, then I won't be responsible. But we've got to pull our boots up on this case, and you require a clear head for that."

A long silence. "It's Helen. Lately, she's giving out with all these hints that she thinks I'm running around."

"Are you?"

"Aw, come off it, Danny. You know me, look but don't touch."

"Maybe Helen's getting nervous that looking might lead to more."

Larkin gave him a long, appraising look. "You're giving me marital advice, now?"

"No, just making an observation. Have you talked to her about this case?"

"Sure. If I don't, Meg will. But Helen only focuses on my comments about women. She thinks Carla Maxwell may have whet my appetite for loose women."

"You do go on about her, sometimes, Frankie."

No answer.

"So, it appears our killer is dead," Larkin said at last. "Where the hell does that leave us?"

"With another killer to track, one who went to great lengths to leave the body where it was easy to find and difficult to reach." When Larkin said nothing, Danny added, "almost like someone was sending a message. Question is, a message for whom?"

"Damned if I know."

But Danny knew where to turn.

NINETEEN

"God damn it, Danny," Cogan said when he and Larkin walked in unannounced, "I told you to give me some time."

Danny sat down and replied as pleasantly as if Cogan had wished him a happy St. Paddy's Day. "Frankie and I have stumbled across some additional information which we thought you might find helpful." He handed Cogan the reservation list and explained the check marks. "Among the unchecked, there are two Toms and one Nick, but I suspect if our guy is on the list at all, it's under a different name. I need you to check out all of them."

"There must be a hundred names here."

"A hundred and eight," Larkin replied, as if being helpful.

Danny fought to keep a grin off his face and explained what the check marks meant. "And one other little detail we thought you'd like to know. Nick, or Tom, or whatever his name is, was found dead on a little islet in the Hutchinson River this morning, one gunshot wound to the head."

"At least we think it's him," Larkin added, "because he was missing his left thumb and fit the description, including a bent nose. But you never know."

"We're not expecting you to have everything we need," Danny said, "but this whole thing reeks."

Cogan studied the list. "Nothing rings a bell. Let me investigate and see if I can find anything. Who discovered the body?"

Danny told him about the fisherman. "We'll be talking to him next. It made no sense to Frankie that a fishing boat was heading upriver.

"I agree," Cogan replied.

"One other thing," Danny said. "When I initially asked you about racketeering in the Bronx, you mentioned cops being on the pad."

Cogan held up a hand. "If we had any information regarding rackets in the Bronx. The point was to warn you to step lightly."

"Which you wouldn't have done if you didn't think I was approaching a land mine. Frankie did some digging. Turns out there was something going five years ago, when Giuseppe Calvino was running things, including a bookmaking racket right under the noses of the 51st Precinct."

"Gravedigger Joe," Cogan said. "He fled the country shortly before the bust. Back to Sicily, I believe."

Larkin snorted. "Tipped off, no doubt."

"Very likely," Cogan replied.

Good. The chess game was over. "Why did he flee if the cops were on the pad? And why then?"

"His racket being busted indicates there were enough who weren't being paid off." Larkin pulled a Lucky Strike from his pack and offered one to Cogan.

The agent accepted the cigarette. "Thanks, Frank. And you're right, but it goes deeper than that. Calvino had some connection with Anthony Anastasio, also known as Tough Tony, who runs the Brooklyn docks."

Danny stopped him. "Can we slow down a moment? We're talking about the Bronx."

Cogan leaned forward and lowered his voice. "Ever hear the term 'the Combination' referring to the rackets?"

"No," Danny replied. "What's it supposed to mean?"

"There is a theory that all the rackets, from the waterfront to prostitution rings in Manhattan, numbers games in Queens, and bookmaking in the Bronx, are ultimately run by an exclusive group."

"How small?" Larkin asked.

"No one knows for certain. There are a lot of variables to consider, like geography, the nature of the criminal activity, and the flow of money."

"You mean to cops on the pad?" Larkin asked.

"No," Cogan replied. "That's just a tiny piece of the puzzle. I'm talking about the flow of money from the street up through the levels of organization to the ultimate bosses."

"Sounds more like US Steel than a crime organization," Larkin said with a chuckle. "How could something like that be kept a secret?"

But Cogan remained dead serious. "That's why officially, no one accepts the theory."

Danny jumped in. "What about unofficially?"

Cogan glanced at the door, as if he was sorry he hadn't closed it. "The director doesn't want to hear about it, and my boss is skeptical, asking questions like the ones you just asked, although recent events have left him more open to the possibility."

"What recent events?" Danny asked.

"You've heard of Murder, Incorporated?"

"Sure," Larkin said. "Who hasn't? A bunch of Guineas and Jews in Brooklyn who hired themselves out as killers back in the thirties. Didn't they break up two years ago when a bunch of them were convicted?"

Cogan hesitated, then stood and closed the door after glancing around for anyone watching or listening. When he returned to his desk, he took a deep breath. "Murder, Incorporated was run by Tough Tony's brother, Albert Anastasia."

"Wait," Danny said. "Isn't Tough Tony's last name Anastasio?" Emphasizing the oh.

"It is, and Albert's given name is Humberto. For some reason, when he Americanized it to Albert, he changed the last letter on his last name. They have multiple differences. Tough Tony fancies himself a swell. Likes expensive suits with broad double-breasted jackets, and silk shirts with white ties. Very dapper. Those who buy into the Combination theory suspect that Murder, Incorporated was their enforcement arm. Since Tough Tony runs the Brooklyn docks, he works hand-in-glove with Anastasia. Word is that anytime he wants to intimidate anyone, he mentions 'my brother, Albert'."

"In Brooklyn," Danny said.

Cogan sat back, his frustration apparent. "Fellas, you need to stop thinking in terms of Brooklyn and the Bronx being separate. To the Combination, they're just different branches of the same business."

"If the Combination exists," Larkin said.

"It exists, all right," Cogan replied. "And Anastasia's enforcement crew still exists, even if the newspapers have retired the title, Murder, Incorporated."

Danny waved for Cogan to slow down. "I don't understand why Anastasia didn't get sent up the same time the others did."

"I'll spell it for you," Cogan replied. "The case against Anastasia involved the murder in 1937 of a union reformer named Peter Panto, for which other members of Murder, Incorporated were convicted. The DA's star witness was a guy by the name of Abe Reles, also known as Kid Twist. He gave lots of evidence on the others, but before he could detail Anastasia's role in it, he took a header off a sixth-floor balcony of the Half Moon Hotel in Coney Island."

"Suicide?" Danny asked.

"That's what it was ruled," Cogan replied, "absent direct evidence to the contrary."

"But why wasn't he being protected?" Danny struggled to keep his voice low.

Cogan's answer came out as a growl. "He was."

Larkin shook his head. "Jesus, Mary and Joseph."

"I'm understanding your insistence on secrecy about this stuff," Danny said. "But I'm still not seeing the link between Bronx rackets and Anastasia's thugs on the Brooklyn docks."

"The entire New York waterfront, and, for that matter, the docks in every city on the East Coast, is controlled by the ILA—the International Longshoreman's Association—which supposedly protects the longshoremen by negotiating contracts with the ship lines. In practice, the ILA controls all the hiring, which is supposedly done daily, depending on what ships are arriving or departing."

"What do you mean, supposedly?" Danny asked.

"Each dock or group of docks has its own local, and each local is dominated by a gang of toughs who run the rackets. Tough Tony runs six locals on the Brooklyn waterfront, and when Peter Panto became too troublesome, he turned to Anastasia to take care of it."

"So, where's the connection to the Bronx rackets?" Larkin asked.

"Some illegal activities on the waterfront, such as the numbers game, are also found in other parts of the city. The newspapers act like Murder, Incorporated is gone, but Anastasia still has his men, and their activities likely extend beyond the docks, along with the other rackets. That's why the theory of a Combination is viable, with Anastasia the head of its enforcement arm. Giuseppe Calvino's Bronx operation may have been conceived on the docks, and that suggests there is a line to be drawn from the docks to local rackets."

"I can't believe this system is allowed to exist," Larkin said. "Even with cops on the pad."

"When Bill O'Dwyer became the Brooklyn DA," Cogan said, "he made solving the murder of Peter Panto a priority. But waterfront cases are almost impossible to solve because there are rarely any witnesses. The men are knowledgeable about the rackets and the under-reported murders, including Panto's. They are terrorized into silence."

"Isn't O'Dwyer in the army now?" Larkin asked.

"Yes," Cogan replied. "Took a leave of absence from being the DA. The army made him a general. Anastasia's in the army, too. Enlisted last year to gain US citizenship."

Danny saw it. "So, with Reles dead and O'Dwyer out of the picture for the duration, Anastasia had nothing to worry about. And now he's in uniform, pretending to be a loyal American soldier. Meanwhile, Calvino's racket in the Bronx had long since been busted and he'd returned to the old country."

Cogan spread his arms. "His connection to Anastasio remains a mystery to us. All we know is Calvino was involved in union work on the part of Brooklyn waterfront managed by Anastasio back in the twenties."

Danny's sole concern right now was the Bronx. "So, someone replaced Calvino because someone always does. Charlie Lavery—you remember, he helped with the Bronx burglaries last year—was in the 51st when they moved on Calvino. Disliking what he saw, he transferred out."

"He told me he didn't know what was going on at the time and was determined not to find out," Larkin added.

Cogan's eyes met Danny's. "And we can assume that if he was so intent on not knowing, he already knew something." He handed a sheet of paper to Danny. "A colleague of mine in our Organized Narcotics Division sent me that. They think a guy named Armand Lombardo is running the Bronx rackets these days. He also has some connection with Tough Tony, maybe from the Brooklyn waterfront, but he keeps a low profile."

"Wait," Larkin said. "What does any of this have to do with narcotics?"

"Longshoremen have easier access to vessels than anyone, so the union bosses press them into service to unload illegal narcotics and get them onto trucks before they can be detected. If the workers resist, they don't get assigned to work gangs and don't get to work. But if they get maimed on the job, they're usually left on their own. Sometimes the union will take up a collection for the injured worker, but his family sees little of the money, if any."

"A fella can lose a thumb on the waterfront," Danny said.

"And arms and legs," Cogan replied. "Let's not get ahead of ourselves. First, we have nothing solid on Lombardo, other than the fact that he's dropped out of sight in Brooklyn and there's been a vacuum of mob leadership in the Bronx. I'm guessing Detective Lavery may be able to give you more than he already has. Tell you what: I'll pass on everything I get when I get it, you pass on anything you learn. We want to keep current on these guys."

"What involvement does your narcotics division have?" Larkin asked.

"Mr. Hoover doesn't want to hear it, but the narcotics boys think that the guys running the rackets may also run the drug trade," Cogan replied. "Why wouldn't they? They already have the apparatus up and running for large-scale operations."

"What about your boss?" Danny asked.

"He never expresses an opinion contrary to Mr. Hoover's unless he knows he's on very firm ground. I may have someone else for you to speak with, but I need to look into it, first. Call me at the end of your shift, today, and I'll let you know."

After leaving Cogan's office, Danny called the Joe and Joe Restaurant and spoke to the fellow who'd provided the reservation list, asking if everyone who showed up for the party on New Year's Eve had to give a name, and if they'd turned away anyone who wasn't on the list. The answer was that they'd stopped checking once things got hopping.

Just as Danny had feared. "Time to talk to Lavery again."

TWENTY

Lavery placed his coffee cup back on its saucer with exaggerated care. Then he turned and glanced around the coffee shop, making sure no one was in any of the other booths or otherwise within earshot. "Frankie, I thought I said to forget it."

Larkin nodded toward Danny. "And I told you he wouldn't."

Danny took charge. "We're not after cops on the pad. That's someone else's headache. We're after a stone-cold killer."

"He's dead, for Christ's sake." Lavery spat the words in a harsh whisper.

"I'm not talking about Tom Thumb. I'm talking about whoever killed him, and whoever ordered him killed." Danny didn't wait for a reaction. "What do you know about a guy named Armand Lombardo?"

"Never heard of him." Lavery's expression suggested he was baffled. "Who's he supposed to be?"

Seeing Larkin about to reply, Danny beat him to it. "Just a name we came across, a possible replacement for Giuseppe Calvino."

Lavery failed to hide the look of recognition.

"I think I hit the bullseye, Frankie."

"Well," Lavery replied, "forget it, Danny. This leads nowhere good, I can tell you. It's a map you don't want to get on. Think of your family…"

Danny held up a hand. "Stop right there. My family is my worry. If you know something, tell me now. No one would associate you with anything since you left the 51st five years ago."

"Anything I could tell you would be second hand, and mostly speculation. And your natural response would be to ask where I got it. True?"

Danny fought the impulse to deny it. Lavery wasn't a criminal. "Probably, yes."

Lavery stood. "So, let's not kid each other. You know I won't point the finger at another cop. You don't even know the name of the dead guy."

"But someone does," Danny replied. "And I'd wager that half the cops in the 51st could tell you based on his description."

"Less than half." Lavery winced immediately.

Danny pointed to the seat Lavery had vacated and waited until he took it before continuing. "Just get me his name. Then I can go back to Bill Cogan for additional leads."

"And the moment you do, Cogan will tell your lieutenant who will ask you where you got it."

"Cogan's the one who told me to step lightly."

"What about Greco?" Lavery asked. "He'll surely want to know. Ya see, Danny, you tell three people, swearing 'em to secrecy, and then they each tell three people, swearing *them* to secrecy, and the next thing you know it's on the front page of the *Daily News*."

"He's got a point, Danny boy," Larkin said. "If he gives you the name, you can't be telling Greco."

Danny thought it over.

"If you can give me your word that you won't tell anyone other than Cogan," Lavery said, "I'll see what I can do to get you the name."

But Greco would eventually find out. And he'd be furious.

"You've got my word," Danny said at last.

***

Larkin didn't say a word as Danny drove back to the precinct. An overturned horse cart in the middle of West Tremont Avenue caused a minor traffic snarl.

"You thought I wouldn't agree to not tell Greco." Danny didn't make it a question.

"No, I knew you'd agree. And I know that when you tell Cogan—assuming Charlie comes back with a name—you won't tell him where you got it."

"Oh, Charlie will give us a name. For all I know, he might already have it. Or at least suspect it. But I have to let him decide in his own time. Meanwhile, we need to be getting over to the coroner's office and see what we can find out about our John Doe."

Larkin lapsed back into silence.

"Frankie, talk to Helen and sort things out."

"I'm working on it."

"No, you're not. Ye can't think that some glib denials and a Hail Mary will make it disappear. Take time off, spend time with her, and reach an understanding."

A humorless laugh. "Danny Brady, married a scant nine months, and giving out with marital advice. Tell me, then, me bucko, if I take off, who watches your back? Vinnie Rossi? Young McHugh? It'll all come to no good."

Danny finally pulled around the fallen cart. "If you're trying to tell me something, you're making a bags of it."

"You must do something you once agreed not to do, and then stick to it."

"You mean not telling Greco."

"I do not." Larkin hesitated, and when he continued, it was in a softer voice. "I mean you can't tell Meg. You can't reveal anything more about this case than you already have. I know you have an agreement with her, and I'll even agree it's a good way to go. But in this case, it could get her, your son, and several other people killed. Whoever this new guy is, he's replaced a guy they called Gravedigger Joe, and it wasn't because his first job was at a cemetery. These bastards don't play, and you need to know that."

"I can't lie to her, Frankie."

"Maybe. But you don't dare tell her the truth."

TWENTY-ONE

After Larkin had left for the day, Danny received confirmation from the coroner that John Doe's cause of death was a single gunshot wound to the left side of the head. The weapon, a .45, was fired at point blank range, and another wound to his scalp and several bruises on his arms and around the rib area suggested there had been a struggle.

A call to the Coast Guard had yielded the call letters of the fisherman who had called in the body sighting on Goose Island. Additional digging had provided the boater's name and an address on City Island.

Before leaving, he called Cogan. "Any luck?"

"Yeah. Curt Ramsay is an ADA in the Brooklyn DA's office. He was involved to some degree in the Panto case and he has rather extensive knowledge of the waterfront rackets."

Danny wrote the number Cogan gave him. "Can I mention your name to him?"

"Yes, but make sure he understands my office is not involved in this investigation."

"But you are."

"Only unofficially," Cogan replied. "When O'Dwyer went into the army, Thomas Hughes stepped up to take his place. We don't know where Hughes stands on this stuff."

"And you don't want to risk someone from Hughes' office dropping a nickel on Tom Donegan." Donegan was head of the FBI's New York office, Cogan's boss.

"Correct. One thing more. Don't mention Ramsay's name to anyone, or say that I gave you a contact with the Brooklyn DA."

***

As Danny drove over to Horace Harding Hospital to see Meg, he tried to determine how he could stop giving her information without losing her trust. By the time he parked the car, he still hadn't decided.

It was still visiting hours, so he was glad to be able to keep the conversation light. But the echoes of both Lavery and Larkin haunted him.

Think of your family.

You can't tell Meg.

This leads nowhere good.

Think of your family.

"Hey," Meg said, "is everything okay? You seem kind of distant, like you have something on your mind."

He tried to shake it off. "Just a long day. How's little Paddy doing?"

She laughed, as he'd known she would. "We agreed not to call him that. It's either Pat or Patrick. And he's doing fine. We both come home tomorrow. I hope that fits with your schedule."

"And if it didn't, I'd make it fit." He bent down to kiss her goodbye, relieved she hadn't asked about the case. "I'll be here at nine." He kissed her again.

She grinned at him. "You can fill me in on the case when we get home."

***

Frank Larkin parked in the driveway of the house on Lincoln Road and killed the engine. Although it was still light out, the windows were lit with lamplight. Frank shuddered, anticipating an unpleasant greeting.

"Home on time, for once," Helen said as he entered.

"I'm home on time whenever possible." He was immediately sorry.

"You mean when there are no attractive females to interview."

He fought the overwhelming temptation to pour himself a Jameson's, understanding it would be a grave error. "Most people I interview are not attractive females. Most of them are just ordinary people."

"You wouldn't know it from the way you describe them."

"I'm sorry, Helen. I only described them that way because I thought you'd be interested."

"Why on Earth would I be interested in the objects of your lust?"

"I don't lust after them. I was just describing them. You wanted to know more details about my work, so I was providing them."

"You know damned well those aren't the details I wanted. I was concerned about you, about your safety. I needed to know how close to widowhood I was coming."

Where the hell did that come from? "Well, let me set your mind to rest. You are nowhere near widowed and not likely ever to be. The city currently has a lower crime rate than it did before the war."

"If that's the case, why are you investing so much time interviewing other women?"

"The victim was a woman who worked in an office with other women, and she had women as neighbors, and Danny and I had to interview them. That's all."

She stared at him. "You're holding something back."

Yes, he was. But he wasn't about to tell her. "No, not a thing. Honest to God."

She turned back to the stove, where dinner was cooking, giving no sign she believed him.

TWENTY-TWO

Friday, May 21, 1943
"Admiral Isoroku Yamamoto, Commander-in-Chief of the Combined Japanese Fleet, who reportedly had boasted he would dictate peace terms to the United States from a seat in the White House, was killed in April, according to Japanese Imperial Headquarters in a communique broadcast domestically this morning by Tokyo. The announcement stated the admiral had been killed while engaged in combat. Admiral Mineichi Koga, formerly commander of Japanese fleet units in Chinese waters, has been appointed as Yamamoto's successor and is already in command."

***

The ringing phone woke Danny out of a sound sleep. Daylight was visible beyond the bedroom window. The clock showed five minutes after six.

It was Lavery. "All right, I found someone who might be able to help, if you can tolerate his conditions."

"Such as?"

"He's a detective in the 51st who can provide some information, but he's very concerned about his safety."

"Is he on the pad?"

"Jesus, Mary, and Joseph, Danny. What the hell…"

"Just give it to me straight, and with a minimum of shite. I'm picking up Meg and the baby at the hospital in a couple of hours."

"Okay, okay. His name is Declan Fagan, and he's certain he knows some of what you're looking for. He hasn't told me because I still don't want to know. But he's desperate to get out from under this mess and thinks your FBI connections might help him and his family get out of range."

"Well, if you insist on staying out of this, how am I supposed to get his information?"

"He wants to meet this afternoon at 1:30 at a bar on Webster Avenue, east side of the street, just south of 197th Street. Corner table in the back." He gave the address and then the line went dead.

So much for spending the day with Meg.

And he couldn't put off telling her any longer.

***

Meg couldn't help laughing at Danny's stunned expression as the nurse thrust little Patrick into his arms at the door of the hospital with a breezy, "Good luck!"

Danny looked terrified as he clutched the infant while Meg slid into the passenger seat, an expression that instantly changed to one of relief as she took the baby back in her arms.

She waited until he was in the driver's seat. "Okay, honey, you can breathe, now."

Why wasn't he laughing?

"I'm fine, and I'll have you home in no time."

Still no smile. "What's the matter?"

"Nothing. I told you, I'm fine."

"Not with that tone of voice, you're not." No reaction. "Danny, this is supposed to be one of our happiest days. We're bringing our first child home from the hospital. So, whatever it is, can you please tell me now so we can get it out of the way and enjoy the rest of the day?"

"I have to go in, today, to interview a witness in this murder case."

Relief. "Okay. What time are you leaving?"

"I'm scheduled to meet him at 1:30 near Fordham University."

"Well, at least you can spend a couple of hours with Patrick and me before you go. Are you coming right home afterward?"

"I don't know. I'll try. Will you be okay?"

"I'll be fine. I can always call my mom or my sister if it gets to be too much."

There was no missing the concern in her voice as he turned off Queens Boulevard, and he didn't say another word until he was parked in front of their apartment. He rushed around to open the door for her, then took Patrick in his arms while she lifted herself out of the car. As soon as she took Patrick back, he turned on his heels and quick-marched to the door.

Patrick stirred and started to cry as they entered the apartment. Danny watched as Meg warmed a bottle of formula and then showed him the correct way to hold both the baby and the bottle. He said nothing, giving only a tight nod of understanding.

She placed a clean diaper on her shoulder and began burping Patrick. "Just a light patting of his back. Sometimes, he spits up a little, but it's nothing to worry about."

Another tight nod.

She laughed, even as her concern deepened. "Okay, if you don't want to talk parenthood, why not tell me how the murder case is going. You haven't talked about it at all lately, and you know I like to know everything."

"What do you do after he burps?"

Not what she was expecting him to say. "I'll put him down for a nap. It will be awhile before he does anything but eat, poop, and sleep."

No response.

She laid Patrick, already asleep on her shoulder, in the bassinet they'd placed in the living room as Danny watched. Satisfied, she turned back to Danny. "So, who is this witness and why is it so important you meet with him today?"

"I can't tell you that."

The words struck her with physical force, softened only by his pained expression. And something else. She'd seen him angry, frustrated, determined, disgusted… but she'd never seen in him what she was certain she saw now: anxiety. "Danny, you promised me a year ago you'd always tell me, that you'd never keep me in the dark and make me worry."

"I know. But this case is unique."

"Are you in danger? I mean, any more than you usually are?" When he didn't answer, she said in a harsh whisper, so as not to awaken Patrick, "Don't put me through this, Danny. You promised."

He gestured to the couch, and they sat together. "It's not the danger to me that concerns me. To a degree, I'm almost always at some level of risk. But if I tell you, I put you in danger, and I can't bear to do that."

She thought she might cry, but the tears wouldn't come. "You can't leave it like that. What have you done? How can you be placing me in danger?"

"Because once you know, you'll turn around and tell Helen, and she'll tell Yolanda, Vinnie Rossi's wife, and perhaps Rebecca Stoneman. And who knows who will hear about it afterwards? You said yourself, wives need to know. And I can't allow that to happen. Not on this case."

"Why not?" She watched as his internal struggle continued to rage.

When he finally spoke, it was in a near whisper. "If I tell you, you must promise never to say anything at all to another soul. Not to Helen or Rebecca, not to your sister or your parents, not to the priests at St. Sebastian's. Not a single soul. Ever."

"I can't tell Helen? Isn't Frankie in the same danger you are? Doesn't she deserve to know?"

"He is, and she does, but it's up to him to tell her."

"But he won't. He never has. Helen is my closest friend."

He took her hands in his. It both reassured her and frightened her. "I know he won't. But you can't, and you must promise me you won't."

"But why?"

"Once I tell you, you'll understand."

"All right, I promise. Not a word to anyone. Ever."

After he laid out what he suspected about Carla Maxwell's death and what he'd learned from Bill Cogan, she said nothing except, "Hold me."

TWENTY-THREE

"So, Meg and the baby are fine?"

Larkin's question, delivered with his usual breezy tone, unnerved Danny. "They are. Meg gave me my first lesson in baby care."

"Don't tell me she's got you changing diapers!"

"Not yet. You know this fella, Fagan?"

"Met him once, as I recall. Thin, almost gaunt. Family hails from Belfast."

"He'll be a Bushmills man, then." Danny found a parking space on Webster Avenue. It was exactly 1:30 when they entered the tavern. Danny and Larkin each took a stool at the empty bar.

Danny, noting the bar had Eichler on tap, ordered a beer; Larkin did, too. As the bartender drew the beers, Danny glanced around and spied a solitary figure at the corner table in the back. He dropped a dollar bill on the bar, and they joined the bar's only other customer.

"I believe you know a friend of ours," Danny said. When Fagan nodded, Danny introduced Larkin.

"I can help you with at least some of what you need. Charlie claimed you would be able to help me get out of this mess."

"I told him I'd talk to someone I know at the FBI. I can't guarantee anything except for putting you in protective custody if you…"

"Fuck protective custody. Didn't do nothing for Abe Reles. I ain't ending up like him. Not gonna wind up a dead witness."

"We're not exactly from the commissioner's office," Larkin said.

Fagan glared at Danny. "Around these parts, you are known as the commissioner's boy."

Danny had no time for this. "What do you want?"

"I want out. No mention of my name anywhere in this case, nothing in your private notes, nothing to suggest I ever even met you guys. Twenty years from now, when I apply for my pension, I'll worry about the formalities. I have a Pennsylvania property, but I won't reveal its whereabouts. Bought it under an assumed name and I'm not leaving a forwarding address. No trace, you understand?"

"Fine with me," Danny replied. "I'll not reveal your name to the FBI or anyone else. In my notes, you'll just be Mr. X, no mention of where you worked or where we met. Fair enough?"

"Okay. The guy who bumped off the bun lady is Nick Gervin."

"Wow," Larkin said. "So, Nick was his real name."

"What of it?"

"Nothing," Danny said. "Apparently, he revealed it to Carla Maxwell. Or, at least, his real first name."

"Yeah, he really had it bad for her. That's what got him into trouble. He told her all kinds of things he shoulda kept to himself."

"Did you know him, personally?" Danny asked.

Fagan hesitated. "You gotta promise I stay outta this. You mention my name to nobody. And I skate on anything illegal I mighta done."

A promise Danny knew he had no authority to make, so he risked becoming an accomplice to whatever Fagan had done if he made it.

***

As soon as the phone rang, Meg knew it would be Helen. She was tempted to ignore it, but Helen would worry and drive over to make sure everything was okay, meaning Meg would have to do her first dissembling face to face.

Meg couldn't risk it. She answered on the fourth ring.

"I hope I didn't get you from anything." Helen's voice lacked her usual cheery tone.

"No, Patrick's asleep and I was dozing." The fib came easily.

"I thought about stopping by, but maybe you're not in the mood for company today."

"Thanks, but I'm fine. It's good to be home."

"At least you have Danny to keep you company."

Decision time. Frankie would probably tell Helen that Danny had gone in, so Meg said it, first. "I did, but he had to go in. Something about getting a report. He promised not to be late."

"Wow. That's not like Danny."

Meg forced a laugh. "He's still trying to balance being a cop with being a new dad."

***

"Armand Lombardo moved in on the Bronx rackets after Gravedigger Joe took off," Fagan said. "He originally worked on the Brooklyn waterfront. He rose to running shape-ups, then graduated to running some rackets on the side."

"What the hell are shape-ups?" Danny asked.

"Twice each day, all the longshoremen looking for work gather on piers, and a hiring boss, a union official, picks out who works on each pier based on how many ships need to be loaded or unloaded. With an excess of men and limited job openings, the system is plagued by rackets."

Danny remembered Cogan saying the ILA controlled all the hiring. "What kinds of rackets?"

Fagan snorted. "You name it: theft, kickbacks from the members in return for work assignments, numbers games—they call them policy lotteries—and loan-sharking of members who can't afford the lotteries… Sometimes they're forced to buy wine grapes regardless of whether they make wine. Some are told what barbers to frequent for haircuts, at exorbitant prices. Getting in good with the boss is the only way to be selected in the shape-up. Promise to kickback part of your pay, pay an outright bribe, play the policy lotteries, buy tickets to the annual ball…"

Larkin broke in. "How's a guy supposed to do that if he can't get work?"

"Easy. Take out a loan from the friendly loan shark. And that 'annual ball' isn't always a union function, although Joe Ryan's Foundation throws quite a wing-ding. But sometimes it's for the Brooklyn Democratic Club, held at the Hotel St. George." Fagan waited for recognition to dawn, which didn't take long. "That's right. The politicians play ball with these guys because they want union support come election time. You need to remember that, Danny, because if Lombardo doesn't stop you, the politicians probably will."

Danny tried to ignore the sinking sensation in the pit of his stomach. "How did Lombardo move from Brooklyn to the Bronx?"

"When Gravedigger Joe took off, Lombardo sold Anastasio on the idea of replacing him, no doubt figuring running the rackets away from the waterfront would be less of a bare-knuckles proposition."

"And Anastasio was okay with it?" Danny asked.

"Sure. Lombardo was in good with Anastasio, always buying a ticket to the Democratic Club dinner I mentioned and always getting seated at a prime table. Anytime his guys came across someone looking to do some stevedoring, they'd funnel them to the Brooklyn docks. Anastasio would occasionally return the favor, providing Lombardo with muscle guys who'd gotten a little maimed on the docks. That's how Gervin came to be working for Lombardo. He'd gotten his left hand slammed by a load of lead ingots in the hold of a freighter and lost his thumb. Anastasio didn't trust him as a dockside enforcer, so he sent him up here."

"What didn't he like about Gervin?" Danny asked.

"His mouth, for one, and a brain that didn't know when to keep it shut."

"And how do you know all this?" Danny had to know how it all fit together.

Fagan stared at him. "We have a deal?"

Despite his certainty that he was making a deal with the devil, Danny nodded.

"I worked for Gravedigger Joe in his day, and I work for Lombardo, now. He had me shadow Gervin and report back anytime he strayed from the straight and narrow. See, Lombardo was sure Anastasio had stuck him with a bad egg, probably as a favor to his brother…"

"Because Anastasia handled the rough side of Anastasio's operation before he enlisted," Larkin said.

"Yeah," Fagan replied, "although there may have been more to it. I don't know. Lombardo wanted to minimize the damage Gervin might do. Turned out he was right. Gervin loved it when people called him 'the Thumb' and he encouraged it. Thought it made him more of a tough guy. But it just showed he had shit for brains. I mean, he never even knew I was tailing him."

"Go on," Danny said.

"He met the bun lady at a New Year's Eve bash at the Joe and Joe. He crashed it, of course, and he wasn't there for over five minutes when he spotted her. Made a beeline for her and that was it. Drove her home and made it with her in his car in front of her house at four in the morning. She was hot to trot, let me tell you. After that, he saw her constantly, and he couldn't stop running his mouth about all the shit he was doing for Lombardo."

"And you reported this back to Lombardo?"

"That's what he was paying me to do. I also told him Carla was repeating at least some of what Gervin told her to her friends. Finally, Lombardo called Gervin in on the carpet, told him he was putting everyone at risk, and that he had to make absolutely certain that she'd repeat nothing he'd told her. Gervin tried telling Carla to cool it, but she blew up at him. In the end, she gave Gervin no choice."

"Did you see him do it?" Larkin asked.

"No, but I saw him follow her into the churchyard. She proved she was smarter than him, because when he talked to her in the bar, she figured out right away where it was going. That's why she ran. She was trying to get into the church, but it was locked. I didn't see him again until he ran down the street. I stayed hidden because there was a patrolman out on St. Ann's Avenue. When Lombardo saw the bun lady splashed all over the newspapers the next day, he split a gut."

"Tell me straight," Danny said as Fagan halted his narrative. "Did you kill Gervin?"

"No. Lombardo ordered me to do it, but my previous offenses had only been taking money to look the other way, squelching the occasional investigation, and keeping tabs on Gervin. I wouldn't risk a murder rap for anybody because Lombardo would sell me out at the first opportunity. So, I said nothing, but that afternoon, I shipped my wife and kid off to my place in Pennsylvania. Told 'em I'd be there as soon as I could."

"Why didn't you go with them?" Larkin asked.

"I figured once I didn't report in, Lombardo would sic his goons on me. I didn't want my family with me if they caught up with me, which so far, they haven't. Charlie Lavery had told me you were sniffing around the Bronx rackets, so I told him to call you and set this up. I figure if you guys are investigating Lombardo, it will keep him on the defensive while I slip out of town."

"One other question," Danny said. "If you didn't kill Gervin, who did?"

"I don't know, but I'd guess it was one of Lombardo's trusted lieutenants from his days on the waterfront. The FBI might be able to help you on that."

TWENTY-FOUR

Ray Walker wasn't home when Danny and Larkin called, but his wife gave them the address of the bait and tackle shop he ran on City Island Avenue. No customers were in the shop when they entered.

Larkin walked over to a display of fishing rods. "Nice rods." He picked one and hefted it.

A man in his forties stepped from behind the counter. "Can I help you? That one's a beauty."

Danny flashed his badge as Larkin placed the rod back in the display. "We're looking for a Ray Walker."

"I'm Walker. Something wrong?"

"You notified the Coast Guard yesterday about a dead body on Goose Island?" Danny asked.

"That's right. I'd been fishing for blues in Manhasset Bay. I was coming back to the marina." He nodded in the general direction of the water beyond the shop.

"Bluefish this time of year?" Larkin asked.

"Sure, blues run pretty much all year in these waters."

"How many did you bag?"

Danny considered interrupting but decided against it. Larkin might be flaunting his fishing knowledge, or he might have a deeper purpose. Best to wait and see.

"Five," Walker replied. "Why?"

"Not a bad haul for a spring morning," Larkin said. "Is that typical around here?"

"It varies." Walker glanced from Larkin to Danny and back. "Why?"

Larkin shrugged. "Just curious. So, you often fish early in the morning this time of year?"

"I usually go out around dawn or a little before, depending on the tides and weather."

"How often?" Larkin sounded less like an interested fisherman and more like a cop.

Walker lost some of his open, friendly demeanor. "Typically, two to three mornings a week."

"And always out on the bay?"

"Mostly, yeah. Sometimes across the East River to Little Neck Bay or Manhasset Bay. Why is this important?"

Larkin flashed a friendly grin. "It's good to know where the hot fishing spots are for my trips." He gave Walker a moment to lower his guard. "How did you end up heading north on the Hutchinson River yesterday morning, past Pelham Parkway and the railroad bridge, when your marina is right here on the bay?"

Danny jumped in. "After all, it's not like there's promising fishing upriver. All that industry."

Walker looked like he'd been punched in the stomach. "Hey, I called it in. Now you're making it sound like…"

"We just need to understand the underlying circumstances," Danny said. "You were right to report it, but our lieutenant will ask these questions of us."

"He's very picky that way," Larkin added. "Nothing to get hot about."

"Oh," Walker said. "Okay. As I said, I was heading back to the marina when I saw a boat coming out of the Hutchinson River at high speed. I got curious, so instead of heading in, I turned upriver to see if there was some kind of emergency. I noticed something unusual on Goose Island, so I slowed down and approached for a closer look. That's when I spotted the dead guy and radioed the Coast Guard."

"What kind of emergency did you expect to find?" Danny asked.

"I don't know, exactly, but…"

"What did you expect to do about it?" Larkin asked.

"Just what I did—call for help."

"It's just a wee bit odd," Danny said. "You see a boat on the water—hardly an unusual occurrence—and you assume there's an emergency, and lo-and-behold, there is one."

"How far upriver were you planning to go?" Larkin added.

"Hey, wait a minute," Walker said. "In the first place, I got curious because I usually see nothing but tugs and barges coming down that river. There's nothing for a pleasure-boater to see up there, and there's no good fishing up there. So, seeing a boat coming out at high speed made me suspicious. Last year, there was a major news story about Nazis attempting to bomb Penn Station. I wondered if the boater could be snooping around unauthorized areas."

Larkin turned to Danny. "Nice that he remembers." Then to Walker. "He's the guy who cracked the saboteur case."

Walker stunned Danny by grabbing his hand. "Let me thank you for doing the city and the country a great service."

"Just my job," Danny said. "But, to clarify, if you were looking for spies or saboteurs, how did you spot the guy on Goose Island?"

"It's all rock, with little soil and almost no vegetation. The dead guy was wearing a red jacket, and the rising sun lit it up like a flare."

Danny made some notes. "That explains it. Anything else you can tell us?"

"Like I said, Goose Island is a collection of rocks. I've never been upriver before. I was careful not to get too close because it's impossible to tell where the submerged rocks extend. Only someone well-versed in the waters and skilled in boating could have dumped the body there."

"Any chance the guy was killed on the island?" Danny asked.

"I suppose it's possible. One guy would have needed to keep the boat steady while the other guy and the victim got out. As I see it, it was probably hard enough to keeping it steady long enough to dump the body."

"Two guys?" Larkin asked. "Did you see two guys?"

"I only got a quick look at the boat. A Chris Craft Utility, twenty-one-footer, nice, polished finish. I'd say five-to-ten years old. I thought I saw someone's head near the rear seat, but I couldn't be sure through the spray the boat was throwing. She was moving at a good twenty-five or thirty knots."

"Ever see the boat before?" Danny asked.

"I've seen several like it. We have two right here in the marina, but not as well kept as this one appeared to be. I mean, the finish was perfect, like it was brand new. Look, Detective, if I had more information for you, I'd say so. I only got a brief look."

"Did you notice anything else about the boat's appearance?" Danny asked. "Anything that would distinguish it from similar boats?"

Walker closed his eyes for a moment. "Yeah. The seat cushions at the stern were bright yellow. Other Utilities I've seen have all had cushions that were sea-foam green."

"Which way did he turn after you saw him?" Larkin asked.

Walker picked up a map from the counter and unfolded it. "I was here, off Belden Point, on my way back from Manhasset Bay and heading northwest toward the marina, here." Walker pointed to a spot on the opposite side of the bay. "He was over here, passing Palmer Inlet."

"There are marinas over there," Larkin said. "Couldn't he have come out of one of them?"

"Not likely at that speed, and besides, the waters were real calm yesterday morning, and I could see his wake leading upriver. And, to answer your probable next question, I only saw him continuing south-southeast as far as Weir Creek, and then I lost sight of him as he turned west. I had already increased speed and headed upriver. My best guess is that he was following the coastline to Throggs Neck before turning west into the East River."

"Or he could have…" Larkin stopped before saying any more. "No, never mind."

"One other question, Mr. Walker," Danny said. "How's your business these days?"

"How do you mean?"

"Any problems? I mean, with the war on, and all, I guess people don't do as much fishing as they used to."

"Actually, business has been rather good, since gasoline rationing only applies to autos. Some folks are going out on party boats hoping to catch a glimpse of a U-boat."

"Sounds like fun," Larkin said.

"Any unexpected difficulties? Unanticipated expenses?"

"No, things are going fine. Why?"

Danny closed his notebook. "Just asking. Crime is generally down, but there are still problems with vandalism and burglaries. Some businesses find security is a problem. Some even pay extra for security."

"Nothing like that around here," Walker replied.

"If anything changes, you call us, okay? Thanks for your time."

TWENTY-FIVE

Meg's first thought when the bell rang was dread. It could only be Helen, and as much as she missed her friend, she really didn't want to talk to her today, because she still didn't know how she was going to handle the inevitable questions.

But as she peered out the front window, it wasn't Helen. It was an army officer.

Hal.

***

As soon as they were back in the car, Larkin said, "He certainly was eager to prove he had nothing to do with it." When Danny said nothing, he added, "Or do you think he did?"

"There are three possibilities of involvement," Danny said at last. "He could have been the killer, the one who drove the boat and dumped the body, or just someone trying to hinder our investigation by making sure we knew Gervin was dead. The first two seem plausible because he knew so much about the island and the difficulties of dumping a body there. But, by that thinking, his explanations would also make us suspicious of how he knew all that."

"And the third?"

"That's why I pressed him about his business. It occurred to me he might be paying protection money and that Lombardo or someone working for him might have offered a little discount in return for a favor. But I've ruled that out."

"Why? It makes perfect sense to me."

"Only if there's a logical reason for us to know sooner rather than later about Gervin's death. But, by all the saints, I can't think of one."

"How about keeping us from probing into Lombardo's operation?"

"Tell me, Frankie, has everything we've learned so far make you more suspicious of racketeer involvement, or less?"

"More. A lot more."

"Right."

"But that includes what we learned from Fagan. And Lombardo most likely wouldn't have expected that."

Danny considered it. "Okay, so forget what Fagan told us. Just the discovery of the body and our talk with Walker."

"You're right. I'd still have to say more. Walker's probably a good guy, acted responsibly, and now is slightly nervous that he may be punished for it. Can't say I blame him."

Danny had one more question. "What were you going to ask Walker before you said to forget it?"

"If he thought the boat was heading for the marina on the other side of Throggs Neck, Locust Point. But I decided it's best to keep that just between us, just in case."

"A wise move." Danny drove in silence until they arrived at the Locust Point Marina. "Let's see if anyone keeps a Chris Craft Utility here."

***

Hal rang the bell several times, and Meg was afraid he'd wake little Patrick. She put her face up against the screen and called down, "Please stop ringing the bell. My son is sleeping."

"I just want to talk."

"We have nothing to talk about."

"Please, Meg."

"Go away." She watched him turn and walk back to the sidewalk, pausing to glance at her window once more before continuing down the street, waiting until he was beyond her field of vision before returning to her easy chair and her book.

***

"We have two Chris Craft Utilities here," the manager of the Locust Point Marina said, "both still in drydock from the winter months."

"Can we see them?" Danny asked.

"I'm afraid there's not much to see of a boat in drydock. Neither is for sale, to the best of my knowledge."

Danny glared at the manager. "Can we see them?"

"It's important," Larkin added.

"Certainly. Step this way."

"We'll also need the names and addresses of the owners," Danny said. "And a signed affidavit from you stating the date they were drydocked and attesting that neither has been in the water since."

Back in the car, Larkin said, "That's it for Bronx marinas west of Eastchester Bay. Continuing west, our best bet is in Queens. I can think of six. Two are on Little Neck Bay, but that would be straight across the river going southeast, and Walker said the boat turned west, so let's rule them out. There are three in College

Point and one on Flushing Bay, built for the World's Fair back in '39."

Danny drove toward the four-year-old Whitestone Bridge. "And if we come up empty on all four?"

"Then, boyo, the most likely spots to check would be on the Hudson, either in Manhattan or headed upriver toward Yonkers."

"Where our good Mr. Maxwell happens to reside."

***

The bell rang again. This time he held his finger on the button so that it rang continuously.

Meg returned to the window. "If you don't stop that right now, I'll call the police."

"Please, Meg, I have a gift for the baby."

She saw nothing in his hands, which sent a chill down her spine. Memories flashed from that awful time in her life, months after the rape, when Hal had accused her of being complicit in it, turning to drinking and, finally, hitting her in his drunken rages until she'd finally had enough.

"I want nothing from you, and I don't want to talk to you. Go away, or I'll call the police." She assumed her threat would be enough, so she didn't watch him leave. She returned to the easy chair.

And the bell ringing resumed.

***

They'd worked their way around College Point, but none of the three marinas had a Chris Craft Utility that fit the description. As they pulled into the parking lot of the World's Fair Marina, Danny said, "I don't know about you, Frankie, but I'm getting jaded."

"I suggest we call it quits if we strike out here."

But that would mean another day for the boat to be moved.

Or destroyed.

"Let's see what we find, Frankie."

The manager was friendly until Danny asked if there were any Chris Crafts at the marina. "Why would you ask?"

Danny turned severe. "Are there?"

"After all," Larkin added, "it's not like you have anything to hide."

"No, of course not," the manager said. He opened a black-covered notebook. "You said it was a Utility?"

"That's right," Danny said. "A twenty-one-footer."

"We have one."

"In the water? Let's see it. And the name and address of the owner, please."

The manager walked them out onto the dock and pulled a tarpaulin off one of the boats.

"That's some nice finish," Larkin said as Danny studied the boat. "It practically gleams."

"Yes, we did that over the winter," the manager replied. "We're very pleased with it, as is the owner. We replaced the seat cushions at the same time."

Danny stared at the cockpit. The cushions were a vibrant red. "When was this most recently taken out?"

"I don't know. We don't track our members' comings and goings. I know the owner took her out last Saturday, because he had us fill her up on gas."

Danny checked the card with the boat owner's name and address: Ronald Trent of Howard Beach. As they walked back to the car, Danny asked, "Frankie, you know a lot about boats. Why would a guy living on the shores of Jamaica Bay keep his boat in Flushing Bay?"

Before Larkin could answer, the radio crackled. "Dispatch to Car 28."

Larkin grabbed the microphone. "Car 28 to dispatch, go ahead."

"Message for Detective Brady from Lieutenant Greco: proceed to 108th Precinct and see Detective Klein immediately. Repeat, immediately."

TWENTY-SIX

He'd wanted to call Meg and check in with her, but the directive "immediately" ruled that out. What the hell had happened?

"Will you calm down?" Larkin said. "The message said nothing about Meg."

"It's my home precinct, and I spoke to Klein on Tuesday and asked him to monitor that gobshite of a former husband of Meg's. What in God's name could it be?"

"The message didn't even mention Meg."

"Exactly. It said to go see Klein. Not call, go see. So, something must have happened to her."

"For God's sake, Danny, you live in Sunnyside Gardens, not Hell's Kitchen."

He drove on in fuming silence, following the Grand Central Parkway around to the Brooklyn Queens Expressway and getting off at Northern Boulevard.

"I'm sure it's just that Klein has news about Corwyn. It's possible they picked him up, as you wanted."

He followed Northern past 48th Street, resisting the temptation to turn off to go check on Meg and the baby.

"Isn't that where the old Madison Square Garden Bowl was?" Larkin asked. "A lot of terrific bouts there, like when Braddock beat Max Baer for the heavyweight title."

Larkin was trying to distract him. Good partner. Good friend. Danny owed it to him to play along. "It is. They tore it down last year. They're building some kind of army supply depot there now."

He continued into Long Island City, crossing Queens Boulevard and onto Jackson Avenue. When he reached 50th Avenue, he turned and found a parking spot.

Walking into the precinct, he recalled his last visit, nearly two years earlier, when he'd first met Meg. She'd supplied a detailed description of her attacker and later spit in his face at a lineup at Danny's precinct. But she'd also taken his breath away, although it had been many months before he'd admitted it, even to himself.

Klein was waiting for him. "We have Corwyn in an interrogation room."

"Where did you pick him up?"

"Outside your building. Meg called us. He'd been ringing your bell, trying to get her to let him in. He claimed to have a present for the baby, but he had nothing on him when we arrested him. Once we picked him up, I called Greco knowing he'd contact you. We told him we're charging him with menacing. If you decide to press charges, that is."

"Let me talk to him."

Larkin put a hand on Danny's arm. "Don't do it, Danny boy."

But Danny ignored him. "Which room?"

"Danny!" Larkin again.

"I agree with Frankie," Klein said. "It's best if you…"

"I appreciate your concern, both of you, but I know what I'm doing. Morris, if you would?"

With obvious reluctance, Klein led them to an interrogation room and opened the door. Hal Corwyn sat at a table in handcuffs in his slightly wrinkled second lieutenant's uniform.

"Frankie, you wait out here. Morris, take his cuffs off and wait outside with Frankie."

Both looked alarmed but said nothing. Klein removed the cuffs, and they retreated.

Danny waited for the door to close before addressing the visibly trembling Corwyn. "What the hell do you want from that woman? What are you after?"

Corwyn swallowed but couldn't answer.

"You know what?" Danny said, "don't bother. I don't care what you want. I have no interest in what your problem is. We have you cold on menacing. And when you're convicted, the army will almost certainly hand you a dishonorable discharge. In fact, considering how much time you've been spending stalking my wife, time you probably should be doing whatever you're supposed to do for the army, they might court-martial you just for good measure."

"Probably."

"You don't want that, and I can resolve this minor problem myself."

"What do you mean?" It was almost a wail.

"I'm a cop. I could kill you here and now, and every cop in this building would swear it was self-defense. Or I could beat you senseless, and they'd say you fell down a flight of stairs trying to run away."

Corwyn blanched and said nothing.

Danny took a step toward him, and Corwyn leaped to his feet and backed into a corner.

Danny grabbed Corwyn's shirt with his left hand, cocking his right arm and forming a fist.

Corwyn gasped and closed his eyes.

"Look me in the eye, you whimpering fool." Danny shook him.

Corwyn opened one eye.

"You're pathetic. No wonder Meg was so glad to be rid of you." Danny released his grip and shoved him back against the wall. "I will not waste the city's time and resources prosecuting you, and I will not sully my hands by thrashing you, at least not today. But I'll be lodging a formal complaint with your commanding officer, and you can take what comes."

"Thank you." It came out a whisper.

"But it's with the clear understanding, between you and me with no witnesses, that if you ever come within a mile of my wife again for any reason, I will kill you. Am I clear?"

Corwyn could only nod.

Danny took a menacing step toward him. "Am… I… clear?"

"Crystal." It came out as a gasp.

Danny opened the door. "Morris, let this filthy gobshite go."

***

Robert Maxwell had nearly finished an amended tax return for a client when the doorbell rang. He glanced at the clock. It was five to three. The children would be home from school soon.

The anxiety that gripped him as he approached the door turned to cold fear when he saw who it was—the fedora man with the black-rimmed glasses. His visitor grinned, which made Robert tremble, and tipped his hat. "Afternoon, Bob. May I come in?"

"All right, but my children will…"

The man strode past him. "Oh, this won't take long. I'm informing you the job is done."

"What job?"

"The man guilty of your wife's untimely demise was found dead yesterday over by Pelham Bay Park. I told you it would be resolved."

"I didn't know what you meant. You mean you…"

The visitor's friendly demeanor evaporated. "I mean exactly what I tell you, nothing more. I'm just a messenger, and the message is that this business is finished. You are to tell the police nothing about it, and their investigation will reveal very little. Understand?"

Robert nodded but said nothing.

The visitor's friendly manner returned. "Excellent. Which leaves only the matter of the fee."

***

Meg snatched the phone on the first ring. "Danny?"

"No, it's Helen. Are you okay? You sound upset."

"I'm fine. Just anxious to hear from Danny."

"Do you know what they're up to today? Frankie said something about interviewing a witness, but that sounded fishy."

"No, that's what Danny said, too. They were supposed to meet him at 1:30."

That pulled Helen up short. "So, Frankie was actually telling the truth? How about that? Did Danny tell you what it was all about?"

Oh, no. She couldn't lie to Helen, but she also couldn't betray Danny's trust. "He didn't say much."

"Then why are you so upset?"

She told Helen about the latest with Hal, relieved at the change of subject. "I called Detective Klein, and they picked him up just down the block. The last I heard, Danny was on his way over to the precinct in Hunters Point."

"You've always handled him before, Meg. Why so upset this time?"

"He said he had something for Patrick. I'm certain he was going to hurt him." She heard the front door open and footsteps on the stairs. "There's Danny, now. I'll call you later, Helen. Thanks."

Danny took her in his arms. "Problem solved. I got him alone in a closed room at the 108th and explained things to him."

He'd used that phrase before as a euphemism for someone being beaten. "Danny, please tell me you didn't do anything…"

He laughed. "No, I told you. I just explained things I would do if he ever came near you again for any reason. Then, I sent him on his way and called his commanding officer to complain about him. It turns out he requested a transfer to the army's new supply depot on Northern Boulevard. His commanding officer assured me the army would deal with him."

"Did he say how?"

"Transfer elsewhere. I think he said Biloxi."

She burst into a giggle. "Mississippi?"

"Yes. Also, his file would be duly noted. I'm guessing he'll be a second lieutenant for the duration, assuming he remains an officer at all."

"How did your meeting go?"

"About what I expected. We also talked to the guy who reported the body to the Coast Guard. But I'm not sure he was telling us the whole truth."

TWENTY-SEVEN

Saturday, May 22, 1943

Danny awoke to the baby's crying. It was just before six. "Didn't we just do this a few hours ago?"

Meg grinned as she changed Patrick's diaper. "Four, to be exact. Our little guy has quite an appetite." She finished and carried him into the kitchen.

Danny followed. "Need a hand?"

"Thanks, just take him while I warm his bottle." She extracted a baby bottle from the ice box and placed it in a pot of warm water. "My mom was shocked to learn I wasn't breast-feeding him."

He cast a glance at her bosom, then turned to Patrick, "I guess you're sorry, too, little guy. You surely wouldn't have starved."

"Danny!"

But he continued speaking to the baby. "Well, that's all right. They're my territory, anyway."

"That's quite enough of that." A few moments later, she handed him the bottle. When he hesitated, she said, "You said you wanted to help."

It was then he noticed the circles under her eyes. "I guess you can use a break."

She kissed him. "No, it's not that. I just need to get this into a routine. Helen says it comes together in a couple of days. Tell you what, in the morning, if your schedule allows, you can feed him while I make you breakfast."

"In other words, I feed him and you feed me. Has Helen been asking probing questions?"

Meg's smile vanished. "Yes, but not out of curiosity about the case. It's more to verify whatever Frankie is telling her about his whereabouts."

"I don't get it. They've been married for, what, fifteen years? Why the sudden suspicion? He really hasn't been fooling around."

"That's the funny thing," she said as the coffee perked. "Instead of being reassured when she learns he's telling the truth, she seems more agitated. Almost like she's disappointed."

Danny burped the baby, as Meg had shown him. "Sounds like she's turning into a header." When Meg shot him a questioning glance, he added, "Mentally unstable."

"I don't think that, necessarily, but something is driving this suspicion of hers. It's almost as if she wants it to be true. Maybe she wants out of the marriage." She pondered that. "Maybe seeing me break free of Hal, and us being so happy together, has made her want something similar."

"By all the saints, Frankie's a damned sight better man than Hal."

"Frankie has very little to do with it. This is Helen's problem." Meg shook it off. "Anyway, my mom is coming for a visit today."

"While Frankie and I visit a yacht owner."

***

"Office of Price Administration is now issuing tickets to motorists alleged to be violating the federal ban on pleasure driving because of the gravity of the current gasoline shortage on the East Coast. Federal agencies are also preparing for further curtailment of home deliveries by various business establishments. It is hoped that the renewed ban on pleasure driving will turn up leads for Federal authorities on black market activities, which have been one of the contributing causes of the discrepancy between outstanding ration coupons and available gasoline supplies."

***

Danny pulled up at the address on 97th Street in Howard Beach the marina had provided and switched off the radio.

"Mr. Trent appears to live a quiet life," Larkin said. "Tidy little house, quiet street, and more docks within walking distance than you can shake a stick at."

"That's why we're here."

Danny rang the bell. When a woman in her forties answered, he flashed his badge. "Does Mr. Ronald Trent live here?"

"Yes, why?"

"May we speak with him, please?"

"Why? What's this about?" There was no mistaking her tone of alarm.

"We'd rather discuss that with him. May we come in? Or should I return with a warrant?" He had no grounds for a warrant, but she didn't know that.

"No, no, please come in." She called out for her husband as she led them into a small, tidy living room.

In a moment, Mr. Trent entered. "Yes? What's the matter?"

Danny regarded him for a moment. Only about five-eight, not very heavy but with a little pot belly, graying hair, pushing fifty or perhaps a little older. "Mr. Trent, you own a Chris Craft Utility, which you just had refinished this winter and keep in a marina in Flushing?"

"Yes, why?"

"Did you take the boat out Thursday morning?"

"No."

143

"Did you give permission to anyone else to take it out?"

"No."

Larkin broke in. "Do you allow anyone else to use it regularly?"

A flicker of the eye. "No."

Danny caught it. "You had to think about that one?"

"No, I'm just a little nervous. Why are two police detectives questioning me about my boat?"

"We're investigating a crime," Danny replied, "in which a boat was used. A boat for which yours is a perfect match. And if it was yours, and you don't tell us about it, that makes you an accessory."

"So," Larkin added, "you maybe want to reconsider your answers?"

Mr. Trent pulled himself up, slightly more erect. "No, I told you the truth."

"Enlighten me," Danny said. "Why would someone living near the water keep their boat ten miles away on the other side of the island?"

"I prefer boating on the East River and Long Island Sound. The channels around the marshy islands of Jamaica Bay can be tricky to navigate. I don't enjoy going outside in a boat that small."

"Outside?" Danny asked.

"He means the Atlantic," Larkin said. "Afraid of U-boats?"

"No," Mr. Trent replied. "The waters can be very rough, and I don't have full use of my right arm."

Danny softened his manner. "Sorry to hear that. War injury?"

"No, a work accident. Is there anything else?"

Danny made some notes in his little book. "No, I think that takes care of it. We'll come back if we think of anything else." Mr. Trent ushered them to the front door, where Danny stopped. "Oh, one other thing, just out of curiosity. What line of work are you in?"

"Odd jobs."

"What kind of odd job were you doing when you hurt your arm?"

"He was a longshoreman," Mrs. Trent said, "and I'm glad he's out."

"Dangerous work," Danny said. "Doing odd jobs is a lot safer. Where did you work? I might know some fellas who worked with you."

"I doubt it," Mr. Trent replied. "It was ten years ago."

"Before you bought the boat?" Larkin asked.

"Yes."

"How did it happen?" Danny asked.

"We were unloading a cargo ship. I was down in the hold when a cable broke, and a falling crate hit me. I was lucky I didn't lose the arm."

"The union was very generous," Mrs. Trent added. "They helped us get through."

"I'm glad," Danny said. "I think that's all. Thanks for your help." But, again, he stopped. "You worked on one of the Hudson River piers?"

"No," Mrs. Trent said. "Brooklyn."

TWENTY-EIGHT

"I wonder how an injured longshoreman could afford a house and a boat," Larkin said. "But the injured arm story also gives him an alibi. How could he dump a body?"

"It does, at least for now," Danny replied.

"The wife was a bigger help than he was."

"She was, indeed. Which tells me she was eager to throw us off the track. 'The union was so generous' translates to 'please don't look for sources of our income.' I doubt she thought about it long enough to realize that the longshoreman's union only takes care of their higher-ranking leaders like that, or that those leaders have other activities they'd rather we not discover."

"Maybe she doesn't know that part."

Danny nodded. "Probably not. I'm sure Trent never shared the gory details. And when I asked if he'd worked in Manhattan, she was happy to say it was Brooklyn, thinking we were looking for a Manhattan link."

"So, where does that leave us?"

"I don't think he dumped Gervin's body, but by all the saints he knows who did, or at least who arranged it. I didn't think the bait and tackle guy was telling us the whole truth yesterday."

"What else do you think he lied about?"

"That's what we're about to discover."

***

Mom gazed down at her sleeping grandson with a beatific smile.

"I told you he was an angel, didn't I, Mom?" Meg said.

"He is. I can't wait until he's awake so I can hold him."

"I must warn you; he becomes considerably less angelic when he first wakes up."

"They all do. How are you managing? With Danny's hours, it must be difficult sometimes."

Meg led her back to the kitchen and poured two cups of coffee. "Sometimes, but he does his best to minimize the disruptions."

Mom looked Meg up and down. "I must say, you look remarkably well for a new mother."

"I take it easy, especially when Patrick's asleep. Danny takes care of any heavy work around the apartment." She tried not to notice the look of discomfort Mom usually displayed whenever Danny's name came up. "He's a wonderful man, mom."

Mom placed her cup on its saucer with care. "I know, darling, and I'm glad you're happy at last."

"It's not 'at last'. I've been happy ever since I divorced Hal."

Mom winced at the word. "Are you going to have Patrick baptized?"

"Of course. Why wouldn't we? Just because Danny and I can't receive doesn't mean Patrick can't be raised a good Catholic. We go to Mass every Sunday and all the Holy Days of Obligation. We observe Advent and Lent. I say the Rosary at least once a week. We figure we'll wait until Patrick is about a month old to have him baptized."

"So, you'll be churched by then."

Meg had suspected this was coming. "No, Mom. I do not need to be purified."

"That's just the old interpretation, darling. Now, it's considered a blessing for the mother and a thanksgiving for a safe delivery."

"If the priest at St. Sebastian's wants to give me a blessing at Patrick's christening, that's fine. But the notion that a new mother needs to be purified before she can re-enter the church is medieval. The ritual is purely ceremonial, and I'm not going through it."

Mom shook her head. "You always have been willful."

"It's one of the things Danny loves about me."

***

The bait and tackle shop was empty, and Walker started when Danny and Larkin entered.

"Hello again," Danny said.

"Bet you didn't expect to see us back so soon," Larkin added.

"No," Walker replied. "Something wrong?"

Danny pulled out his little notebook. "Not at all. Just need to clarify a few things. Are you color-blind?"

Walker grew wary. "No. Why?"

"Because you lied to us about the color of the seat cushions on that Chris Craft you saw." Danny flipped several pages in the notebook. "Ah, here it is. You said they were bright yellow. In reality, they were not." He snapped the notebook closed and waited. If Walker admitted to the lie, it would mean they were on the right track. "I don't like people lying to me. It makes me wonder what else you're hiding."

Walker glanced around to make certain no one else had entered the shop. "I'm not hiding anything. I told you the truth about everything…"

"Except the seat covers," Larkin said. "Which was a key point in identifying the boat."

"He means," Danny added, "we were unlikely to locate the correct boat looking for the wrong seat covers. That means you've obstructed a police investigation, which is a crime."

Walker broke into a sweat. "Look, you gotta understand. Everything about this smells like a racket's involved. Whoever dumped that body saw me as clearly as I saw him. I got a wife and kids, and I want to keep breathing. It sounds like you located the boat even with my wrong description."

"We believe we have," Danny said. "But if anyone has threatened you, we need to know that, too, along with any remaining little details you may have kept from us."

"I told you all I know. I reported the body's location, did my duty as a citizen. If I'd wanted to throw you off, I'd have given you misinformation about the make and model of the boat."

Danny reopened the notebook. "So, tell me again, what color were the seat cushions on the Chris Craft?"

"But you already know that."

"I want to hear you say it."

Larkin spoke up. "It's called probable cause, and you need it for a search warrant."

Walker heaved a deep sigh. "The new cushions were red. Bright red."

***

Back at the precinct, Lt. Greco listened to Danny's report with mounting irritation. "You want me to ask Monroe for a search warrant based on seat cushions?" Dennis Monroe was an assistant district attorney in the Bronx DA's office. He and Danny had worked together often in the past. "And nothing else to link the boat to the murder?"

"Except that it fits perfectly the description Walker gave us," Danny replied. "You know, the eyewitness who called in his discovery of the body. The ADA can word it broadly enough to cover any physical evidence connected to the crime."

"Except that if you're right," Greco shot back, "that evidence is probably long since wiped clean. Your search will tip off whoever is behind the killing that we're on to him."

"If Trent hasn't already done that," Larkin said.

Danny wished Frankie would keep his gob shut for once. "I didn't ask him for permission to search the boat for precisely that reason. Let him think he fobbed us off. He doesn't know what we know about him, or how we might be able to connect him."

"And how might we do that?" Greco asked.

"Trent got a sweet deal after he got hurt stevedoring on a pier run by Anthony Anastasio. Lombardo once did shape-ups for Anastasio. If that doesn't make your nose twitch, Lieutenant, then I think you need a checkup."

"We already know Gervin was connected with Lombardo's operation," Larkin said.

"Sounds awfully tenuous to me," Greco replied.

"That's why we need to probe it." Danny waited for a response.

"Okay," Greco said at last. "I'll call Monroe and try to get you a search warrant by Monday. What about you two?"

"End of tour for me," Larkin said.

"I just have some housekeeping to do before I leave," Danny replied. "Enjoy your day off." He pulled out his notepad to check the number for Curt Ramsay, the contact Cogan had given him.

TWENTY-NINE

Sunday, May 23, 1943

"A forty percent cut in truck, bus, and taxicab mileage in thirteen states of the eastern gasoline shortage and the drastic curtailment of deliveries of such commodities as beer, liquor, soft drinks, ice cream, and flowers were decreed by the Office of Defense Transportation to meet the gasoline shortage caused by military demands and the washout of pipelines and railroad beds by western floods. In New York, the Price Administration Office delivered a blow to the black market, one of the causes of the gasoline supply crisis in the east, by shutting down fourteen service stations whose operators admitted illegal dealing in counterfeit ration coupons."

***

It was just a little past noon, and Ramsay was waiting by the entrance to Feltman's Restaurant, Bar and Grill on the boardwalk at Coney Island, wearing a beige sport shirt with wide brown stripes running down on both sides of the buttons, as he'd said he would. He was slightly shorter than Danny, and he bore an uncanny resemblance to George Raft, looking less like an assistant district attorney and more like a criminal.

Danny approached him. "I'm Brady."

"Yes, I know who you are." Ramsay's manner remained cool but extended his hand.

Danny shook it. "Nice to meet you." He nodded toward Feltman's. "Shall we?"

"Not inside. Let's walk down the boardwalk. Does your partner, Detective Larkin, or your supervising officer, Lieutenant Greco, know you're here?"

"They do not. Does Tom Hughes know you're here?" It was fine that Ramsay was letting him know he'd been checking up on Danny, but best to make sure they were meeting as equals.

Ramsay broke into a bitter grin. "No. Hughes knowing would not be helpful to either of us. What's this about, anyway?"

"Bill Cogan told me about your involvement with the Panto murder case…"

"A SNAFU of biblical proportions. The hand-picked team of Bill O'Dwyer's hand-picked police captain, according to their statements afterward, all slept like babies while O'Dwyer's star witness plunged six stories from the Half Moon Hotel." He pointed up the boardwalk. "The dome of the hotel is clearly visible from here."

"Kid Twist. I know the story."

Ramsay stopped to light a cigarette. "So, tell me, what's a Bronx detective who lives in Queens doing poking around the Brooklyn waterfront?"

Danny recounted the murders of Carla Maxwell and Nick Gervin.

"Never heard of either of 'em outside of what I read in the papers."

"Gervin had been working for Armand Lombardo," Danny said.

Ramsay took a long drag. "Him, I've heard of. One of Anastasio's guys. Moved up to the Bronx when…"

"When Giuseppe Calvino left town."

Ramsay laughed. "Gravedigger Joe. He was a character. Tough on the outside, yellow on the inside. A lot more common with these guys than you think. So, you're going after Lombardo?"

"We don't have enough information at the moment. I need to know how Lombardo fit in with Anastasio's organization, or with Anastasia, to determine if I should look closer at him. Also, anything you can tell me about a guy named Ronald Trent would be a big help."

"Trent? The name doesn't ring a bell but let me review my files and I'll see what I find."

"He would have been on the docks in the late twenties, early thirties. Apparently, he was injured on the job and got a sweet deal from the ILA. Lives in Howard Beach a block from the water but keeps his boat in Flushing."

They walked several more blocks in silence. Danny wondered if Ramsay had lost interest.

But he hadn't. "If he was well enough connected to get that kind of deal, he was probably one of Anastasio's fair-haired boys. Which means he wasn't really a longshoreman. Where are you going with all this? Who are you really after?"

"Like you, I want everyone responsible for these murders either in the chair or in prison."

They'd reached the Half Moon Hotel. Ramsay pointed up at a balcony. "There it is. Abe Reles' final diving platform."

"You think he jumped?"

Ramsay snorted. "Yeah, with a little help." He turned, and they began the walk back to Feltman's. "You're a tough boy. You ran down that rapist who killed the Sunday School teacher, then bagged those Nazis before they could blow up Penn Station. And you whipped a bunch of law enforcement departments in line in both cases to do it. But you need to know you're in a different ballgame, here. Very different."

"So I hear."

"Hearing is one thing, understanding what it means is another. Your biggest problems in chasing those Nazis were getting things organized and thinking a couple of steps ahead. The FBI and the NYPD bigwigs might have been slow to come around to your way of thinking, but they were at least on your side. If you're going after Anastasio and those guys, you must understand how much power they have in the system."

"I'm not after Anastasio or anyone like that. But if Armand Lombardo is behind these two murders, I am going after him."

Ramsay took a last drag and flicked the butt away. "That's just it. Lombardo is a subsidiary of Anastasio's operation."

"The Combination."

"That's one word for it."

"Which may or may not exist."

"Oh, it exists, all right. J. Edgar Hoover refuses to admit it, and Fiorello La Guardia does his best to ignore it. Bill O'Dwyer knows it, but he ran off to the army, not out of any sense of patriotism, but because he didn't want to admit there wasn't anything he could do about it because the party that got him elected is in bed with these guys."

"The annual Democratic Club dinner," Danny said.

Ramsay laughed without humor. "That's only part of it. You may recall early last year that French passenger ship caught fire and sank?"

"The Normandie. It was docked at Pier 88 in Manhattan being converted to a troopship. There was a lot of talk about sabotage."

"And that was four months before your Nazi saboteurs landed out on Long Island. There were rumors that Anastasia was behind it, an attempt to push the Navy into a deal with the ILA whereby Charles 'Lucky' Luciano would be transferred from Dannemora upstate, to a minimum-security prison, while the ILA would promise to prevent sabotage on the New York waterfront."

"I thought they determined that the fire was started by a welder's torch and spread because the ship's sprinkler system had been turned off."

"Correct. But Luciano was transferred out of Dannemora to Great Meadow in Comstock in May, and the ILA promised they would prevent any attempts at sabotage and that there would be no strikes by longshoremen for the duration of the war."

"In other words, the Navy recognized the rackets run the waterfront." Danny took a couple of blocks to consider matters. "Anastasia is Anastasio's enforcer, correct?"

"Yes. Or at least he was until he enlisted. These days, he's training draftees to be longshoremen. But Tough Tony has other guys he can call on."

"If Lombardo is Anastasio's Bronx subsidiary, doesn't that mean he can call on Tough Tony to provide the muscle?"

Ramsay nodded with satisfaction. "You catch on fast. Let's put it this way: if Anastasio decided Lombardo had become a liability…"

"Meaning that his illegal activities could be tied directly to Anastasio himself."

"Exactly. In that case, he would likely have one of his guys address the problem. But if you're asking if Anastasio or his people were responsible for Gervin's murder, I would say definitely not. If Tough Tony was behind it, you never would have found the body."

Danny remained silent.

"What?" Ramsay asked. "You don't believe me?"

"If Trent was one of Anastasio's fair-haired boys, and Lombardo was behind Gervin's murder, that means Lombardo had access to Trent's boat. That suggests a stronger connection."

Ramsay chewed on that for a moment. "You might be right. Give me a number where I can reach you, and I'll let you know when I find something out. Don't worry, I'll call you from a pay phone. And if you need to call me, please do the same."

"Understood."

"And remember you don't know me, you never heard my name, and this conversation definitely never occurred."

THIRTY

Monday, May 24, 1943

Danny was just finishing his breakfast when the bell rang.

It was Larkin. "I'm driving in today and I thought I'd give you a lift."

"Is everything okay?" Meg asked.

"Sure, why wouldn't it be?"

"Because," Danny said, "you never just drop by unannounced to drive me to work."

"It's nothing. You ready?"

Danny kissed Meg goodbye, then gave Patrick a little pat on the head. "I'll call when I get a chance."

Once in the car, Larkin lit a cigarette "How much have you told Meg about the case?"

"Why?"

"Because Helen is more suspicious about me than ever. She thinks I told you not to tell Meg anything, and that's why Meg's not telling her."

Danny laughed. "You did tell me that." Then he turned serious. "And I told Meg all the reasons."

"Aww, Danny!"

Enough was enough. "Frankie, you can't rearrange basic understandings in my marriage to make it easier on yours. For what it's worth, Meg begged me not to keep her in the dark, and I don't. I haven't told her everything, but I've made it clear that whatever I hold back is for her safety, not mine. It bothers her she can't tell Helen, but I think she's handling it the best she can."

Larkin drove for several minutes in silence. When he stopped for a red light, he lit another cigarette with the smoldering butt of the first. As he approached the Triboro Bridge, Danny broke the silence. "If ye don't mind me saying so, it looks to me like things are getting worse between you and Helen, not better. If you want to stop the rot, you need to sit down and have a good, heart-to-heart talk. Maybe go see a priest."

"What good would he do?"

"Serve as a referee, if nothing else."

"Hear anything further from Cogan?"

The question took Danny by surprise, so much so that he remained silent.

"What's the matter, boyo? Cat got your tongue?"

"You're just trying to change the subject."

"And you're not?"

"We were discussing your situation with Helen."

"We finished that. You've given me your advice. Time we turned to more pressing matters, don't you think? Cogan must have told you something, otherwise you would've come out and said he didn't, or that you haven't heard from him. Out with it."

Danny stared out at the East River. Cogan had told him not to mention the Brooklyn DA's office, and Ramsay had insisted he not mention his name.

"You tell three people and swear them to secrecy..." Fagan had said.

But Larkin was his partner, and as soon as Danny told him what he'd learned, and if he learned anything further, Larkin would demand to know. "Cogan gave me another contact, under the condition that I do not disclose the name of that contact or where he is to anyone. I met with him yesterday." He told Larkin about the information from Ramsay.

"Jesus, Mary, and Joseph," Larkin said. "I guess you won't be telling Greco."

***

As soon as the phone rang, Meg knew who it was.

"Did Frankie stop by you this morning?"

"Yes, Helen. He picked Danny up, and he's driving him in. Are you okay?"

"Fine. He spent the entire afternoon out yesterday, listening to baseball at a local tavern. Or, so he says."

"Why would he lie about something like that?"

"Because he lies about everything. Besides, he's a Yankee fan, and the only team they'd be listening to in a tavern around here would be the Brooklyn Dodgers, who he hates."

Meg gave a silent prayer of thanks that she and Danny didn't have problems like this. "You need to ask him to talk to you and to listen to what he says."

"Just tell me one thing, Meg. Is Danny telling you about this case they're working?"

"Some things, but not everything. He told me it's for my own protection, and he didn't mean from worry. Apparently, there's something they're dealing with that they can't afford to become widely known. Next, you'll ask me what, but please don't, because then I'll either have to break my promise to him or lie to you. I love you like a sister, Helen, and I hope that you and Frankie will still be Patrick's godparents."

***

Greco was standing in the doorway of his office when they walked in. Charlie Lavery was inside, but he was wearing s sport shirt and no jacket—clearly off-duty.

Despite the alarm going off in his brain, Danny kept it light as Greco closed the door. "Slumming on your day off, Charlie?"

"Declan Fagan is missing," Lavery replied. "I spoke to him Saturday night. We were supposed to meet yesterday morning, and he never showed. I stopped by the fleabag joint where he's been staying, and no one had seen him, but he hadn't checked out."

"Maybe he took off for his place in Pennsylvania," Larkin said.

"Unlikely. He was specifically avoiding joining his family until he was convinced he was out of danger, and that won't be until this case is resolved."

"Cases," Danny said. "And, no, don't ask. Did you file a Missing Persons report?"

Lavery's eyes went wide. "Shit, no. We'd wind up helping them find him."

Greco spoke up. "We're now at the point in the conversation Charlie and I were at when you two walked in."

"My wife has taken the kids to her mother's place in Connecticut," Lavery said. "I'm staying at a boarding house close to the precinct at the moment, but I'll be moving around on a weekly basis." He turned and left.

Greco glared at Danny and Larkin. "Have we stumbled into a minefield, here?" When Danny remained silent, Greco pressed him. "Danny? Something? Anything?"

"Did you get the warrant?"

"ADA Monroe promised me he would apply for the search warrant when he received a signed affidavit from you laying out all the details of your probable cause." Greco didn't look any happier saying it than Danny felt hearing it.

Larkin exploded. "What kind of shite is that? Since when is he strictly by the book?"

"Calm down, Frankie," Danny said, his voice quiet. "He doesn't know everything we know about this case."

"Maybe it's about time you filled him in," Greco said.

Which would begin the process of information seeping out, unstoppable. "Frankie, get the Crime Scene guys on the horn and let them know we'll need them to move as soon as we get the search warrant."

"I don't know any Crime Scene people in Queens."

"No, here in the Bronx," Danny said.

"Aw, hell, Danny," Greco said, "that just opens up a jurisdictional tug-of-war."

But Danny had no time for this. "They can sue me later. We'll need the results fast, which means without the red tape, and that suggests pulling a favor. Frankie will probably need you on the horn to back him up once he tells them the location. You can say it's related to a Bronx homicide."

***

ADA Monroe sat back in his chair as Danny explained the chain of events. "You should have alerted me the moment you learned there was a connection to the rackets."

"And yet you already suspected something." When Monroe's eyebrows shot up, Danny added, "You must have, because you suddenly went all by the book on our search warrant request."

"Okay, yeah. The body turning up on Goose Island set my alarm bells off. And that tells me you can't just continue this investigation on the fly. Be as organized as you were last year when handling the Sunday School teacher's murder and the saboteurs. I don't see anything like that here."

"And you won't." Time for some facts of life. "Rackets mean cops on the pad, which will torpedo most investigations." He considered mentioning Ramsay's comments on the politicians but decided against it since it would only make Monroe's position more difficult. "The only positive turn of events we've had is a crooked cop who wants to leave and sought me out."

"From the 51st?"

"Not saying."

"Jesus, Danny, I'm on your side!"

"Yes, but you can't be certain about everyone out in this office. This cop, whom I've promised to call Mr. X, gave me some background on Lombardo, but now he's disappeared, and my intermediary with him doesn't think it was part of his plan. On Saturday, I spoke with the owner of the boat we suspect was used to dump Gervin's body. The disappearance of Mr. X suggests that said owner may have tipped off Lombardo or one of his lieutenants that we're on his trail."

"And your intermediary is Detective Charles Lavery, correct?" When Danny only glared, he continued, "It only makes sense. Lavery used to work in the 51st, and we know lots of guys there were on the pad. With a roster of the detectives still there, I could probably pick out your Mr. X." Seeing the look on Danny's face, he quickly added, "Don't worry, I won't. How do you think this all plays out?"

"The boat owner, Trent, is a former longshoreman who injured an arm. Frankie Larkin thinks it's possible he wouldn't be able to control the boat well enough to get it close to the island for someone to dump the body."

"So, then, what are you…?"

"We're looking for prints that aren't Trent's. We're also looking for any evidence that Gervin was on that boat. If we get it, we can squeeze Trent for more information."

"But you still may not get enough to link it to Lombardo. What do you do then?"

"That depends on what we find on the boat."

Monroe took the affidavit. "I'll do my best to get you the warrant."

THIRTY-ONE

When Danny returned to the precinct, there was a large group congregated around Officer Sean McHugh, who was grinning from ear to ear.

"Our boy just got his gold shield," Larkin said.

"Out of the bag at last," Rossi added, referring to the police uniform.

The badge of a detective. Danny shook McHugh's hand. "Well deserved, and not a moment too soon. Have you told Rebecca?"

"Not yet. I just found out." McHugh still looked stunned.

"Well, tell her. We'll all go out one of these evenings together." Danny saw Vinnie Rossi and waved him and Larkin over. "I'm waiting for the search warrant from Monroe, and then I'll take McHugh with me for the search. In the meantime, it occurs to me we should probably touch base with our aggrieved widower, who should be glad to know his wife's killer has been dispatched. If you two would handle that, I'd be forever in your debt."

***

Monroe finally arrived with the warrant after two hours of convincing the judge about the probable cause. Danny immediately alerted the Bronx Crime Scene unit and signaled McHugh. They were soon speeding across the Whitestone Bridge.

Danny presented the manager with the warrant before the team from the Bronx unit arrived.

The manager picked up the receiver from the phone. "I'll have to phone Mr. Trent about this."

Danny reached over and depressed the switch hook. "That's fine, after we get access to the boat."

The manager waved an employee over and together they walked out onto the dock, one of three forming a large E. Danny pointed to the next dock over. "Sean, please cross to the next berth and check for anything unusual on the hull."

"Like what?"

"Goose Island is a collection of rocks, and one of the guys on the scene said it would be difficult to get a boat close enough to dump a body without hitting the rocks. Maybe whoever did it got too close."

The Crime Scene guys arrived as a boatyard employee pulled the tarp off. But before they could begin dusting for fingerprints, Sean called out, "Hey, Danny! You'd better look at this."

Danny rushed over to the dock where Sean stood, pointing. On the boat's starboard side, there were several light splotches.

"That's gotta be damage to the hull," McHugh said.

Danny raced back to the boat, waving his arms. "Hold it. First, we do a complete sweep of the interior of the boat, then I want it pulled out of the water so we can examine the hull."

"I can't do that without the owner's permission," the manager replied..

"You have until these guys finish their work to get it. But, if he refuses, we're impounding the boat."

***

"Whoa." Frank pulled behind another parked car on Robert Maxwell's block and shifted into neutral.

"What is it?" Rossi asked.

"You see that maroon car pulling out up there? It's a '37 DeSoto. I've seen it before." Before Rossi could reply, Frank counted to five and then pulled out.

"You're following him?" Rossi asked.

"Only long enough for you to get his license plate number."

After half a block, Rossi said, "Okay, got it."

At the next corner, the DeSoto turned left. Frank slowed and then made a right.

"Where have you seen it?" Rossi asked. "And what's this about?"

"When Danny and I first interviewed Maxwell, he claimed to be waiting for a client, and when we came out, that car was sitting there."

"So," Rossi said, "he probably had to come back as part of their business."

"Yeah, but what business, exactly?" He made three more right turns and pulled up in front of the Maxwell home. When he rang the bell, there was no answer.

"I guess the client didn't find him at home," Rossi said.

"I don't believe for a minute he's a client, and I suspect that if he didn't find Maxwell at home, he'd camp out and wait. And that's exactly what we'll do if he doesn't answer the door." Frank checked his watch. "His two kids will be home from school in a couple of hours. If he's gone somewhere, he'll be back by then."

***

Robert Maxwell was still shaking, and the ringing bell so soon after his visitor's departure made it worse. He'd never come back once his visit ended and his message had been delivered. But a glance through the living room window revealed it was not the visitor at all, but two other men, one of whom he recognized. He was a detective who'd questioned him about Carla.

A surge of relief! He could tell the police everything, and they could protect him and put an end to this nightmare.

But no. The visitor had warned him specifically not to contact the police or else there would be serious consequences affecting the children.

Sweet Mary and little Ken.

Other thoughts grappled for his attention, desperate for a way out.

Pay the money. He could raise it, although it would be difficult. Pay it and be done with it.

Although he suspected it wouldn't stop with one payment. They'd keep squeezing him and he'd keep paying until there was nothing left.

Take the children and run. Move out of state. Sell the business if he could find a buyer. Make a new start in some other place.

But his client list was meager and not worth paying for. And wherever he went, they would likely follow, and the consequences would be worse.

He could buy a gun and shoot the visitor the next time he showed up.

Someone else would kill him and probably the children, too.

***

It was just a brief flicker of movement behind the curtain, but Frank was certain he'd seen it. "He's home. He's just not answering the door."

"Why would he do that?" Rossi asked. After thinking about it, he continued, "Of course. Whoever that guy was probably scared the shit out of him."

Frank pounded on the front door with his fist. "Mr. Maxwell? Police!" Moments later, he pounded on the door once more, shouting, "Open up, Mr. Maxwell."

Maxwell, pale as a ghost, opened the door. "Please don't do that."

Frank's demeanor turned friendly. "May we come in? This is Detective Rossi." They stepped inside. "Sorry to be so insistent, but I saw you had a visitor who just left, so I assumed you were in."

Maxwell's eyes went wide. "You saw… I mean, yes, I had a client here. I was just cleaning up some papers, which is why I couldn't answer the door when you first rang."

"Who was he?" Frank asked.

"As I said, he was a client."

"I need a name."

"Why would you need that? He's just a client of mine."

"Because he was the same client you were expecting the last time I was here. I recognized the car."

"Perhaps he was, but I still don't see any reason to tell you. I mean, it's not as if I'm involved an anything illegal."

"Then you have no reason to withhold the name. And the longer you do, the more I smell something fishy."

"No, no, there's nothing fishy at all. His name is John Bartley."

"Thank you. And his address?"

"705 West 252nd Street."

"North Riverdale?" Rossi asked.

"That's right," Maxwell replied.

"And what was his business with you?" Frank asked.

"Just clearing up some questions I had on the financials for the concern I'm auditing."

***

Danny held the paper bag containing the .45 caliber shell the search of the boat's interior had turned up. Officers had swarmed over every surface dusting for fingerprints, turning up several.

"How many people?" Danny asked the sergeant.

"Looks like five."

One set would certainly belong to Trent, but the presence of others meant that, without an eyewitness to the contrary, they wouldn't be able to place him on the boat on Thursday morning. "At least some of those would likely belong to your employees, correct?" Danny asked the manager.

"Perhaps."

"Get prints of all of them," Danny said to the sergeant. "Then let's get the boat out of the water."

"I couldn't reach Mr. Trent," the manager said.

"Okay, do we just pull it out and look, or do we impound it and order a police boat to tow it?" Danny dangled the search warrant in front of the stunned manager's face. "Up to you."

"I'm certain, under the circumstances, Mr. Trent would prefer you leave the boat here."

"Good. My partner and I will interview your employees as they're fingerprinted."

THIRTY-TWO

Danny remained silent all the way back to the precinct. Too much remained unresolved, and it irked him he'd had no word from Larkin since they'd split up.

"Want to stop for a late lunch before we go back?" McHugh asked.

"No. Too much to do."

But he wasn't prepared for the first thing Larkin said when they entered the station house. "I think we have a problem."

"Well," Greco said, coming up behind him, "then I suggest we all repair to the conference room, and you can tell me all about it."

Danny hated it when Greco did this, but then Greco probably hated it when Danny and Larkin made sure they had their stories aligned before they briefed him.

As soon as the door closed behind them, Greco pounced. "Okay, Danny, what did you turn up on the boat?"

"If you don't mind, Lieutenant…"

"I do mind, Danny. Here's the agenda: first, the boat; second, Larkin's accountant; third, next steps."

There was no missing Larkin's distressed expression, but there was nothing Danny could do about it. "Okay, Lieutenant. We dusted the boat for fingerprints, and it will take two or three days to process them, possibly longer to find out who they all belong to. The hull showed clear signs of damage, suggesting a collision with a very hard, irregularly shaped object. Now, Frankie, what are you on about?"

Before Greco could react, Larkin said, "We saw the DeSoto again, pulling out just as we were turning onto Maxwell's block. We followed until Vinnie got the license number."

"It's 9-B-648," Rossi said. "New York 35 plates. We haven't had time to check the Motor Vehicle Bureau records, yet."

"That's odd," Danny said. "What the hell are 1935 plates doing on a 1937 car?"

"Maybe you got the year wrong," Greco said. "Maybe they were '37 plates."

Rossi shook his head. "Yellow plate, raised black lettering."

"Yeah," Greco replied. "Same as '37, and the same numbering scheme."

But Rossi held his ground. "Except the 'NY 35' label was on the bottom of the plate. The '37 plates had the state and year on top."

"This guy knows his license plates," Larkin said, sotto voice.

"Did he see you following him?" Danny asked.

Larkin shrugged. "Not likely. I was only behind him for half a block. Chances are he never noticed, and if he did, there are no markings on the front indicating police."

"If he noticed you, he might remember the last time we were there," Danny said. "What about Maxwell?"

Larkin recounted the conversation. "He was covering up something, no question. But he gave us the name and address of the client. 705 West 252nd Street."

"Wait a minute," McHugh said. "I used to walk a beat in North Riverdale. There is no 705 on that street. The last address is in the high 600s."

Larkin pounded the table. "Goddamn it. I knew he gave it up too fast."

"Sean, research the name and the license plate registrant," Danny said. "But I'm sure they won't be the same."

"Great," Greco snorted. "Just terrific. Danny, how certain are you that the boat you checked out today was the one used to dump the body?"

All eyes turned toward Danny, but he had to answer truthfully. "All I can prove is that it hit something hard, and recently, and a .45 was fired by someone on board at some point. The damage to the hull was fresh. I can ask Trent, but he'll either give me some shite about it or claim not to know anything."

"Either way, you'll have tipped him off you know," Greco said.

"He knows we know, anyway," Danny replied. "Because he knows we searched the boat, including pulling it out of the water."

"So, what's next?" Larkin asked.

Danny considered it for several moments. "If we do nothing, he'll probably assume we suspect him and are looking to build a case without his help. That might prompt him to act impulsively, exposing either himself or whoever is in charge, possibly providing us with another clue. At worst, he'll keep his head down, keeping him out of our way. I say leave him until we have more information."

"What about Maxwell?" Greco asked.

"Him," Danny replied, "I want to question again. I'm wondering if maybe he's involved."

Greco all but exploded. "What?"

But Danny remained calm. "Lieutenant, if your wife was murdered, what would you do?"

"Find the sonofabitch who did it and kill him." Seeing Danny's grin, he added, "Well, that would be my first reaction, but..."

"Thanks, Lieutenant, but your first reaction was exactly what I was looking for. We know Gervin was a big talker, so maybe someone in Lombardo's organization wanted his mouth shut for him. But it didn't happen until after he killed Carla Maxwell."

"So," Greco said, "you think Maxwell paid to have Gervin killed?"

"That would only make sense if he knew Gervin had done it," Larkin said.

"Tell me, Frankie," Danny said. "Do you believe anything Maxwell has told us?"

Larkin thought about it.

"Exactly," Danny said. "Lieutenant, I'm not ruling anything out. I'm going to stop and see Cogan tomorrow to bring him up to date on Trent and the boat." He checked his watch, thinking of Meg. "I need to be on my way."

"I'll give you a lift," Larkin said.

As they approached the car, Danny said, "This is new for you, driving in every day."

"Might as well enjoy the benefits of my profession." Under the gasoline rationing system, most car owners had "A" cards, restricting them to 4 gallons of gasoline per week. Members of certain professions considered critical to the war effort, including police, had the coveted "X" card, which allowed unlimited fill-ups.

"That must not sit well with Helen."

"Nothing sits well with her these days. She has a right puss on her most of the time. But I'm the police officer, not her."

When Larkin pulled up to the apartment, Danny thanked him for the lift but said nothing else. He climbed the stairs, looking forward to a cheerful greeting from Meg.

But he found her waiting, ashen-faced. "Lieutenant Greco called ten minutes ago. He said for you to call him as soon as you got home, that it was urgent."

THIRTY-THREE

Detective Declan Fagan's body had been found in a wooded area behind the station house, just off University Avenue, after the desk sergeant had received an anonymous phone call complaining of a foul odor in the area. His tie was wrapped and knotted tightly around his neck as if he'd been strangled, but he'd been shot in the head with a .45. A half-eaten bun had been left near his body.

McHugh was already there. "The guy from the coroner's office says he was probably killed early this morning. The lady living in the house nearest these woods says she has seen no one prowling around all day. Neither has anyone else. And no one admitted calling in the complaint. No signs of any nibbling by wildlife, either."

"Too early for that," Danny said. "But I'm surprised the bun is still here. Any signs he put up a fight?"

"No. Which surprises me. Unless he was jumped from behind."

"I doubt it. He was in hiding someplace and they found him, probably someone he knew who invited him to go somewhere for a chat. Once isolated, they killed him without a struggle."

"That they left the bun kinda gives me the willies," McHugh said. "The reference is obvious."

Danny nodded. "Too bloody obvious."

Greco joined them. "After talking to Meg, I left a message for Larkin, but he hasn't gotten back to me. What's your next move when he gets here?"

If he got there, which Danny doubted he would, because he was certain Larkin wouldn't get the message. "I've been waiting for Cogan to provide me with additional information. McHugh and I will head down there now to see him."

"What about Larkin?" Greco asked. "Helen said she'd tell him when he got in."

There was no way Danny was going to bring Frankie's marital problems into the discussion. "I think they had plans for tonight. I don't recall what. Anyway, let's not hold things up for him. If he joins us, he can gather all the information from the coroner and about the crime scene. In the meantime, I'll stop in and give Cogan the latest."

Greco's eyes narrowed. "Is there something going on with Larkin you haven't told me?"

Danny flashed a disarming smile. "No, Lieutenant, not to my knowledge."

***

Making a cold call on Cogan was risky after six, but Danny, aware of Cogan's late work hours, wanted to ensure there were no casual listeners around. He was grateful that Greco hadn't asked him why he was so anxious to see Cogan tonight, since that would have provoked another battle.

The FBI's office on East 69th Street was almost deserted, but Cogan was still there. "To what do I owe the pleasure?"

Danny recapped the details about Fagan's disappearance and subsequent murder.

Cogan sat back and pondered it. "So, you think Lombardo is sending you a message to back off?"

Good, no mention of Curt Ramsay. Best to keep that one dark. "At first, yes. But leaving the bun with the body was too outlandish. It leads me to believe someone wanted to make it look that way, someone who knew the details of Carla Maxwell's murder."

"Wait," McHugh said. "You don't think Lombardo was behind Carla's death?"

"I'm thinking there are a lot of different variations that could be in play, here. We now have three deaths that are connected, but to what degree? The one thing I'm certain of is that Mr. X's death and Gervin's death were carried out to call attention to the rackets. Also, I'm convinced if Lombardo had wanted Mr. X killed for squealing, he'd have done it as quietly as possible."

"What about as a warning to other cops on the pad?" McHugh asked.

"His disappearance alone would have done that," Danny replied. "This calls attention to it, and it raises the possibility of a departmental crackdown."

"Upping the ante for keeping cops on it," Cogan said. "I have to agree with you, Danny. How do you propose to respond?"

Danny pressed him. "Can you find out if anyone is trying to shove Lombardo aside?"

"I can try, but it will take time."

"A luxury we don't have. When news of Mr. X's murder hits the papers, we may lose any control we have over this investigation."

"Now that he's dead, can you tell me Mr. X's real name?"

Might as well, since it would be in the papers within the next twenty-four hours. "Detective Declan Fagan. One more thing: I need the address where can I find Lombardo."

***

The social club Armand Lombardo called his "office" was on Arthur Avenue, just off 187th Street.

"On the same street as the Roosevelt Beer Garden and Pizzeria," McHugh said.

"Sounds like the perfect place for a fine Irish lad and his Jewish girlfriend," Danny said with a laugh as they crossed the Third Avenue Bridge back into the Bronx.

"Yeah, I've taken her there a few times. She likes it."

"Boyo, you could take her to a stable for a dinner of oats, and she'd think it was the Ritz."

McHugh turned serious. "What, exactly, do you have in mind when we meet with Lombardo?"

"We are not meeting with Lombardo. I am." Danny needed to forestall McHugh's objections. "This must be low key. I want you to remain outside in the car. If you see any signs of a disturbance, call for backup. The same if I'm not out in thirty minutes."

"You might be dead by then."

"No. Lombardo has an empire to protect, and there's already a dead detective who was on his payroll. Keep in mind, Sean, racketeers buy cops, they don't kill them unless it's a shootout, which they do their best to avoid. If I'm right, Lombardo will be as eager to nail whoever is behind these deaths as we are."

"What if you're wrong, Danny?"

He parked a few doors down from the social club. "That's why I set the time limit before you call for backup."

THIRTY-FOUR

Conversation in the social club abruptly stopped when Danny, the lone Irishman, entered. As he made his way to the bar, a powerfully built man slightly shorter than Danny followed two steps behind, saying nothing.

"Can I help you, friend?" the bartender asked.

Danny laid a five-dollar bill on the bar. "I'll have whatever's good on tap."

The bartender drew a glass of Knickerbocker, placed it in front of Danny, picked up the sawbuck and laid four dollar bills and three quarters next to the beer.

"Keep it," Danny said.

The muscle-bound bouncer drew closer.

"What's the gag?" the bartender asked.

Danny took a sip of the beer. "No gag," Danny replied with a calmness he didn't feel. "I'm looking for Mr. Lombardo."

"He ain't here."

"Then please call him." Danny pulled out his badge. "Tell him I'm here on unofficial business." The bouncer clamped a hand on Danny's arm, but Danny kept calm and said, "You wouldn't want to do that, me bucko. My business could become official quickly, and none of us wants that."

The bartender gave a quick shake of his head, and the bouncer released his grip and walked away. "What should I say your unofficial business is?"

"Unofficial."

The bartender reached under the bar. A moment later Lombardo emerged through a door next to the bar. He was a compact man, only five-nine, with an oval face that with his goatee trimmed to a point appeared longer. An old scar along the edge of his jaw, his black hair slicked back, and thick high arched black brows over glaring eyes gave him a devilish appearance that his tailored suit, white shirt, and striped tie in a perfect Windsor knot did nothing to dispel.

In short order, his glare gave way to a grin and a quick snort of a laugh. "A little far from Sedgwick Avenue, aren't you, Detective Brady?"

***

It was after eight, and still no sign of Danny. Normally, Meg wouldn't be worried because she'd gotten used to this sort of thing. But Danny's warnings about the case took this out of the normal routine.

The phone rang, making her jump. She snatched the receiver, glad that Danny had called.

"Mrs. Brady, this is Lieutenant Greco. Has Danny gotten home, yet?"

"No. Why? When did he leave?"

"Just before six, but he was making a stop in Manhattan, so…"

"Where in Manhattan? Why?"

"I'm so sorry to have disturbed you, Mrs. Brady. Just please have him call me when he gets in."

"Wait, Lieutenant…"

But the line went dead.

She immediately called Helen to ask if Frankie was home, yet.

"Yeah, he got in around six-thirty. Why?"

"Can I talk to him, please?"

"Sorry, hon, but he only had time for a quick fight with me before he ran out again. He's either at a bar or out on a date, possibly both. It's not enough the bastard leaves me without a car during the day, he has to take it at night, too."

"Did he say anything about Danny?"

"No. He never mentions Danny anymore because whenever he does, I remind him how a proper husband treats his wife." Helen stopped. "Wait. What's wrong?"

"Danny's late, and I haven't heard from him. And then Lieutenant Greco called a few minutes ago asking if he was home, yet."

"Well, I warned you what you were in for." It only took a moment for her to add, "Oh, I'm sorry, Meg, that was heartless of me. I'd offer to come over, but without the car..."

"No, that's okay. I'm sure he'll be home soon." She replaced the receiver and started for the kitchen. But she turned for the bedroom, instead.

She stared down at little Patrick, fast asleep. She stroked his back and whispered a prayer. "Dear Lord, please keep Danny safe."

***

Danny settled into the seat opposite Lombardo's desk in the tidy little office that gave no clues about the affairs of its occupant.

Lombardo broke into a disarming grin. "You seem surprised I recognized you."

"Not at all. I suspect if we put all our cards on the table, we would each discover much the other knew."

180

"You think I was behind the murders of Mrs. Maxwell and Mr. Gervin."

"I suspected you, initially. But the murder of Detective Fagan has caused me to think again."

Lombardo's expression didn't change, and his hesitation was only momentary. "I don't believe I know a Detective Fagan."

Already fencing. Not a good sign. "He told me you knew him very well. I won't go into how." Danny studied him for a moment. "You didn't know he was dead, did you?"

Another hesitation. "As I said, I don't know any…"

"Mr. Lombardo, his dead body, along with a half-eaten bun, was left on land behind our station house, and we received an anonymous tip by phone. You're too smart to have a detective killed and then thumb your nose at the police that way. And if you had arranged for the untimely demise of Nick Gervin, you certainly wouldn't have left his body out in the open. Those actions reek of an amateur's panic."

"Why do you think that?"

"Whoever was responsible wanted to curtail the police investigation of Carla Maxwell's murder. But any clear-thinking person would realize it would have just the opposite effect. And you are a clear-thinking person."

"So, if you don't believe I was responsible—and you're correct, I wasn't—why are you here?"

"Because whoever was responsible has gone to great lengths to make you look guilty, suggesting that someone is trying to use the police department as a tool to take you down."

Lombardo broke into the slightest of grins. "A reasonable suggestion."

"Here's another one: you might know who is behind it."

The grin grew wider. "In which case I may take care of it in my own way and in my own good time."

"Ah, see, that's where we run into a problem. Because if you do that, you only make yourself look complicit in the whole mess."

Danny added a grin of his own. "And, who knows, you may be, and my hunch may be all wrong. Perhaps we should investigate you, after all."

"You're welcome to investigate."

Danny took another moment to assess him. "Mr. Lombardo, you knew who I was the minute you saw me. So, you must know you don't scare me. I came here because I think we have a mutual interest in seeing these murders solved. If I'm right, you'll tell me what I need to know and won't frustrate my work afterward, while I'll do what I must while leaving your operations as undisturbed as circumstances allow."

"And if you're wrong?"

Danny glared at him and held it until Lombardo's grin vanished. "Am I?"

Lombardo's grin returned. "No. But you will understand if I can't reveal to you what you need to know."

"Not directly. But I'm sure you can point me in the right direction. Some innocent remark with a hidden meaning."

"I'm sorry, Detective, but you realize that change is constant and some of us adapt better than others. Such is the way of the world."

Danny considered it, then slowly nodded. "Thank you."

"I must remember," Lombardo said, "never to play poker with you."

THIRTY-FIVE

Tuesday, May 25, 1943

"Allied air attacks on the German city of Dortmund have brought the total bomb load dropped on Germany to date to 100,000 tons. In Washington, several officials have resigned from the Food Price Division of the Price Administration Office in a major dispute over policy. Observers are calling for President Roosevelt to intervene. Meanwhile, the OPA crackdown on violators of the pleasure driving ban continues with many holders of A cards losing coupons."

***

Danny stormed into Greco's office as soon as he arrived at the station house. "Why the hell did you call Meg last night?"

"I was trying to reach you. I wanted to know what you found out from Cogan. Besides, what are you all steamed about? I'm not allowed to call you at home?"

"Not when the radio spews reports that a detective was found murdered behind our station house. She was a wreck when I got home."

"Well, maybe it's not the best idea to go off on your own and not tell anybody. It's bad enough I've already got one detective with his head up his ass. What the hell is wrong with Frankie, anyway?"

"Don't change the subject," Danny said as he did so himself. "Did we get anything back on Trent's boat?"

"Yeah. Lots of fingerprints and palm prints. They're still working through them. They found one palm print on a railing that was too smudged to be able to read, like the person had grabbed it and then moved his hand while holding on. But you'll be interested to know it was a left hand with no thumb."

"So, they used Trent's boat to take Gervin's body to Goose Island, and it may even have been where he was killed."

"Or, he might have been on it some other time."

Danny narrowed his eyes. "Are you volunteering for the Trent Defense Team?"

"Jesus, Danny, I'm just trying to test your theory. Ease up, will ya?"

"Sorry," Danny said. "Anything on the hull?"

"They found a few fragments of the same rocks as Goose Island. Crime Scene is going out this morning to see if there are any traces of wood that match the Chris Craft."

"If they find any, we can pick up Trent and squeeze him." Danny left Greco's office. McHugh had arrived. "Come on, Sean."

"Wait," Greco called. "Where are you going?"

"To see Cogan again," Danny replied.

"You still need to tell me what you two talked about last night."

"I'll brief you when we get back. Meanwhile, when Frankie comes in, please have him follow up with Crime Scene to learn what they come up with."

***

"Good Christ," Cogan said with a sigh. "Don't you guys ever go home?"

"First things first." Danny took a seat and McHugh followed. "I met with Lombardo last night. He fenced for a while, but he gave me a clue about who we're looking for."

"A clue?" Cogan asked. "You mean he didn't just tell you?"

"He's playing his cards very close to the vest." Danny repeated what Lombardo had said about adapting to change. "That suggests there is someone working for him at a high level who also worked for Giuseppe Calvino, and who doesn't like the way things are going."

"Was that all he said?" McHugh asked.

"Wait," Cogan said. "You weren't together?"

"No," Danny replied. "I had Sean wait in the car. I figured two of us might spook Lombardo, and I needed someone outside to call for backup if things went to hell. And, yes, that was all he said. Which makes me think that there may be more than one potential rival. Bill, I'm hoping your guys can give me a clearer picture."

"Ever stop to think he might've just been throwing you a curve?" Cogan asked.

"I considered that, but I don't think he is. He's happy to have us working to take out a rival who's getting at him from the inside, providing he doesn't place any of his operation at risk."

Cogan reached for a cigarette and lit it. After a thoughtful drag, he said, "If Tom Donegan gets a hold of this, it'll be my neck."

The mention of Cogan's boss didn't surprise Danny, nor did it deter him. "You can blame me. Just say I requested information connected with a cop killing but provided no background. I need to know who in Lombardo's operation previously worked for Gravedigger Joe and where they fit. I also need anything you have on Trent, and I need it today."

"Is that all?" Cogan asked.

"I should think that would be enough for now," Danny replied. "Please leave a message at the precinct when you have them, but don't reveal any information to anyone. Not even Lieutenant Greco."

Cogan flashed a grin. "You're learning."

***

Frank Larkin hadn't waited for Greco's answer when he asked him to have Rossi follow up on the evidence found on Trent's boat and that he was checking out another lead. Calling from a pay phone meant he didn't have to worry about Greco calling him back.

He rubbed his cheek where Bridie, the raven-haired barmaid at his favorite local bar who hailed from County Clare, had slapped him last night. The physical pain was gone, and now only guilt remained. He'd known her for years and they'd always enjoyed a gently teasing relationship. But last night, he'd done the unthinkable, driven by frustration from his latest tussle with Helen, this time in front of their daughter, fear at the sense of a case spinning beyond the control of even the likes of Danny Brady, and too many shots and beer chasers.

The pass had been clumsy, dripping with poorly disguised innuendo. The slap was immediate and heads all along the bar had turned. It was an unwritten rule: customers never made passes at Bridie. Frank had skulked out of the tavern.

Greco didn't know where Danny was headed, but Frank knew. And the possibility of young McHugh supplanting him as Danny's partner gnawed at him as he was already reeling from the news of Declan Fagan's death. He set out on his own, driving out of the city, a cigarette dangling from his lips, seeking his own kind of redemption.

They hadn't heard from Charlie Lavery since Fagan's disappearance. He'd said his wife and kids were staying with his in-laws in Connecticut. Frank rechecked the address and continued up US-1.

***

"Where the hell is Larkin?" Greco shouted the moment Danny and McHugh returned to the precinct. "He called in and then went off on his own without saying where he was going or why. Since he's driving his own car, we have no way to reach him."

"So, where to, now, Danny?" McHugh asked. "Think he went to pick up Trent?"

"Until we hear from the lab about the splinters and the fingerprints, we don't have probable cause on the Gervin murder. Frankie knows that as well as we do."

"So, where is he?"

"I wish I knew."

Danny's phone rang. It was Ramsay. "Meet me at the information booth at Grand Central at one o'clock, sharp." It was followed by a loud click. Danny checked his watch. 12:15. The subway was his best bet, but the timing was going to be tight.

"Where are you going?" Greco demanded as Danny stood to go.

"To see a fella about a racehorse. Sean, you keep the pressure on the lads at CSU while I'm gone."

THIRTY-SIX

Danny climbed the stairs from the Lexington Avenue Line's 42nd Street stop to the interior of Grand Central Terminal. There were lines at every ticket window and travelers dashed about, including many men in uniform. Announcements of departing trains droned over the loudspeaker system. Danny checked his watch against the enormous clock looming over the information counter.

It was 12:58. No sign of Ramsay.

Danny struggled to hold his annoyance in check. If this was just a wild goose chase…

"Hello, Dan." A voice from behind.

Ramsay.

"Hello Curt."

"Headed for the subway? Me, too."

They walked back toward the stairs. After they passed through the turnstiles, Ramsay held out an envelope. "I copied this information from our case files. You are not to show this to anyone. After you've read and digested it, burn these notes."

Danny grinned at him. He must be joking.

But Ramsay remained steely-eyed. "There's nothing funny about this, Dan. I'm risking my career by even telling you this information exists. I'm counting on you to keep it absolutely confidential."

Danny turned serious. "What if I need it for my investigation? What if my lieutenant asks me where I got it?"

"Tell him you got it from an anonymous source."

"That's not probable cause."

"Welcome to my world. Do you want the information with my conditions or don't you?"

Danny took the envelope. "Okay."

Ramsay relaxed. "Good. Watch yourself, Dan. You've got Meg and Patrick to think of." He turned for the stairs to the downtown trains.

Danny grabbed the next Woodlawn-bound train. On the ride back, he replayed the odd exchange in his head, focusing on the mention of Meg and Patrick.

It sounded like a threat.

***

The Norwalk. Connecticut neighborhood where Lavery's in-laws lived was quiet. As Frank pulled up, he noted that Charlie's car was nowhere around. Not a good sign.

Peggy Lavery answered the door after the second ring. A petite blond, her usually cheerful face was creased with worry. "Oh. Frankie. Hi, how are you?"

"Fine, thanks, Peggy. Is Charlie around?"

She stepped outside and closed the front door behind her. "No, he isn't. I haven't seen him since he dropped us off here on Sunday. He called last night saying he was okay, but he wouldn't tell me what's going on. Do you know?"

"Did he say where he was staying?"

Some of the color drained from her cheeks. "I assumed he was calling from home. You mean he isn't there?"

Too late to do anything about that. "I called but got no answer."

"How did you know I'd be here?"

"He mentioned it yesterday morning. Has he talked about the job at all, lately?"

"Come on, Frankie. You know we wives are the last to know anything. Do me a favor: just tell me what is going on. What has he done and who is he hiding from?"

"He's done nothing wrong, but some fellas he worked with in the past may have."

"Like what? Taking money to look the other way?"

Frank shrugged. "It happens. The next time he calls, will you please ask him to call me? Better yet, Danny Brady."

"You mean he's mixed up in this, too?"

"We're trying to get to the bottom of it."

She nodded back toward the house. "My kids are missing school. I may just take them back."

He placed his hands on her shoulders. "For the love of Mary, please don't do that."

***

When Danny returned to the precinct, Greco was waiting for him. "What have you been up to? I was about to send out the hounds."

Ramsay's warning flashed through his mind. "Chasing down an anonymous tip."

"Concerning what?"

"Doesn't matter, it was nothing."

Greco glared at him. "Where the hell is Larkin?"

"Ah, well, you see, Lieutenant, as I wasn't here when he called in, and I haven't spoken with himself since yesterday afternoon, I'm afraid I can't help you there."

"All right, then, can you at least shed some light on what's eating him these days?"

McHugh approached. "Heard from the lab. They found hairs that match Gervin. They were found sticking to a pointed edge, and the coroner's report says Gervin had a deep wound to the scalp on the back of his head where hairs were missing."

"So, we have Gervin on the boat and the boat at Goose Island," Greco said. "Excellent. So, why the long face?"

"Two sets of fingerprints from the boat match employees of the marina," McHugh replied. "One matches Gervin's."

"Great," Danny said, seeing a chance to get out before Greco asked more about his anonymous tip. "Let's go pick up Trent."

"Hold it," Greco replied. "You still don't know if you can put him in the boat."

But Danny was already pulling McHugh toward the door. "It's his boat. If he wasn't on it, he knows full well who was."

THIRTY-SEVEN

"Is someone going to tell me what this is all about?" Trent asked when Danny and McHugh walked into the interrogation room. They'd returned with him under arrest and left him cooling his heels after being fingerprinted. It had taken time to get a report back on whether Trent's prints were among those lifted from the boat.

They weren't, and now Greco was joining him and McHugh with Trent while Rossi waited outside for some word on Larkin.

Danny opened his file and made a show of studying its contents. "Nick Gervin."

"Never heard of him."

Danny flashed a grin. "Of course not. However, he was murdered on your boat last Wednesday."

"That's preposterous."

The grin gave way to a look of sincerity. "Oh, no. Not at all. He was shot in the head with a .45 caliber pistol, and we found a spent .45 shell casing in the cockpit of your boat. We also found some of his hairs there, apparently the result of a struggle before he was killed, as well as his fingerprints and a palm print of his left hand, the one with no thumb."

"And whose fingerprints did you find besides his?" Trent asked.

"Two marina employees and two others we are still looking to match."

"But not mine, which you just took."

"No."

"So, why am I here?"

Danny turned to McHugh. "Interesting, isn't it? He knew we hadn't found his prints on the boat."

"Because I haven't been on it," Trent said.

"Except for a week ago Saturday, when you filled it with gasoline and took it out," Danny said. "Fascinating that you knew to wipe it clean of your fingerprints." Before Trent could answer, Danny added, "You also neglected to provide details about your prior work history with the ILA."

"International Longshoremen's Association," McHugh added.

"You knew I was a longshoreman."

"But you performed a great deal more work for the union, under Antonio Anastasio, running policy lotteries, better known as numbers rackets, on the docks, than you did loading and unloading ships," Danny said. "And they took care of you when you got hurt, even let you get out of the rackets."

"I didn't think anyone ever retired from the rackets," McHugh said.

"Maybe he didn't retire," Danny replied. "After all, he let them use his boat to settle a score. Anything for his old pal, Armand Lombardo."

"Who?" Trent asked.

"You know," Danny said. "The guy who ran the shape-ups on the pier you worked. You collected the kickbacks from the poor slobs forced to pay to get picked for work. Turned the names of the non-payers over to the goons who convinced them to pay up their agreed amounts. Got yourself assigned to a regular work gang, but never had to show up to work. You got hurt when you had to work a shift for appearances' sake when a detective came sniffing around about the union's rackets. Anastasio and the boys took care of you." When Trent protested, Danny held up the closed file folder. "It's all right here."

"Bullshit."

"Not at all. But I can't understand why you turned on Lombardo after he took such good care of you. Or didn't you know it wasn't Lombardo who needed a boat?"

A momentary flicker of alarm. "I have no idea what you mean."

"Yes, you do. You got a call from someone asking to use your boat and claiming it was Lombardo's request. Naturally, you said yes, no questions asked. Why would you? After all, you get requests to use the boat all the time, what with moving stolen goods and contraband."

"That's ridiculous."

"Is it? Pilfering and smuggling are rampant all throughout the harbor, and the stuff gets moved using small boats and trucks, and no one's the wiser." He glanced inside the folder. "I'm guessing that the call came from one of two individuals. All I need from you is the name."

"Who are the two individuals?"

Danny closed the file. "That's not how it works. You tell me, or else you're an accessory to murder."

"I assure you I'm no such thing."

Danny leaned forward. "And I assure you, Mr. Trent, that you are and will be charged as such unless you cooperate fully with this investigation. Who contacted you about the boat last week?"

"Nobody. I wasn't aware of anyone using my boat."

"Oh, you have an understanding with someone that they can use it whenever they need it?" Danny asked.

"No. Nothing of the sort. As for my fingerprints not being found, that's because I always wear work gloves on the boat. I don't like getting callouses."

Danny turned to McHugh. "Imagine that. A longshoreman afraid of callouses."

McHugh stood and walked around the table, behind Trent, as if he were leaving, but he stopped and swung a hard right at Trent's head. Trent instantly raised his right arm, fending off the blow.

"Seems that arm is still in pretty good shape, Mr. Trent," Danny said. "Sean, take him down and book him for accessory to murder."

***

Greco gestured for Danny to follow him into his office, then closed the door. "What exactly do you have in that file?"

"What do you mean, Lieutenant?"

"Who provided the background information on Trent? Why is this the first I'm hearing about it?" Before Danny could answer, Greco added, "Let me see that file. Now."

Danny handed it to him, silently relieved that he had already burned the notes Ramsay had given him.

Greco turned page after page… the report from the fingerprint unit, the ballistics reports, the coroner's reports on Carla Maxwell, Nick Gervin, and Declan Fagan… "There's nothing here about all that stuff you brought up to Trent. Nothing but your notes on your previous interview with him." He slapped the folder down on his desk. "What the hell are you pulling? And don't give me any of that Irish blarney bullshit."

"Not in a month of Sundays, Lieutenant."

"Goddamn it…"

Enough was enough. "I got it from the anonymous tip I told you about earlier."

"I thought you said it was nothing."

Danny heaved a deep sigh. "I didn't want to go into it before we questioned Trent."

"But you were reading from the file. I saw you."

"No, you saw me looking at the file. But if I convinced you I was reading, then I must have convinced Trent, too, and that's good."

Greco's eyes narrowed. "You trying to tell me you faked all that? That it was just one big bluff?"

"Yes and no. I bluffed that I was reading, but not about what I knew."

"When and how did you learn all this? Don't tell me Cogan had it. Besides, you said it was an anonymous tip." Greco studied him for a few moments. "But it wasn't anonymous, was it? Goddamn it, Danny, I shouldn't have to interrogate my own detectives."

Decision time. "No, you shouldn't. I can't tell you my source, other than to say he's well-positioned to provide the information he gave me."

"Damn it, Danny…"

"I recall something Charlie Lavery said when Frankie and I first talked to him about this case: that if you swear people to secrecy about something confidential, they'll tell someone and swear them to secrecy, and that's how things get out that shouldn't. I won't tell you who gave me this, but I will tell you it wasn't Cogan."

"Is there anything else this source of yours told you I should know?"

Hell would host a snowstorm before Danny revealed the political connection. "Just one."

THIRTY-EIGHT

Frank entered the station house just as McHugh was leaving with Trent. Inside, he found Danny in Greco's office.

"Where in God's name have you been?" Greco said.

"Looking for Charlie Lavery. No one knows where he is. He took off after Declan Fagan went missing."

"What the hell for?" Greco asked. "And why is it suddenly your problem to find him?"

Frank closed the door to Greco's office. "He sent his family to stay with his in-laws in Norwalk, and even his wife doesn't know where he is. And it's my problem, Lieutenant, because I dragged him into this thing. It's already gotten Fagan killed and…"

Danny made a sweeping gesture with his right arm. "Hold it, Frankie. Fagan came to us, not the other way around, and he was killed because he was trying to get out from under." He turned to Greco. "But I disagree with you it's not our problem to help Lavery. He set us up with Fagan and he almost certainly knew how Fagan's disappearance would end."

"Okay," Greco replied. "So, what do you want to do about it?"

"Lavery's wife said he sometimes calls her," Frank said. "I thought we might want to put a tap on her in-laws' phone and then trace the next call he makes to her."

"I doubt Connecticut will take too kindly to the New York Police putting a tap on the phone of one of their residents," Greco said.

"And we need to be careful," Danny added, "not to lead anyone to Lavery who might hunt him down."

"You mean like Lombardo?" Greco asked.

"No," Danny replied. "There are two associates of Lombardo's who worked for Gravedigger Joe. One is a guy named Carl Villano; the other is Jocko Messina. If we're going to tap anyone's phones, it should be those two."

Frank stared at Danny, wondering where he got that piece of information.

But Greco just nodded. "Have McHugh locate the numbers and I'll see to it. In the meantime, let Lavery come to you if he wants help. If he's found himself a haven, it's best to leave him there."

"But his wife wants to take the kids back home," Frank said. "They're missing school. And Charlie moved them because he was afraid to leave them at home."

Greco was adamant. "Lavery's responsible for his family. Unless he asks for help, that's it."

It wasn't right, but unless Danny put up a fight, it was pointless to press it. He followed Danny back out to their desks. "Where did you get that about Villano and Messina?"

***

Ramsay had sworn him to secrecy. But Larkin was his partner. "I can't tell you who…"

Larkin spoke in a harsh whisper. "For God's sake, we're partners. Was it somebody Cogan gave you?"

198

Danny dropped his voice to a whisper as well. "It was. You're the one who was so on about keeping this close to the vest. If we want the complete picture, we need to understand there are others who may be at risk, too. Look at Fagan and Lavery. By all the saints, I'm not even mentioning any of this to Meg."

"Okay, okay. What can you tell me?"

Danny repeated everything he'd learned about Trent's connection to Lombardo and Anastasio. "I won't name my source, but he is someone who was involved with the Panto murder case."

"NYPD or Brooklyn DA's office?"

"Sorry, Frankie, that's as far as I can go."

***

Charlie Lavery turned the corner heading back to the Foster Hotel on Seventh Avenue after mailing a letter to his wife.

But his path was blocked by a familiar face wearing black-rimmed glasses and a fedora. "We meet again."

Charlie tried to push past him.

The man grabbed his arm with an iron grip. "Don't be in such a rush, Detective. We know Fagan went to you for protection, and that you referred him to one Detective Brady. You also know enough from your stint at your former precinct that you could share information with Brady anytime. You'll understand why that would make some folks very nervous."

"But I've said nothing to anyone. And I won't."

"Of course not. You wouldn't want to endanger Peggy and your children. Now, if you'll come with me, we can go somewhere quiet and work out the details." He gestured to the familiar red 1937 DeSoto sedan parked a few feet away.

THIRTY-NINE

It was late in the afternoon when Rossi strode up to Danny's desk. "I got something on that license plate. Registered to a guy who lived in Brooklyn and who died in 1935. Suicide, according to the Brooklyn Coroner's Office. Jumped out a window. I tried to get details from the local precinct, but all I got was the run around."

"Which is enough to set my siren blaring," Danny replied.

"Are you kidding? It gets better. The guy in question was…"

"Let me guess," Larkin said. "A longshoreman."

"Give the man a cigar," Rossi said with a laugh.

But Danny wasn't laughing. "We need to track that car down."

"We could put out an all-points," Larkin said.

Danny waved it away. "That's the worst thing we could do. They'd know about it before we got another patrol car on the road. No, this needs to be just among us."

"Geez, Danny," Larkin said. "You don't trust cops at all anymore?"

Danny shot him a warning glare. He'd stepped over the line, and only a short while after the warning. "Right now, Frankie, I'm not sure who to trust."

***

As soon as the group dispersed, Larkin lit a fresh cigarette using the last remains of the one he'd been smoking when he'd arrived at the precinct and asked Danny in a whisper, "Were you referring to me?"

"Of course not. Why would I?"

"I dunno. First, you wouldn't tell me your source, then that comment. I just get the sense I'm on the outs these days."

"You should have let me know you were off chasing Lavery. And you've been detached lately, so McHugh has been standing in for you. If you don't mind me saying so, I think you're all wrapped up in whatever's gone wrong between you and Helen, and you need to take care of that. Use these next two days off to do it."

They were interrupted when ADA Monroe walked in and pointed to Greco's office. Danny and Larkin followed him in.

"Danny, did you guys arrest Ronald Trent today?" Monroe asked in a low voice.

"We did. Nick Gervin was murdered on his boat, and his boat was used to dump the body on Goose Island. But how did you…"

Monroe glanced at Greco and back. "Did you find any evidence on the boat proving he was the murderer?"

"We did not. He claims to have been wearing gloves when last he was on it."

"So, you can't prove conclusively he was the killer."

Danny tried to make eye contact with Greco, who wouldn't meet his gaze. "We're not charging him with murder, only as an accessory. It was in the booking."

"But you can't prove he was on the boat, or that he gave permission to whoever was. So, you have zero proof he abetted the crime."

"At the moment, yes," Danny replied, "but…"

"You don't have a case against him, period. I've ordered his immediate release."

Larkin all but exploded. "You did what?"

"Easy, Frankie." Danny was working to hold his own temper. "With all respect, Counselor, we hold criminals while making a case against them all the time. This one is connected to a conspiracy that killed a detective."

But Monroe remained unfazed. "You don't know that for certain, either. All you have is a painfully weak circumstantial case against an ILA delegate…"

"How do you happen to know he's an ILA delegate?" Danny asked. "From the same guy who told you all the weak spots in our case?"

"That's not important. What is important is that we're in the middle of a world war, the success of which depends in large part on America shipping desperately needed supplies to our allies overseas. The last thing anyone wants right now is a labor problem on our own waterfront. If you get enough to make an airtight case against Trent, I'll sign the affidavit for the arrest warrant myself. Otherwise, lay off."

For a moment, Danny was tempted to reveal what Ramsay had told him about the deal between the Combination and the Navy assuring there would be no labor problems on the waterfront. But that would mean outing Ramsay to Monroe and Greco, both of whom had already raised questions in Danny's mind about trust.

He stormed out, but Monroe followed him. "Sorry, Danny, it's not personal."

"Okay, just tell me one thing: who ordered you to do this?"

"That's none of your concern. But I'd advise you against digging any deeper. Carla Maxwell's killer is dead. Leave it at that."

"And how about Declan Fagan's killer? Or the guy who ordered it? And what about the fate of Charlie Lavery? I know you don't want to hear this, but you need to." Danny gestured toward the street. "It's about to turn into Dodge City out there."

***

After signing out, Danny tried to relax as he took the subway home. As he walked down the stairs at Grand Central from the Lexington Avenue Line to the Flushing Line, he caught a glimpse of a man in a blue short-sleeve shirt and a snap-billed cap, the brim pulled low over his brow, several steps behind him. Something about him was familiar, like Danny had seen him before.

The man did not make eye contact, and when Danny boarded the Flushing-bound train at the front of a car, the man in the cap boarded the same car at the rear. But as the train emerged from the tunnel in Hunters Point, Danny decided he was letting his nerves get the better of him and put the man in the cap out of his mind.

He had almost relaxed as he left the train at the Bliss Street station when he caught a glimpse of the cap man getting off, too.

Walking home, he glanced around several times, seeing nothing further of the cap man.

But that didn't change his conviction he was being shadowed.

FORTY

Thursday, May 27, 1943

"President Roosevelt ordered striking workers in Akron, Ohio rubber plants to return to their jobs by noon today, calling the strike a blow to the war effort. Meanwhile, the National Railway Labor Panel recommended a general wage increase of eight percent for more than a million railway employees, calling the increase, 'the minimum non-inflationary adjustment necessary to correct gross inequities and aid in the effective prosecution of the war'. The cost of the increase is estimated to be $204 million."

***

Two days off put Danny in a better frame of mind. Helping Meg with Patrick and focusing on family relaxed him, and he tried to put the cap man out of his mind, along with the conundrum facing him. He was tempted to return for another visit with Lombardo but sensed it would be the wrong move. Lombardo might be thrilled to have the NYPD chasing down someone looking to unseat him, but he wasn't about to lift a finger to help.

He was shaving when the phone rang. Meg answered it, and all he heard was, "Okay, Frankie, I'll tell him." A moment later, she appeared at the bathroom door, ashen-faced. "That was Frankie. He won't be able to pick you up this morning. Helen has the car. She dropped Dorothy at school before driving to her folks, where she and Dorothy are staying."

"Jesus, Mary and Joseph. How far away are they?"

"Not far, just over on Argyle Road in Flatbush. Did you know things had gotten that bad?"

"I did." He dried his face.

"I feel like it's partly my fault. I haven't had the chance to talk to her, lately."

He kissed her. "Nothing to do with you, Meg. She's gotten it into her head that Frankie's running around on her. And, I must say, he doesn't do much to help himself."

"You mean Helen might be right?"

"I do not. I mean he retreats when he should be engaging. Now, she's doing the same thing."

"They really should go talk to a priest," Meg said.

"That's just what I told him. But Frankie won't hear of it. After all, he might have to admit he's partly at fault."

She cast a wary eye at him. "Partly?"

"Indeed. From Frankie's side of it, she's quick to accuse and slow to listen. I understand her fears, and Frankie does nothing to calm them, even though he could. That's his own doing. But you'd think after all these years, she'd give him the benefit of the doubt. Do you have her mother's phone number?"

"No, but I can look it up. I'll call her today. Meanwhile, you take care of yourself and be careful."

***

"You look like shite," Danny said as Larkin walked in. When he got no response, he added, "What the hell happened?"

"I got in late the night of your dust-up with Monroe. I stopped off for a drink or two..."

205

"Or three or six."

"Jaysus, Danny! You too?"

"Frankie, you're in this mess because you've been ducking the problem. Pretty soon it will be too late."

"It already is. Helen wants a divorce. The last thing she said to me before she took Dorothy off to her mother's place was, 'If Meg can get a divorce, so can I.' What the hell am I supposed to say to that?"

"You could compare yourself to that useless gobshite Meg dumped instead of running off to stare into the bottom of a whiskey glass. You could tell her how wrong you've been to talk about other women and assure her no one could ever take her place in your life. Go see a priest and if she won't go with you, go see one yourself. Do it today. Tell the desk sergeant you're coming down with something and going home."

***

McHugh arrived a few minutes after Larkin left. Greco still wasn't in, so Danny took McHugh with him, using his own car. He left word at the desk he'd check in periodically by phone.

"No need," the sergeant said. "Lieutenant Greco won't be in until sometime this afternoon. Emergency trip to the dentist."

Good. One less headache.

"Where are we going?" McHugh asked once they were on the road.

"Yonkers. I want to see if we can spot Maxwell's 'client', and if so, to question the little bollocks." But something about McHugh wasn't right. "Are you jaded?"

"No, I'm fine."

They cruised Maxwell's neighborhood for two hours but saw nothing of the elusive DeSoto. Danny finally parked across the street and a couple of hundred feet down the block from

Maxwell's house. "I'm talking to him. If the DeSoto pulls up, honk the horn twice."

"Got it."

Maxwell was surprised to see him. "What can I do for you, Detective?" He gestured to Danny to come inside.

"Thank you. I was curious if your Mr. Bartley has been by lately."

"Who?"

"John Bartley, your alleged client who wears black-rimmed glasses and drives a 1937 DeSoto sedan registered to a man who's been dead for eight years."

Maxwell paled. "I don't know whom you're talking about."

"Sure, you do, although I'm not surprised you've forgotten the fake name you gave me the last time I was here. Did you kill your wife?"

Maxwell's expression turned to one of horror. "Of course not. I could never have harmed a hair on her head."

"Even though she was cheating on you? And don't tell me you didn't know."

He collapsed in a chair. "I didn't want to know. I wanted to believe whatever she told me. There was extra money coming in, so I accepted she really was working late all those nights."

Danny stopped him. "Extra money? How much and how often?"

"I don't know. When we were first married, whenever she went shopping, she'd press me for money. But not long after she started with the late hours, she was buying lots of new clothes and things, saying that she was enjoying the fruits of her labor, as she called it."

"And when did that start?"

Maxwell swallowed hard. "Not long after the first of the year."

Dany tried not to chuckle. "So, what about New Year's Eve?"

"What about it? As I told you, she went to a party with her coworkers. I was sick and couldn't go, but I told her she shouldn't miss out. She'd been so looking forward to going out with her friends and having a good time."

"What time did she get home?"

Maxwell looked away. "I don't know. I was asleep."

"Like hell. You didn't want to know. Probably kept your eyes clamped shut, or turned away from the clock so you wouldn't see. Possibly both. But you knew all the same. After four in the morning, wasn't it?"

"How did you know that?"

"Because I spoke to someone who was tailing her brand-new boyfriend, whom she'd met that night."

"Who? Why was he tailing…?"

"Never mind. He also saw what they did together in the car before she came in."

Maxwell broke down. "Stop it! Why are you doing this to me?"

Danny sat back and waited until Maxwell stopped sobbing. "The man who strangled your wife was a penny ante hoodlum named Nick Gervin. He had some connection with a known racketeer. I suspect your Mr. Bartley, or whatever his real name is, probably works for the same racketeer. Also, Gervin turned up dead last week, shot in the head. All of which suggests that you may have paid to have either Mrs. Maxwell or Mr. Gervin whacked."

"No!"

"Then why has the guy you call Bartley been here? I'm getting a subpoena for your bank records." He'd only just thought of it, and he was certain Monroe would never agree, but Maxwell didn't know that. "If I see any suspicious withdrawals, I'll know you're lying. You can save us all a lot of time and trouble by telling me the truth now, which would be a refreshing change."

Maxwell stood. "Detective, I've answered your questions as well as I can, and I've shown you every courtesy. Now please leave."

FORTY-ONE

McHugh told Danny he hadn't seen the DeSoto, so the only logical course was to see ADA Monroe about the possibility of a subpoena for Maxwell's bank records. "We checked with the phone company, and he pays his bills from a checking account at Manufacturers Hanover Trust, and they have a branch in Yonkers."

Monroe eyed Danny with suspicion. "Why? What's the charge?"

"We've revised our theory of the murder of Carla Maxwell. Her husband admitted to me he knew she was cheating on him, and that's a handsome motive. He has an alibi for that night, so we know he didn't kill her himself, but we think he may have paid a local tough to have her killed."

"You mean he paid Nick Gervin?"

"Or someone who ordered Gervin to do it."

Monroe tossed the pen he'd been holding onto his desk. "Goddamn it, Danny, I told you to steer clear of this thing."

"I'm a cop, Counselor. And I don't like leaving crimes unsolved, especially murders. If Maxwell paid to have his wife snuffed, then he's as guilty as Gervin." Danny paused, got up and closed the door, and returned to his seat. "We've always gotten on well together. And you got as much credit as I did for putting a serial rapist and murderer in the chair."

"As I recall, you didn't approve of my decision not to prosecute him for the rapes. But then, you had an emotional investment in that case."

"Meg and I weren't involved yet when that happened. But I knew how badly she wanted to accuse him in court." Danny allowed himself a grin. "Then again, your decision set in motion the dissolution of her marriage to that gobshite, so I suppose it worked out for the best. Now might be an excellent time for you to follow my advice."

"And that is...?"

"There's enough stench around this case for a barrel of week-old fish. You've been ordered by higher-ups to stifle it, and don't tell me otherwise." For a moment, he considered revealing some of what Fagan and Ramsay had told him about politicians and the rackets but decided that would only inflame matters. "My gut tells me you're as concerned about that fish stench as I am, and maybe almost as eager to dig out all the facts. I don't know what Robert Maxwell is up to, but I know he's scared to death, and it's connected to that shady character in the car registered to a dead man."

"And what do you think his bank records will tell you?"

"I don't have the foggiest notion. All I'm asking is for the chance to find out. I'll share what I find with you, and we can decide what to do then."

***

Frank Larkin pulled up to Charlie Lavery's in-laws' house in the squad car he'd signed out wondering if this was just a waste of time. Though Danny suggested he spend the day reconciling with Helen, he couldn't turn his back on his friend in trouble.

Especially since he was convinced the boat had already sailed on his marriage.

Peggy Lavery answered the door. "No one's home. My mom took the kids to the playground. Please come in, I have something for you."

He followed her into the living room, where the well-stocked bookcases and comfortable furnishings reminded him of Helen's parents' home in Flatbush.

She handed him a letter. "I got this in this morning's mail."

His sense of impending loss of Helen suddenly intensified. It was a letter from Charlie:

Dear Peggy,

I know you're worried, so I wanted to let you know I'm okay. If you see either Frankie Larkin or Danny Brady, either of whom might come looking for me, you can tell them this week I'm at the same hotel where they arrested the Sunday School teacher's killer. They'll know the place.

There's much you don't know about things I've seen in my time on the force, things I never wanted you to worry about. I thought I'd gotten free of them when I transferred precincts, but I was wrong. I realize it's hard for you and the kids right now, but I need to lie low until a certain problem has blown over. Then, we'll be able to move on with our lives. If it all goes wrong, which I suppose it might, please know that I love you all more than anything.

Charlie

"What's this all about, Frankie? That's a farewell note, and you can't tell me any different. I deserve to know."

It hit him like a punch in the stomach. "Yes, you do. I know the hotel he's talking about—the Foster Hotel, a fleabag joint in the Garment District. He's been adamant about not letting us know where he is. So, him asking you to tell us can only mean he's in trouble. I'll check it out and let Danny know, too."

"But what's it all about?"

"Danny and I caught a murder case that appears to be connected to racketeering in the Bronx. A detective Charlie knew in the 51st has since been killed. Charlie put us in touch with him before he died, so Charlie must think he's next. I'll let you know what I find out."

***

The bank manager in Yonkers resisted showing Danny the records for Robert Maxwell's account until Danny shoved the subpoena under his nose. "I still don't understand why New York Police are interested in the bank records of a Yonkers resident."

"And the beauty of it," Danny replied, "is that you don't need to understand. Just comply."

The manager produced the file with Maxwell's records and allowed them the use of an empty office. They started at the beginning of 1938, each taking a year at a time. Danny was near the end of 1940 when he noticed McHugh was staring down but not reading. "Find something?"

McHugh started. "Um, no, not yet." But he was still on 1939.

"Come on, Sean. You need to concentrate on this."

"Yeah, sorry." He returned to the listing of checks and finished reviewing 1939. "Nothing jumped out at me here."

Danny picked it up. "Tell you what: you review them, and I'll check."

Twenty minutes later, McHugh reached the end. "Nothing jumped out at me."

Danny picked up the last page. "How about this? A $5,000 cash withdrawal on May 25th. Nothing else even comes close in the past four years."

McHugh blushed. "That sounds low for a contract killing."

"Might be a first installment." Danny returned the file to the manager. "Mr. Maxwell made a $5,000 withdrawal two days ago.

Here's my card. If he takes out any additional large amounts of cash, anything over a thousand dollars, please call me to let me know."

"Is Mr. Maxwell in some kind of trouble?" the manager asked.

"He may be, and not with us."

***

If Frank expected a twinge of nostalgia upon entering the Foster Hotel, it was lost in his growing fear for his friend, combined with guilt. He had dragged Charlie Lavery into this mess and, through him, Declan Fagan.

"Can I help you?" the desk clerk asked.

"Yeah." Frank flashed his badge. "I'm looking for a guy I know is staying here."

"What's his name?"

"That doesn't matter because I'm sure he didn't register under his real name. It's for me to guess what name he might have used, but I know his handwriting. So, please let me see the register book." When the clerk hesitated, he added, "Don't make me make you give it to me."

The clerk placed the register on the counter.

"Thank you." Frank went slowly, line by line, working backwards. He stopped when he saw it: Vito Redden, in Lavery's wild script. "This guy. Is he still here?"

The clerk paled. "I don't know."

"Has he checked out?"

"No."

"Then he must still be here."

"I dunno."

Frank grabbed him by the shirt, near the collar. "Don't fuck around with me, you little prick. Where is he?"

"I really don't know. I haven't seen him since Tuesday, I swear."

Frank pulled him harder, twisting his fist to tighten the collar to near-strangulation. "Where did you see him? Who was he with? Tell me, or so help me, Christ, I'll…"

"He left the hotel Tuesday morning, and was stopped by some guy…"

"Describe him." A further partial twist.

The clerk's face turned red, and he started to gag, "About six feet, kinda lanky, wearing black-rimmed glasses and a gray fedora."

Frank eased his grip. "Continue."

"They talked for a couple of minutes and then they got into a car together."

"What was the model and year of the car? How about the color?"

"A DeSoto. A dark red DeSoto sedan, about four or five years old."

Frank yanked a little harder "Get the license number?"

"Yeah. At least I think I did. 9-B-648."

"You whisper one word of this to anybody, and I'll come back and burn this place to the ground with you chained to a steampipe in the basement."

FORTY-TWO

When the bell rang, Meg was sure it was Helen even though she hadn't called. But when she answered on the intercom, it was Rebecca Stoneman. Meg buzzed her in. "Forgive me for not coming down to open the door."

Rebecca hugged her. "Not to worry. I just wanted to see if you were okay." She peered into the bassinet where Patrick was sleeping. "Oh, he's such a little sweetheart."

"You should hear him when he wakes up."

Rebecca remained serious. "Helen called me this morning, and she was in a black mood. Is there anything wrong between you two?"

"No, but she and Frankie are having some problems. I offered to listen, but she's rather angry with everyone. I'd love to be able to help her, but I really can't. Danny's tried talking to Frankie, too."

Rebecca fell silent.

"What's wrong, Rebecca?" Meg led her to the kitchen for coffee.

"Is there a reason you've stopped telling me about the case Danny and Sean are working? At first, I figured it was because you were busy with the baby, but now…" She shook her head. "I'm sorry. Maybe Danny hasn't been telling you."

Meg poured two cups and handed one to her guest. "That's part of why Helen is annoyed with me. Danny tells me, because I can't bear to not know, but the nature of the case is such that if any part of his investigation got out, all of us could be endangered."

"Isn't that a little dramatic?"

"No, it isn't. He gave me a choice: I could know what's going on but only on the condition that I tell no one, not even you or Helen, or be kept in the dark. I'm sorry, Rebecca, but I needed to know, and now that I do, I understand why the guys are being so tight-lipped about it."

Rebecca considered it. "But what about us? I need to know just as much as you do."

"I agree. But it's up to Sean to tell you, just as it's up to Frankie to tell Helen."

"He won't. I've begged him. Things have been bad enough with half his family demanding we get married in a Catholic church and the other half saying they won't come even if we do."

"What about your family, Rebecca?"

A teary-eyed attempt at a smile. "Poppa wasn't happy when I told him, but he agreed it was my life and I was entitled to happiness, as long as I promised to raise our children in the Jewish traditions and faith."

"How did Sean take that?"

"He said that we should raise them in both traditions and let them decide when they were adults which to follow."

Meg thought of the priests at St. Sebastian's. "The church might not take kindly to that."

"That's what Poppa said, but Sean just smiled and said that would be their problem, not his."

Meg patted her hand. "Which is one reason you love him so much."

Rebecca's grin faded. "But the stress from this case is making any kind of planning difficult. Can't you at least give me some idea why it's so dangerous? My heart is in my mouth all the time, now. I can't sleep, and I can't stand it."

How far could she go without violating Danny's trust? "It may involve gangsters of some sort. Now, please don't repeat that to anyone; don't even tell Sean you know."

***

Danny and McHugh cruised Maxwell's neighborhood for over an hour but did not see the DeSoto. McHugh hadn't said a word since they'd left the bank.

"How did you miss that $5,000 withdrawal?" Danny kept his voice calm, not wanting to sound accusatory.

"I guess I was expecting a larger number."

"Rule Number One, Sean: never give your partner bollocks. If there's something going on that you're stewing about, and it's interfering with the job, I need to know about it."

No answer.

Danny grinned at him. "This is the part where you tell me what you're so on about."

"Getting a lot of shit about the wedding and where it'll be held, but mostly about how we decide to raise our kids. Like it's any of their business. And Rebecca's been stewing a lot about this case, because nobody is telling her anything—not that I'm complaining. I agree, we can't—but it makes everything else worse."

"Want my advice?"

"Yeah."

"Get married at City Hall, like Meg and I did. Whoever comes, comes, and anyone who doesn't can just feck off. And if anyone asks how you're raising your kids, tell 'em they'll be Druids."

Sean guffawed.

"Now," Danny added, "back to the case."

He continued driving for a bit until McHugh said, "Maybe he only made one payment. Or maybe it was for something else altogether."

"Like what? You think he celebrated his wife's death by purchasing a yacht? Investing in the stock market?"

"Maybe he wants to do something for the kids to take the sting out of their mother's death. I'm sorry, Danny, but he just seemed too broken up to have been responsible for her murder."

True. Maxwell certainly wasn't much of an actor. "Maybe it wasn't for Carla's death. What if it was for killing Gervin?"

McHugh chewed on that for a while. "It's a possibility. But how would a guy like Maxwell know where to find a hit man?"

"Maybe the hit man found him." Danny drove directly to Maxwell's home.

Maxwell groaned as he opened the door. "What is it now?"

"We have more questions," Danny said. "We can discuss them here or we can take you back to the Bronx." He glanced at his watch. Twenty minutes to three. "Your kids will be home from school soon. I'm sure you won't want them coming home to an empty house."

Maxwell waved them in. "This isn't right."

Enough with the delay tactics. "What was the five thousand dollars for?"

"What five thousand dollars?"

Danny grabbed Maxwell by the lapels. "Don't give me any shite, Maxwell. You just took five thousand out of the bank. Who did you pay and what was it for?"

"I… I didn't pay to have Carla murdered."

"I'm sure you didn't. But perhaps you paid to have Nick Gervin murdered."

"No! I didn't even know who he was until after he was dead, when I read his name in the paper. How could I?"

Danny released his grip on Maxwell's lapels. It was finally making sense. "So, why did you pay the five grand to the guy in the black glasses and fedora who drives a maroon DeSoto and isn't called John Bartley?"

"Who says I…?"

For the first time, Danny allowed himself a smile. "Your eyes, Mr. Maxwell. You paid that guy five grand, or my name is Winston Churchill. But if it wasn't to kill Gervin, what was it for? Did you gamble with a client's money and then need a loan from a shady source to pay it back?"

"No, of course not."

"Then tell us, Mr. Maxwell. What was it for? Because I know you paid him that five grand. And whatever it was for, whatever he told you, I can guarantee he'll be back for more."

Something close to terror flashed in Maxwell's eyes.

Danny turned to McHugh. "He's already been back for another dip. I'll bet my pension on it."

"No, it's nothing like that, I swear. He's a client, that's all. And he offered me a chance to invest in…"

Danny growled at him. "Yes, a client who lives at a nonexistent address and drives a car registered to a man who died two years before it was built. It's put up or shut up time, Maxwell. You can be a victim or an accomplice, but you can't be both. Choose. Now."

Maxwell stood in trembling silence. "My children…"

Danny checked the clock on the mantel. "Yes, they'll be home soon."

Maxwell collapsed in an easy chair. "I don't know his name. He came the morning I learned Carla had been killed. He said he knew the man who did it and that he'd pay with his life. All I had to do was keep quiet about it, especially to the police. Then, the day the news broke about the man being found dead on Goose Island, he returned and said there would be a fee of $5,000. He gave me two days to pay, and when I did, he said it was an installment, and he'd be back for another. He's going to keep doing this, isn't he?"

"That's the way the game goes, usually," Danny said. But there was something in Maxwell's eyes. "What else did he say?"

"Nothing about money." He pointed to a framed photograph of the children on the mantel. "But he leered at that and said he thought Mary was so lovely for a girl her age."

FORTY-THREE

Danny and McHugh arrived back at the station house a few steps ahead of Larkin, and they all found Greco, his normal surliness no doubt intensified by his morning in the dentist's chair.

"Will someone please explain what the hell has been going on around here?"

Danny gestured for Larkin to go first, and, after lighting a cigarette, he filled them in on Lavery's letter and what he'd learned about the guy in the DeSoto grabbing him off the street. Danny explained the latest on Maxwell and the circumstantial evidence that the guy who had killed Gervin was now extorting the newly minted widower. "Lieutenant, I think we should ask the Yonkers police to put a guard on the Maxwell home and alert us if this guy shows up."

Greco stared at him. "So, now you suddenly think Maxwell's a babe in the woods, and he needs protection? Other than the car, the glasses, and the fedora, do we have any kind of description on this guy?"

Larkin repeated what the hotel clerk had told him.

"Not enough." Greco all but spat the words. "That description could fit a million guys, except maybe for the car."

"You mean the one registered to the dead guy?" Larkin asked.

Well, welcome back, Frankie.

But Greco wasn't swayed. "Gentlemen, we know Carla Maxwell's killer is dead. Beyond that, you're chasing shadows. Either get me some viable leads or close it out."

"Out," Danny said to Larkin and McHugh.

With Greco turning red, the two detectives bolted. Danny closed the door behind them. "Lieutenant, I don't know what's going on, but I've had all the pushing back I'm going to tolerate. One detective is dead, and possibly two, and you're talking about closing it out?"

"You guys are burning up a tremendous amount of overtime and getting nothing for it. How many times do I have to tell you, the rackets are a low priority?"

"Two dead cops are a low priority?"

"One dead cop we know of, and you said yourself he was on the pad."

"You know full well Lavery has about as much chance of being alive as I have of being elected president. Who's pressuring you?"

"What the hell does that mean?"

"Just what I said. Someone upstairs is giving Monroe shite about this case, and someone is giving you the same. Is it the commissioner? The mayor? Who?"

"Just what are you accusing me of, Detective?"

"Answer me."

Greco turned away. "No one. But this whole mess looks like we're chasing our tails. Get Monroe something he can use besides a weepy accountant's alibi."

***

Danny drove Larkin home, and he was glad the weather was warm enough to keep the windows wide open as Larkin chain-smoked one cigarette after another. Neither said a word the entire way. When Danny parked in front of Larkin's house on Lincoln Road, he turned the engine off. "That was good work today, Frankie. I'm grateful. You haven't been at your best lately, but today was good."

"Thanks,"

"You're not done, yet. This business with Helen has gone far enough. You need to level with her about this case. Tell her everything."

"You can't be serious. You and I agreed…"

"Yes, and I soon found it didn't work. The more secretive we are, the more fearful the girls become. Your secrecy is part of what's killing your marriage."

"And you think that me suddenly opening up is going to solve everything?"

"No. But it's a start. I've been thinking about this all day, and I have a suggestion. Why don't you and Helen come to our place tomorrow night. We'll lay everything out for her about this case, no holds barred. You can say your mea culpas to Helen and maybe you can get back on track, and then you can stop with all the chain-smoking stinking up my clothing. Maybe we'll even invite Sean and Rebecca, too."

"Jesus, Danny, they're not even married, yet."

"Meg and I weren't yet married when I agreed to tell her everything."

***

Danny's usual parking spot, the one right in front of his front door, was taken, so he parked a short way down the block. As he was walking back, he noticed a familiar face in the driver's seat of the 1940 Hudson Sedan parked in his spot.

Ramsay waved him over as he opened the door on the passenger's side. "Pleasant neighborhood you live in, here. What's it called?"

"Sunnyside Gardens. Now, what brings you to my neck of the woods?"

"I was curious about how you're coming along on your investigation. Did you pick up Trent?"

"We did. But the ADA cut him loose. The interesting part was that he knew Trent is an ILA delegate."

Ramsay snorted. "Not surprised. Joe Ryan, the self-appointed lifetime president of the ILA, probably dropped a nickel on the Bronx DA. He's intervened before. He usually stresses the need to keep the port fully functioning for the war effort."

Something Monroe had mentioned to Danny. "Which suggests that our Mr. Trent may be held in even higher esteem than we thought."

"Not an unreasonable assumption. I'll let you know if I turn anything else up. You still going on the theory that whoever is behind this is trying to take Lombardo down?"

"I am, although there's something that keeps nagging at me: when these guys decide to take a boss down, don't they just do it on their own?"

"Yes. And you're wondering why they haven't done so, here. I can think of a couple of reasons. In the overall scheme of rackets, the Bronx is a relatively minor operation, and the beef is from within, not another boss trying to take the territory. Moreover, Lombardo's connections are strong enough that any move against him could bring a swift reprisal."

Danny stared at the ground. "I suppose so."

"Something else?" Ramsay asked.

"It appears Gervin was giving Carla Maxwell money, enough for her to revamp her wardrobe. How would a muscle guy have that kind of money?"

"Normally, he wouldn't." Ramsay paused for effect. "Unless he was skimming collections on loans, or the numbers."

Danny considered it, then turned to another concern. "Someone has been shadowing me, lately. He's pretty good at keeping out of sight, but one develops a sixth sense about such things. You know anything about that?"

"One certainly does. I'm not surprised, but it has nothing to do with me."

***

"I love it," Meg said when Danny arrived home and told her of the invitation he'd extended to the Larkins. "Rebecca was over today and she's worried sick."

"But are you up to entertaining?"

She gave him a peck on the cheek. "He asks after he's extended the invitation. What did Frankie think of it?"

"He said he'd think about it."

The phone rang, and it was Helen asking Meg if the invitation was genuine. Meg assured her it was. "We're inviting Sean and Rebecca, too."

Meg hung up and said, "Helen agreed. Tomorrow night at eight. With luck, Patrick will be down for the night, or at least until two in the morning."

The phone rang again. Meg answered, but her smile vanished. "Just a minute."

It was Rossi. "Danny, I just got a call from a buddy of mine who works with Harbor Patrol. They fished a body matching Charlie Lavery's description out of Spuyten Duyvil Creek. Initial call is a single gunshot wound to the head. The coroner's office will get us the word by noon tomorrow, official report will probably take a few days."

"Did they say how long they thought he'd been in the drink?" Danny asked.

"They think he went in between ten and midnight last night."

"Get the slug to Ballistics, pronto. And if it's by any chance a .45, I want it compared to the slugs recovered from Gervin and Fagan."

FORTY-FOUR

Friday, May 28, 1943
"The Office of Defense Transportation yesterday ordered an immediate twenty percent cut in bus and taxicab service as a step toward the forty percent overall mileage reduction previously ordered in order to deal with the gasoline crisis from Maine to Virginia. The order is expected to result in 'bus-less Sundays' in Manhattan and a reduction in service in Brooklyn.

"In London, the army's Civil Affairs section revealed detailed plans for the occupation of Germany and other countries, providing for a large staff of specialists in finance, health, education, and legal affairs."

***

Taking Friday off was not uncommon as Decoration Day fell on a Sunday. Despite a busy shift at the precinct, the Coroner's Office had only one technician and Ballistics was completely unmanned. By noon, Danny had just one of the pieces of information he needed: according to a crime scene technician, Charlie Lavery had been killed with a .45. The same caliber bullet in the same part of the body in three different murders.

Danny marched into Greco's office and demanded an All-Points Bulletin on the maroon 1937 DeSoto with the license plate number Rossi had seen and the clerk at the Foster had confirmed.

"Won't that just drive the killer underground?" Greco asked.

"It could, and that will keep him off Maxwell's neck and give his kids a little peace. It might also save another cop's life."

"Or maybe he'll just ditch the DeSoto."

"Which is why we'll include the limited description we have of him," Danny replied.

"And then whoever is behind this will simply bring another goon in off the bench."

"I also want that police guard at Maxwell's place just in case he does exactly that. But I'm glad you finally admitted that there is someone behind all this."

Greco sat back and ran his fingers through his hair, making him look increasingly disheveled. "You don't let up, do you?"

"That depends. Are you prepared to share who is pressuring you to back down?"

"No one, but even if someone was, I couldn't tell you, and I'd strongly advise you not to guess."

***

By the time Danny and McHugh arrived in Maxwell's neighborhood in an unmarked radio car, Larkin was on his way to Norwalk to give Peggy the sad news about Charlie. Rossi had made the identification earlier that morning.

Yonkers police already had a patrol car posted in front of the Maxwell home, but Danny was looking for some other activity. Schools were closed, so the kids would be with their friends. With luck, the visible police presence would give them and their father the protection they needed, although who knew what questions the neighbors would ask?

After an hour of cruising the neighborhood, McHugh asked, "How much longer will we stay?"

"One more time around," Danny said.

"What are you thinking?"

"If his boss hasn't picked up on the All-Points Bulletin, he might come to collect the next installment." When Danny saw his questioning expression, he added, "Yes when the kids are off from school. He'll be looking for a way to increase the pressure. That's the 'maybe'. But if he's heard about the APB, he'll want to squeeze Maxwell one last time before he goes to ground. Oh, and I hope you and Rebecca can make it tonight."

"Yeah. What's it all about, anyway? Rebecca was tight-lipped about it."

"We need to talk through some things. It's really for Frankie's benefit, but I think it'll be good for you and Rebecca, too."

***

Frank couldn't believe it. Peggy didn't shed a tear. Her only visible reaction was a simple, hard stare.

Like it was his fault.

Which he already felt it was. "Peggy, I'm sorry about all this. I only went to Charlie for some ideas about where we should look. He kept me in the dark about his subsequent actions, and it wasn't until he mentioned Declan Fagan's disappearance that I learned about any potential danger."

She touched his cheek. "Not your fault, Frankie. He never discussed anything about the job with me. And he never mentioned Declan after he left the fifty-first."

"Did he ever tell you why he left?"

"He had concerns about what was happening there and worried about being involved, eventually."

"Did he ever mention any names, anyone outside the department?"

"No, why?"

It was a long shot. "He registered at the hotel under an assumed name, Vito Redden. I wondered if it meant…"

"Redden or Rodino?"

"Why?"

"Because I remember him mentioning a guy named Vito Rodino back then. I overheard him talking on the phone with someone and mentioning the name. When he got off, I made a joke about it, about the rhyme. He got angry and told me never to mention that name again. Funny thing, if he hadn't reacted like that, I'd have long since forgotten it, but because he did, that name has stayed with me. Does it mean something to you?"

"Not until now. Thanks, Peggy. If there's anything I can do, please let me know."

***

Danny had just reached the end of Maxwell's block, ready to turn back for the station house, when he spotted the DeSoto coming from the opposite direction. The person behind the back-rimmed glasses flashed recognition, and he kicked the accelerator and sped away.

Danny spun in a wide U-turn, hit the siren, and the chase was on.

As the DeSoto turned south on Warburton Avenue, Danny followed close behind. "Sean, radio in we're in a chase with our guy. Keep them updated on our position."

Danny swore as the DeSoto skidded taking a high speed left onto Prospect Street. "He'll head south on Route 9, just as sure as I'm born."

A single long block later, Danny followed the DeSoto in a fast half-right turn.

"You called it, Danny." McHugh radioed in the update.

Danny tried to calculate the percentages. A high-speed chase down a main commercial section meant danger for everyone. A car or cart pulling into the road at the wrong moment might force the fedora man to slow down or stop, but he also could injure or kill innocent people.

With each passing block, he searched for a potential spot to run down the DeSoto, but there was nothing but stretches of stores or homes, with the occasional empty lot. On the sidewalk, people stopped and turned to stare at the two vehicles hurtling by to the tune of a wailing siren.

At 263rd Street, they reached Van Cortlandt Park on their left.

"We're in the Bronx, now, Danny."

"He's got to be heading for the Henry Hudson Parkway."

"And the interchange with the Mosholu Parkway. We could lose him." McHugh pressed the microphone button. "Suspect still southbound, believe he's heading for the Henry Hudson Parkway."

Danny nodded approval. "If they can dispatch mobile units in time, we'll have numbers on him." But as they approached 260th Street, traffic thinned, and the DeSoto picked up speed.

They needed to make a move now. "Slide away from the door," he told McHugh.

"Not much room, Danny."

"Do it!" He floored the accelerator and pulled up on the left side of the DeSoto, slamming into it.

The DeSoto careened to the right, then pulled out of a skid and resumed course.

At 259th, Danny slammed him again, and again he pulled back to avoid skidding.

"There's a little park coming up at Mosholu Avenue," McHugh said.

Danny forcefully turned right at the intersection, slamming the DeSoto for the third time, and driving the other driver into the small park. The few benches were empty, and both drivers hit their brakes, their skids cutting deep ravines in the soft, wet turf. As Danny brought the patrol car to a halt, smashing a park bench, the DeSoto burst through a thin hedgerow and crashed into a tree.

McHugh jumped out and crouched in front of the DeSoto in a two-handed stance, pointing his .38 at the driver as distant sirens grew louder. Danny yanked the driver's side door open and leveled his pistol at the fedora man. "Don't even think about it."

FORTY-FIVE

The alleged Mr. Bartley wasn't talking. Even after McHugh had roughed him up and Danny had called him off and questioned him quietly, he wouldn't give them so much as his name. But he had no choice with fingerprints.

When Larkin arrived, he joined them in the interrogation room, landing a blow to the suspect's head with his own .38 before he even asked a question.

"He ain't talking," Danny said.

Larkin jerked a thumb in the direction of the doorway. Once outside, he said, "Lavery registered at the Foster hotel under the name of Vito Redden." He recounted what Peggy Lavery had told him. "Danny boy, Lavery knew he was in trouble and that time was running out. That's why he wrote to Peggy telling her where he was staying. He knew we'd follow it up, and he left a nice trail for us to follow. Let's locate Rodino, pick him up, and then this guy will spill his guts."

"Not yet. It makes sense to us, but to the DA, I'm guessing it won't be probable cause." Danny was already having qualms about how much he could rely on Monroe.

"What kind of shite is that? We grab him now and fill in probable cause later. We've done it dozens of times before."

"Not with someone like this, we haven't. McHugh is working at getting our Mr. Bartley's prints processed. Once we get an ID on him, we have him for three murders, and we can squeeze him for all he's worth. Meanwhile, I'll call Cogan and ask for all available information he's got on Mr. Rodino, and you can check the name for priors tomorrow morning." He needed to leave the station house for one last call.

A short distance away, McHugh slammed down the phone hard enough to turn heads across the squad room. "The best they can manage is tomorrow morning. Sorry, Danny, I did my best."

"Don't give it a second thought. Put our guest in the holding cell and he can cool his heels until tomorrow. In the meantime, I'll see you two and your lovely ladies at 8:00 tonight."

On his way home, he stopped at a phone booth and called Ramsay. "Does the name Vito Rodino mean anything to you?"

"No," Ramsay said. "Try Rudy Begonia."

"Excuse me?"

Ramsay chuckled. "An old vaudeville routine. Sorry. I'm afraid it doesn't ring a bell, but I'll check my files before I go home tonight to see if I find anything."

***

Meg had Patrick changed, fed, and asleep in his bassinet before McHugh and Rebecca arrived. Seeing the two of them together—Rebecca, with her long, wavy dark hair and soulful brown eyes, and Sean with his mop of red hair and the map of Ireland on his face—Meg couldn't help but wonder what their children would look like.

"Where's Frankie and Helen?" McHugh asked.

"I spoke to Helen this afternoon," Meg said. "She wasn't thrilled about coming with Frankie, but she agreed to it since they'll be Patrick's godparents."

"You told her this was about Patrick?" Danny asked, sounding doubtful.

"She had that impression, and I thought it was better to go along with it until they arrive."

"So, what is this about?" Rebecca asked. "You mean it's not just social?"

Good. Sean had said nothing about it, either. "Danny wants to share important information about the case they're working."

The bell rang, and she welcomed Frank and Helen Larkin.

***

Danny served drinks and then sat down. "I generally tell Meg everything about cases I'm working, because she explained long ago that it's worse for wives when they don't know. And she usually tells both of you." He nodded toward Helen and Rebecca. "In the early stages of this case, I decided I couldn't risk discussing it with anyone other than Sean and Frankie due to the potential risks if the wrong people found out. I've since told Meg provided she doesn't tell you, and I now realize that was a mistake."

There was no missing Larkin's stunned expression, but Danny continued. "The three murders we're working—Carla Maxwell, Nick Gervin, and Declan Fagan—are all connected, and today we added a fourth, Charlie Lavery."

Helen and Meg both gasped.

Danny recounted the sequence of events. "Everything is tied to Bronx racketeering. I've already spoken with Armand Lombardo, who runs the Bronx rackets…"

"You, what?" Meg cried before lowering it so as not to awaken Patrick. "You didn't tell me that."

"Because I eliminated him as a suspect. Someone ordered the killing of Gervin, Fagan, and Lavery, someone looking to push Lombardo aside. More than likely, it's some high-ranking individual in his organization. I believe we have the killer of all three in custody."

"What about Carla Maxwell?" Meg asked.

"Gervin most likely did that on his own, because she wouldn't stop repeating things he told her," Danny replied. "Once Sean, here, gets a hit on our suspect's fingerprints, we can charge him with the three murders and use him to finger the guy he's working for."

"I appreciate you taking the time to tell us all this," Helen said. "But why the secrecy? What danger?" She turned to her husband. "You never said anything about this."

"Helen," Danny replied, "there's one more thing you need to know. Frankie hasn't been stepping out on you. He's as true as any man I know and better than most, and not simply because he's my partner. Secrecy is warranted because the rackets have deep roots in this city. Mobsters buy cops, they don't kill them. They buy prosecutors and politicians, too, when they can."

"Please tell me you're not trying to take them all down yourself," Meg said.

"No, darling, I'm not. This started with the murder of a philandering office worker by her thug boyfriend and grew. But when someone orders the killing of cops, we can't stand idly by. And you know I never would."

Meg's little smile. "I know."

"Please only talk about this case if you are face to face with no one else within earshot. I will continue to tell Meg about it, and I'll ask Sean and Frankie to do the same with you girls. But nothing over the phone. It must be strictly in person."

"Why?" Rebecca asked.

Sean sighed and said, "The bad guys can tap our phones as easily as we can tap theirs."

Phone taps. Something he'd forgotten about that he needed to check on with Greco.

FORTY-SIX

Saturday, May 29, 1943

Helen had breakfast ready when Frank came down dressed for his regular shift. She poured him a cup of coffee as he sat at the kitchen table but said nothing. Just as she'd said nothing coming home from Danny and Meg's.

Meg had taken him aside just before they'd left. "Don't wait for Helen to apologize first, Frankie. Reach out to her. Trust me."

He took a sip of coffee, black as he usually took it. "I'm sorry this all blew up, Helen."

"I just want to know one thing. Why were you constantly spending your time off out, getting drunk in bars?"

"I needed to find a place to be alone. It was a terrible decision, but since you wouldn't listen, I felt I didn't have any other choice. When Declan disappeared, followed by Charlie, I was genuinely worried for all of us, but especially for you and Dorothy. I considered suggesting you and she stay with your folks, but I was afraid you'd think I wanted to split up."

"But you don't?"

"Of course not. In the event you'd like to see a priest to discuss anything bothering you, that would be okay with me."

She thought about it. "No, I think we can handle this ourselves. Promise me if we ever have problems in the future, you'll go."

His relief was instantaneous. "Absolutely. And for starters, I promise never to mention another woman's looks to you." He turned to check the clock. "Damn, I'm going to be late."

"It's early Saturday morning. Traffic won't be bad at all."

"No, but the trains are slower, and I figured you'd want the car."

***

"What the fuck has he been doing in our holding cell since last night?" Greco demanded as Danny walked in. The other detectives hadn't arrived yet.

We're not having this out in the squad room. Danny pointed to Greco's office and strode in without an invitation. "What's the deal with the phone taps on Villano and Messina?"

Greco closed the door a little harder than necessary. "You're getting pretty high and mighty. I'm still the lieutenant around here."

"In name, perhaps, but you've been three lengths behind on this investigation and fighting me at every turn. What about the taps you said you'd order?"

Greco grew defensive. "I haven't had a chance to…"

"Bollocks. You don't want to do it. Who's looking over your shoulder, Lieutenant?" He gestured in the general direction of the holding cell. "We don't know that fella's name, yet, but we know he's the one who killed Nick Gervin and two detectives. We also have a damned good idea of who is responsible." Danny recounted the string of evidence pointing to Rodino.

Greco snorted. "It's all circumstantial."

"Is that from Monroe? Or is it from the DA himself?"

"What the hell is that supposed to mean?"

"You've fought me before on cases, Lieutenant, but you've never tried to snuff a lead like this."

McHugh rapped on the door and Danny let him in. "We got a hit on the fingerprints of the guy we're holding. His name is Rick Tomasso, also known as Rick Thomas. He's done two stretches for aggravated assault. Also, Ballistics says that the gun that killed Gervin and Fagan is the same one that killed Charlie Lavery, and the crime lab found hairs matching Lavery's in the trunk of the DeSoto. Vinnie is down at Central Booking checking Vito Rodino for priors."

"Wait till Frankie gets here," Danny said, "and then we'll confront Tomasso." He turned to Greco. "And not before."

McHugh left the office.

"So, what's the deal with the phone taps?" Danny asked. "Who quashed them? And don't give me any shite about you forgetting to do it."

"All right. I had second thoughts. I didn't want to risk having questions asked I wouldn't want to answer."

"So, I was right. You are getting pushback from upstairs. Care to tell me who?"

Greco looked him in the eye. "Care to tell me the name of your anonymous source?" When Danny didn't answer, he said, "I didn't think so. We all have our little secrets."

"I've noticed someone shadowing me, lately. Do you have any idea who's behind that?"

"No one I know of. You'd better hope it's not Lombardo."

"I'm not worried about him. He sees me as doing him a favor. I'm more concerned it might be someone within the department or the DA's office."

"I doubt that," Greco replied, "but I suggest you don't go asking. It probably wouldn't lead to anything helpful. What do you suggest we do until Larkin gets here?"

"Just need to step outside real quick."

He strode to the phone booth on the corner.

***

By the time Larkin came in, Danny had arranged for ADA Monroe to participate in interrogating Rick Tomasso. With Greco, Larkin, and McHugh all present, the room was crowded, hot and stuffy.

Before Danny could begin, Monroe had a concern. "I understand that this man has been under arrest nearly eighteen hours without being booked. Anyone want to tell me why?"

Danny played it straight, although he was sure Monroe already knew. "He refused to tell us his name, and he had no identification on him when he was arrested. We had no choice. However, fingerprint analysis has now established his identity, and the ballistics evidence in the folder I just handed you, as well as an eyewitness identification, establishes he is the killer of all three victims. In addition, the statement provided by the widower of Carla Maxwell establishes the basis of the charge for extortion."

"We also don't believe he was working alone," Larkin said. "He is clearly part of an organized racket, as was Nick Gervin."

Monroe studied the file. "Three counts of murder and one count of extortion. That will almost certainly get you the chair, Mr. Tomasso. You can help yourself quite a bit if you tell us who you were working for."

Tomasso remained smug until Danny added, "And remember, we wouldn't be asking if we didn't already know."

"And Vito sends his regrets," Larkin added. "So, you're on your own, boyo."

Danny forestalled any comment from Greco with a glare.

"What do you want from me and what will I get?" Tomasso asked, opening his mouth for the first time since he'd refused to tell them his name.

"The DA just told you," Danny replied.

Larkin reached across the table and grabbed Tomasso by the shirtfront. "And it better be the right name."

"Although," Danny added, "personally, I'm fine with him not telling us and sending him to Old Sparky so there's no doubt."

Larkin yanked harder, slamming Tomasso's chest against the edge of the table. "What's it gonna be?"

"Don't I get a phone call?" Tomasso asked.

"Sure," Monroe replied. "Here's a nickel. There's a pay phone out near the front desk."

"Watch him so he doesn't bolt," Danny said to McHugh while Larkin walked behind the main desk and picked up an earpiece he kept hidden from view in the palm of his hand.

While they were waiting, Danny pulled Monroe aside. "I need to know you're going to nail this guy and the guy he's working for."

"Don't worry, Danny. No one wants to see cops getting killed by mobsters. I want this guy as badly as you do."

"You mean if Tomasso had stopped with Gervin and extorting Robert Maxwell, you'd have been okay with letting Rodino walk?"

"You know I don't mean that. I must say, Danny, you've been very accusatory since you took on this case. You act like everyone is corrupt except you."

"There has been a lot about this case that reeks to high heaven."

"I know what you mean. Tell you what. We'll talk after this case is resolved."

The desk sergeant approached. "Detective Brady, you have a phone call."

It was Ramsay. "Sorry I couldn't talk before. I couldn't find anything on your Mr. Rodino. I'll keep looking, but it's likely he's relatively low level and not anywhere in my files."

FORTY-SEVEN

When Tomasso returned to the interrogation room with McHugh, his smug expression had returned. "I just spoke to my lawyer, and he said I shouldn't say anything until he gets here."

Larkin was right behind him, shaking his head.

"Just a moment," Danny said. "What's on your mind, Frankie?"

"He didn't call his lawyer, and the guy he spoke to didn't say that."

Tomasso's face fell. "How would you know?"

Larkin shrugged. "I listened in. Sean, did you get the number he called?"

"Sure did. You were right, Danny. I checked it out. He called Vito Rodino."

"Who told him," Larkin added, "to keep his mouth shut for now and he'd spring him."

"Fascinating," Monroe said. "Did he happen to say how?"

"Nope, just what I told you."

"Okay. Mr. Tomasso," Danny said, "since you called Mr. Rodino, and he told you to keep mum, I'll make a wild guess that he's the one who ordered these killings. I'll also guess this was part of a campaign to take down Armand Lombardo so that Mr.

Rodino, or someone to whom Rodino reports, could step up and take his place. Was Tough Tony Anastasio behind it all?"

Monroe, Greco, and Tomasso all paled.

"I don't know nothin' about that," Tomasso said at last.

"But you were working for Rodino, correct?" Danny replied. "Why else would you call him?"

"Um, yeah."

"I need you to tell us exactly what the arrangement was, including if Mr. Rodino was subordinate to anyone besides Armand Lombardo," Monroe said. "And I need your assurance that you will testify against Rodino at trial."

"What do I get in return?"

"If your story checks out and if you hold up at trial and Mr. Rodino is convicted, I'll knock it all down to three counts of manslaughter if Mr. Maxwell gets his money back."

Greco told them to wait while he got a stenographer to take Tomasso's statement.

***

Monroe asked Danny for a private word in Greco's office while they waited for the stenographer. "Are you nuts? What the hell does Tony Anastasio have to do with any of this?"

"Maybe nothing, but possibly everything. Look at the cast of characters—Nick Gervin, Armand Lombardo, Giuseppe Calvino, Ronald Trent, and probably Vito Rodino and Rick Tomasso. What do they all have in common? They all worked on the Brooklyn waterfront run by Anastasio. Or am I the only one who's been paying attention?"

"You're talking about ancient history, and history that goes way beyond our jurisdiction."

"Yes, but they've been after Tony's brother's hide ever since they took down most of Murder, Incorporated, and the only reason they didn't get him is because Abe Reles didn't live to see the trial. That's probably why Anastasia hightailed it into the military, leaving Tough Tony as the sole man in charge. At least let's see where the evidence leads."

Monroe considered it. "You've been talking to Bill Cogan, haven't you?"

"Naturally. Why wouldn't I?"

"Danny, we're all human, trying to get what we want, and we use others to get it whenever possible. I realize you and Cogan worked together the Babić case with Meg, and the Nazi saboteurs. But don't think he wouldn't sacrifice you to get his way."

"Suppose you let me worry about that and stick with nailing Tomasso and Rodino and whoever they report to for now." It wasn't the first time Danny had considered how Cogan had referred him to Curt Ramsay, conveniently keeping his name, as well as the FBI, out of it. "What I don't get is what's worrying you, why you are so averse to following the trail wherever it leads."

Monroe glanced around, checking if Greco might burst in. Since he wasn't anywhere in sight, he answered Danny's question. "If you found any direct connection to Anastasio, it would complicate things on a scale that would dwarf our murder cases in the Bronx. It would involve things we have no control over."

"You mean the deal the Navy made with the ILA to suppress any labor problems on the waterfront, which involved moving Lucky Luciano out of Dannemora."

"So, Cogan has been talking to you. Yes, that. Any move against Anastasio would need to be made with the approval of the Navy at the direct request of the Brooklyn DA."

"You mean Bill O'Dwyer, currently in the army like Albert Anastasia."

"No, I mean Tom Hughes, who is filling in. The Bronx DA does not desire to engage in a pissing contest with Hughes or any other DA. It's in your best interests to remember that."

"And just where do you stand, Counselor?"

"You should know that by now. We all have limits within which we are required to work. Within those limits, I'll do everything I can to prosecute the cases you bring me. You're testing those limits right now. So, don't say I didn't warn you."

The stenographer still hadn't arrived when Rossi handed Danny a list of Vito Rodino's prior convictions.

FORTY-EIGHT

"Yeah," Tomasso said once the stenographer gave the signal that she was ready. "I've been working for Mr. Rodino for seven years, now. Actually, we both worked for Mr. Calvino back when we first moved to the Bronx."

"What had you done previously?" Danny asked.

"I worked as a longshoreman in Brooklyn."

"Regular work gangs, shape-ups, or muscle work for the union bosses?" Danny pressed.

Tomasso hesitated. "I started before the war with the shape-ups, when there were no regular work gangs, but I started doing favors for the hiring boss when there wasn't enough work."

"What favors?"

"Selling the policy lotteries, arranging for loans for guys who couldn't get enough work, selling tickets to the annual Democratic Club ball, collecting debts."

Monroe leaned over and whispered something to the stenographer, who made a minor correction. Danny was certain the reference to the Democratic Club had just been deleted.

"So," Danny said, "basic muscle work. I guess it beat risking life and limb down in the hold of some ship."

"Yeah. Anyway, a couple years after Mr. Calvino left the waterfront, he asked Mr. Rodino to join him, and Mr. Rodino told me it would be better working with him in the Bronx than staying the waterfront, so I agreed to go."

"With Mr. Anastasio's blessing?" Danny asked, not looking at Monroe.

"I don't know nothin' about that. I never even met the man."

"And who is Mr. Rodino's boss in the organization?" Danny asked.

"No one ever told me. I always figured he took orders from Mr. Calvino."

"And while you and Mr. Rodino were leaving the Brooklyn waterfront, what was Mr. Lombardo doing?"

"He was one of the bosses, like Mr. Rodino. I didn't know him then. I didn't get to know him at all until he replaced Mr. Calvino."

"How did Mr. Rodino react to Mr. Lombardo becoming his new boss?" Larkin asked.

The additional questioner threw Tomasso. "Huh? Um, he was pretty sore. He said we could make huge money in Bronx rackets and although Mr. Calvino had gotten sloppy, Mr. Lombardo was never great on the waterfront and he'd make things tougher on us while keeping most of the profits himself."

"And did he?" Danny asked.

"At first, no. He kept a low profile cleaning up Mr. Calvino's mess, and he built the rackets up even stronger."

"Such as?" Larkin asked.

"I couldn't say, but we made way more money and got paid for it. But then he started expanding the loansharking, and he needed more muscle, so he arranged for The Thumb to come up to the Bronx to help with collections."

"That would be Mr. Gervin?" Danny asked.

"Yeah. Except he was stupid. Couldn't keep his mouth shut. Mr. Rodino is the one who started calling him Tom Thumb, and the jerk thought it was a compliment. When he met that slut,

Carla, he started telling her all kinds of shit just to impress her, figuring she was hot for a gangster, which I guess she was. Fagan told Mr. Rodino about it and…"

"Wait," Danny said. "What was Detective Fagan's role in the Bronx rackets?" Time to investigate if Fagan's story had been whitewashed.

"He started working with Mr. Calvino early on, and Mr. Lombardo continued using him when he got here. Fagan was our eyes and ears in the police department. He alerted us anytime the cops were looking at one of our rackets, and he did his best to gum up the works when the cops got close enough that they might close us down. When Gervin got here, Mr. Rodino said he figured him for trouble, and he had Fagan tail him whenever possible."

"Wait," Danny said. "Rodino had Fagan tail Gervin, or Lombardo did?"

"Rodino told me he did. Anyway, Fagan was at that New Year's Eve bash at Joe and Joe's Restaurant, and he saw Gervin go nuts for the Maxwell dame. He hung close after that, spying on them whenever they were together. Gervin couldn't keep his mouth shut."

Danny hesitated before asking the next question, not wanting to confuse his own investigation. Still, the nagging doubt remained. "Was there anything else Gervin did that would have caused anger within the organization?"

Larkin stared at him, stunned.

FORTY-NINE

Tomasso looked dumfounded. "Like what?"

"Anything," Danny said with a shrug. "You tell me."

Tomasso considered it. "Nothing that I knew of."

If he pressed it, he'd be coaching him, and he couldn't risk Tomasso saying only what he thought Danny wanted to hear.

Larkin filled the awkward silence. "So, why did you kill Fagan? And why Charlie Lavery?"

"When Mr. Lombardo found out about Fagan tailing Gervin, he told him to knock it off, that he'd deal with Gervin himself. But then Mr. Rodino told Fagan to keep right on tailing him, and he'd pay him a bonus for it, but to report only to him, and not Mr. Lombardo. A month later, they were supposed to meet. Fagan never showed. At that point Mr. Rodino had me tail Fagan, and I saw him talking with Charlie Lavery, so Mr. Rodino figured Fagan was either turning himself in or turning state's evidence, probably both. When I saw Lavery meet with you two," he gestured to Danny and Larkin, "we knew we were right. Mr. Rodino ordered me to kill them both."

"And why extort Robert Maxwell?" Danny asked,

"He knew about Gervin screwin' his wife, so we didn't know how much else he knew, what his wife might have told him. The extortion was nothing, pocket change, really, just to scare him into silence with you guys."

Danny held up Robert Maxwell's written statement. "I guess that didn't work, either."

"Yeah. Stupid considering the trouble we took to convince him Lombardo had ordered Gervin killed."

"One other question," Danny said. "What was Ronald Trent's role in all this?"

"Who?"

Danny jumped up. "Don't pull any shite with me. Trent, the guy whose boat you used to dump Gervin's body on Goose Island. Don't try to tell me you know nothing about it."

"I don't. Mr. Rodino, Gervin, and I rode over to the marina in Flushing. Rodino had the keys to a boat."

"Where did he get them?"

"He never said. He just had them. Mr. Rodino told him we needed to talk on the boat because the cops were on to our racket in the Bronx, and he was sure they were tailing us. Gervin was stupid enough to buy it."

"So, what happened next?" Danny asked.

"I circled around Gervin to club him from behind, but he figured it out and lunged at me. I slammed his head against something hard on the boat, knocking him out. Then I laid him out and shot him in the head. Mr. Rodino pulled up to the island, and I dumped him there."

"That's enough for now," Monroe said. "I'll need some additional details later."

"Not so fast," Danny said. "I've been looking over Rodino's record. He got out of Sing Sing in 1935 after serving seven years for armed robbery. The last time I checked, none of the rackets on the waterfront involved stick-ups."

Tomasso was baffled. "So?"

Danny leaned over the table. "So, he likely never saw a longshoreman's hook until he was released from prison, which is probably where he met someone who directed him to the waterfront. It's amazing how many union toughs got their referral to the ILA in prison."

"What's your point?" Monroe asked.

"My point? He wouldn't have enough time on the docks to make any kind of name for himself before Calvino took him to the Bronx. Nor any way of knowing how high a position in the organization Calvino held. I also don't believe that two low-level toughs would have enough juice to pull off three murders like these guys did."

"So, who did?" Monroe asked.

"You say you didn't know Trent, the guy who owned the boat," Danny said to Tomasso. "I believe you. Also, whoever did must have met him during Trent's days on the docks, and he must have held a higher position in the organization. That ain't Rodino. So, who is it?"

"I don't know. I take all my orders from Rodino."

"Sean," Danny said, "book him."

***

Larkin pulled Danny aside before they could all get together in Greco's office. "Why the hell did you ask him if Gervin was doing anything else? What else were you thinking?"

Danny glanced around to make sure no one was within earshot. "Maxwell said Carla was getting extra money. It's why he believed she was working overtime. But she bought herself a lot of fancy clothes, meaning she was getting a lot more than what overtime at the hospital would produce. Not to mention the endless supply of nylons."

"So?"

"Gervin was dumb muscle. A peasant worker. Where would he get that kind of money?"

Larkin laughed. "Um, criminal activity comes to mind."

"What if he was skimming on collections?"

"Okay, what if he was? None of these guys are altar boys."

Danny said nothing.

"Wait," Larkin said at last. "You think Lombardo was responsible after all? That he wasn't being got at?"

"Rodino's almost as low a peasant as Tomasso. He was taking orders from somebody. Maybe Lombardo ordered Gervin killed and either Villano or Messina saw it as a chance to kill two birds with one stone." There, he'd finally put it into words.

"Danny boy, you're chasing your tail, now. I think this case has finally gotten to you."

And now that he had voiced his doubt, it sounded silly. "Yeah, you're right."

At least he hoped Larkin was right.

FIFTY

"You don't need a warrant to arrest Rodino," Monroe said back in Greco's office. "Tomasso's statement gives you ample probable cause. The only thing that bothers me is you listening in on his conversation, especially when he said he was talking to his lawyer."

"Excuse me, Counselor," Larkin said, "but I never believed for a moment he was calling a lawyer. I listened in because I was certain he'd call Rodino, and I was right."

"Suppose you'd been wrong, Detective?"

"Then I would have stopped listening immediately and I wouldn't have tried to use anything I heard."

"Anything else?" Danny asked.

Greco spoke up. "I got a little nervous when you brought up Anastasio…"

"I needed to link them all together. And I left Mr. Monroe's options open to pursue it if he chooses."

But Monroe was stewing about something else. "Danny, when you were pressing him about who might be over Rodino, you sounded awfully certain of yourself."

"I was trying to shake him."

"But you sounded like you already knew the answer. Like you had inside information. If you do, it would be helpful for me to know your source."

The warnings he'd gotten from Ramsay and Fagan echoed in his ears. "I was simply going based on the facts, like I said inside." He turned to Greco. "Please don't release the information about Tomasso's arrest until we grab Rodino. I don't want him to skip town before we can grab him."

"How do you plan to accomplish that?" Greco asked.

"I need to see a friend, first. Come on, Frankie."

***

As Danny recounted the facts of the case and the entire cast of characters, he watched Cogan's frown grow deeper and deeper until it was officially a scowl. "Why so unhappy, Bill? I'd have thought this rated at least a hurrah."

"I told you a week ago I thought you were wandering into dangerous territory. Who'd have expected you to jump in with both feet? Two dead detectives, and you're still pushing?"

"I'm pushing because of the two dead detectives. In case you haven't noticed, Bill, this is now a shooting war, and I'm not about to stand by and watch the mobsters win it."

"You looking to take down Lombardo, too?"

It was a question that had been nagging at Danny since his one-to-one chat with him. "I don't know, yet. It appears his role was limited to requesting additional muscle—Gervin. Rodino's activities were part of Lombardo's enterprise, but thanks to Rodino's actions, Lombardo appears to have had nothing to do with any of the murders."

"If Tomasso is telling the truth," Cogan said.

"Yes. But once we arrest Rodino and get his prints, we can check them with those on Trent's boat. If he was on it, then…"

Cogan finished the thought. "Who was his connection to Trent?"

The weak spot. "Tomasso didn't know, so neither do I. That's another reason I'm here. I need anything you might have on Trent that you haven't already given me."

Cogan chuckled. "And what's the first reason? I'm still waiting to hear it."

"Can you provide Rodino's address before the news about Tomasso's arrest becomes public knowledge?"

"You're learning. Good. Give me a minute." Cogan got up and walked out.

"How would Rodino react if word got out about Tomasso?" Larkin asked.

"I'm not worried about how Rodino would react. I'm worried about how Lombardo would react."

Cogan returned a few minutes later with a few sheets of information. "Address and phone number; make, model, color, and license plate number of car, verified description. Good luck, and good hunting."

***

The address was a tidy, unpretentious house on Radio Drive in the Country Club section of the Bronx. A black 1940 Cadillac with the license number Cogan had given them was parked in the driveway. A light shone in the front downstairs window but there was no sign of any other activity. Danny circled the block, from Radio Drive to Lucerne Street, to Stadium Avenue and then right onto Griswold Avenue, leading back to the curving Radio Drive.

As they pulled up to the front of the house, the Cadillac roared out of the driveway and up Radio Drive onto Spencer Drive. Danny gave chase, and when Rodino skidded into a hard left onto Stadium Avenue, Danny had to cut speed to keep the car from flipping over. But he floored it as he shifted into third gear and was closing when he saw the light on Bruckner Boulevard turn red. He hit the siren.

Rodino entered the intersection with Bruckner just as an army jeep and a large army truck approached from the left. With no room to pass the army vehicles, Danny had to slow down, praying there were no other vehicles behind them.

But there was yet another truck.

Danny drummed his fingers on the wheel with impatience until it passed, but as he resumed the chase, he saw Rodino had turned south on Bruckner and had a half mile lead. Danny sped after him and radioed the information in, but Rodino was soon lost in the early evening traffic.

"We have no choice," Danny said to Larkin. "We need to ask for an APB on Rodino's Cadillac."

But after two hours of cruising, he admitted they'd lost him.

FIFTY-ONE

Monday, May 31, 1943

Danny was changing at Grand Central from the Flushing Line to the Jerome Avenue Line when he saw the now-familiar snap-billed cap. As usual, the stranger's face was obscured by the bill pulled low. Greco had suggested he drop pursuing it, but Greco had been a wagonload of poor advice, lately.

Snap-bill was about thirty paces behind him as he approached the stairs leading up to the Uptown platform. Danny climbed the stairs, keeping his eyes focused straight ahead, as if he had no concern about his surroundings. When he reached the platform, an express was waiting, its doors open. Danny boarded it, walked to the rear of the car, and waited while watching the top of the stairway.

Snap-bill appeared, glanced quickly up and down the platform, then took a step to board the train as the doors began to close.

Danny stepped off and walked directly toward snap-bill, his badge already out. "Police. Stay where you are."

The train pulled out.

Snap-bill gave a bemused smile. "Detective Brady. I guess I shouldn't be surprised you finally noticed me, although I'm usually adept at remaining unnoticed. Then again, it took you until today."

"No, I've been aware of your presence for some time."

"Of course, you would say…"

"Blue sport shirt. Tan windbreaker. Yellow sport shirt. And that's just off the top of my head." Danny decided not to mention the cap.

Snap-bill uttered a rueful chuckle. "Touché."

"You still have me at a disadvantage," Danny said.

"I suppose I do." Snap-bill pulled out a badge of his own. "Inspector Louis Harrison. I suggest we repair to a coffee shop upstairs in the main terminal and discuss things."

"I'd love to, but I'm going to be late for work."

Harrison lowered his voice. "With the amount of your own time you've been putting in, lately, I'm sure you have nothing to fear on that score."

It didn't quite sound like a threat.

***

They had just grabbed a table, and Danny by then had regained his footing. "You mentioned your rank but not your command, Inspector."

"I report to the Chief of Detectives."

"In what capacity?"

Harrison paused while a waitress took their order. When she'd gone, he continued. "That isn't germane to our discussion."

"Which is about what, exactly?"

Harrison pulled a pack of Lucky Strikes from his pocket and offered Danny one.

"No, thanks."

"Oh, right. You never do. I'd offer to buy you a Bushmills at the bar across the concourse…"

"Too early, and I don't drink while I'm working."

"Yes, I know. Perhaps another time, at Gann's, in your neighborhood. Now…"

Time to retake the initiative. "It strikes me as odd that a police inspector would be reduced to shadowing a lowly detective."

Harrison grinned. "Odd in the extreme, I'd say. Perhaps I should add that my shadowing of you is not entirely in connection with my position in the department."

"Perhaps you should explain how it is and how it isn't."

The grin vanished. "I don't have that kind of time, Detective Brady, and neither do you. Whether or not you realize it, you've stepped into the middle of a rather large hornets' nest. You're walking a fine line, one side being the danger of falling victim to the allure of easy money and the other side being the guarantee of frustration of one's efforts, at a minimum."

"And the maximum?"

Harrison exhaled a stream of smoke. "You saw what happened to Charlie Lavery."

"Are you saying someone in the department was responsible for Charlie's murder? Because, if you are…"

"No, nothing of the kind. You have Lavery's murderer in custody, do you not?"

"Yes."

Harrison drained his coffee and checked his watch. "I must be going."

"Fine," Danny replied. "But the shadowing ends here and now."

There was no humor in Harrison's grin. "Of course. It's served its purpose, and you've blown my cover."

"And what was that purpose, exactly?"

"I observe and track officers and detectives in the department whose abilities and attitudes score outside the usual range." He held up a hand to forestall any comment from Danny. "None of what I learn is shared with anyone inside the department's hierarchy, but in cases like yours, it could serve as background for a recommendation on a promotion or decoration."

"What about outside the department?" Danny's glare didn't waver.

Harrison stood. "You ask uncommonly good questions, Detective. It's been a pleasure talking with you. I've already paid the check." He walked away, hesitated, and returned. "Oh, and I must insist you not share the details of our chat, or my identity, with anyone. It would be disastrous for us both. Congratulations to you and your lovely wife on the birth of your son."

***

"The Navy reports that only one Japanese stronghold remains on the Aleutian Island of Attu, and that ultimate conquest of the island is imminent.

"Mayor La Guardia called yesterday's eighty percent reduction in bus service unreasonable and unscientific and said that other changes in bus service would be worked out during the week to achieve the reductions made necessary by the gasoline crisis. With pleasure driving in limbo, inspectors from the Price Administration Office were satisfied, and trolley lines and subways carried more than their usual Sunday loads."

***

Greco snapped off the radio when Danny entered his office. "Still nothing on Rodino."

"And top o' the mornin' to you, too, Lieutenant," Danny said without humor. "Did we get a stakeout team in place at his house?"

"First thing yesterday morning. We're also monitoring Penn Station, including the Greyhound Bus Terminal, and Grand Central Terminal. We have a team outside of Lombardo's social club, too."

"Probably the last place he'd go. He's only got one guy to turn to at this point, either Jocko Messina or Carl Villano, whoever he's working for." Danny considered it. "Whoever it is would likely eliminate him, so no hope there, either."

"Which reminds me, how did you learn of Messina and Villano? You never told me."

"It's not important, Lieutenant. If it pans out, I'll tell you then."

Greco stared at him before finally saying, "Nothing to do, then, but wait for the word. You'll want to be able to move the moment you hear. By the way, you're a bit late this morning. What kept you?"

"Had to wait for a train at Grand Central." Which was technically the truth. "We can't just sit and do nothing. There must be something else we can do; someplace else we can check."

Greco regarded him with arched brows. "I'll be interested to hear a suggestion."

FIFTY-TWO

By the time Larkin arrived, Danny had decided for the time being not to ask Ramsay about Harrison and instead hit upon the idea of cruising the Belmont section, also known as the Little Italy of the Bronx.

"I don't know what you hope to find here, Danny boy," Larkin said after they'd been driving around for what felt like hours, "but I must admit, it beats sitting around the station house doing nothing."

"I reread the material Cogan provided. Rodino has family here. There is no way he's returning home because he must know we're watching his house. Ditto with the train and bus stations."

"What about the piers?"

"I thought of that. But it's not like he can just catch the next ship."

"You said yourself longshoremen have easy access to ships. And while the Queen Mary isn't making regular trips these days, it wouldn't take much effort to sneak him aboard a coastal freighter."

"Contraband is normal business; stowing away is another matter. Besides, he'd need help from one of the gang bosses,

Anastasio or someone close to him, and I'm thinking he's likely not too beloved in those quarters these days. Otherwise, what reason would either Anastasio or Anastasia have to dump him in Lombardo's lap?"

"What makes you think they did?"

"Such a short stint working the docks, and then Gravedigger Joe brings him up here? He's a washout, just like Gervin and Tommaso. And that he was so intent on convincing Tommaso that he was a boss tells me he's been trying to turn himself into something he's not."

"I guess, although it still seems paper thin to me. Besides, I can't imagine he'd just leave his Caddy on the street, and there aren't a lot of places to hide one around here."

"Certainly not on Arthur Avenue." Danny made the sharp left onto Crescent Avenue. After he'd driven three blocks, he said, "Good Lord, don't any of these places have driveways?"

Larkin guffawed. "You've gotten too used to Queens, boyo. But stay to the left as you cross 187th Street. The neighborhood changes a bit as you get closer to Fordham Road."

As Crescent became Cambreleng Avenue, Danny saw what Larkin meant. Most of the houses were attached, but some were semi-attached with walkways between houses. As they crossed 189th Street, Larkin turned serious. "Slow down, Danny. Some of these houses have driveways."

"You check your side, Frankie, and I'll check mine."

Less than half a block from Fordham Road, Danny jammed on the brakes, then threw it into reverse.

"You got something?" Larkin asked.

Danny didn't answer. He only stared at a car parked in the narrow driveway between houses. "A 1940 Cadillac. Check the plate."

Larkin examined the plate, checked it against the number he had written down, then double checked the plate. "That's our boy, Danny. Now what?"

Danny radioed in asking Greco to send McHugh and Rossi to his current location. "In the meantime, we'll make sure Mr. Rodino doesn't go anywhere."

They didn't wait for long. McHugh and Rossi arrived within 20 minutes in another unmarked radio car.

"We'd have been here sooner," Rossi said, "but Junior, here, insisted we not take a regular radio car."

Danny caught a brief expression of minor annoyance crossing McHugh's face. "Proving that Junior knows what he's doing. Okay, Sean, you take up station behind the house, because if we don't grab him, he'll likely sneak out the back. Vinnie, you stay out front in case he comes out on one of the sides. Frankie, you're with me."

After allowing a couple of minutes for McHugh to establish his position, Danny and Larkin climbed the front steps and rang the bell.

A middle-aged woman wearing a frayed, dingy house coat opened the door. "Yes?"

Danny tipped his fedora. "Good morning, ma'am. We were just walking by, and I couldn't help admiring the Cadillac in your driveway. Is your husband the owner? I want to make an offer to buy it."

She glanced toward Larkin and back. "I'm a widow, and the car isn't mine."

Danny turned sincere. "Oh, I'm so sorry. If I'm not prying, who is the owner?"

"My… brother-in-law."

Danny caught the hesitation. "Is something wrong?"

"No, not at all."

"Then, may I speak to your brother-in-law?"

After another moment's hesitation, she said, "He's not here."

Upstairs, a door slammed.

Danny flashed his badge. "Police. Out of my way. Frankie, outside!" He rushed up the stairs with his revolver pulled.

A door facing the top of the staircase slammed shut. Danny kicked it open. The room was empty, the window open, its curtains blowing in the breeze.

Arriving at the window, he peered down and spotted a man climbing down a rickety trellis attached to the house. It had to be Rodino.

McHugh stood below with his revolver already raised. "Keep coming, Mr. Rodino. Nice and easy."

Rodino climbed back a step, freezing when he spied Danny in the window.

Danny aimed his revolver at Rodino, "No way out of this. You can climb up to me or down to my partner, but you're coming with us either way."

Rodino reached for something in his pocket.

"Don't even think about it," Danny called. "Or I shoot."

Down below, Larkin had joined McHugh and had his weapon out as well.

"Keep your hands out where we can see them," Danny added. "Hold the trellis with both hands. That's it. Now, step by step, nice and easy, and nobody gets hurt."

Rodino stared at Danny, then at the men standing in the yard. Rossi had joined them.

"Move it, Rodino," Danny said, "or I kill you here."

As he took a tentative step down, there was a crackling sound.

"That thing won't hold much longer," Danny said.

Rodino resumed his descent at a quicker pace. He was five feet from the ground when there was another crackling sound, followed by a loud snap, and the trellis collapsed.

Danny dashed downstairs, through the front door, and into the backyard. He arrived just as Larkin snapped on the handcuffs.

FIFTY-THREE

Danny didn't hear Monroe approaching, so the first he knew of the ADA's presence was the hand clamped firmly on his shoulder and a sincere, "Well done."

"We're all overwhelmed with awe," Larkin said with a smirk.

"Frankie's a wee bit jealous because he's the one who put the cuffs on Rodino." Danny shook his head, as if in sympathy.

"Load of shite," Larkin said in a mumble.

Monroe gestured to the interrogation room. "Shall we?"

Danny arrived in the room first, and he waited until Monroe, Larkin, and Greco took their seats. "I must say, Mr. Rodino, that for a racketeering underboss, both your tactics and your choice of enforcers leave much to be desired."

Rodino regarded him with a scowl. "What's that supposed to mean? You got nothing on me."

"Not quite nothing," Danny replied. "My partner listened in on Mr. Tomasso's phone call to you."

"Heard every word," Larkin added. "Both sides. You told him to sit tight, you'd get him out."

"So? That ain't a crime." Rodino crossed his arms over his chest.

"No," Danny replied, "but killing three people, including two cops, certainly is."

"I ain't done that."

Danny glanced at Larkin. "Such a well-spoken lad. No, but we have a full confession from the trigger man, your Mr. Tomasso, including the matter of you having given the orders."

"He lied to worm his way out of the mess he's in. I didn't have nothing to do with killing nobody, and you can't prove I did."

"I wouldn't be overly confident," Danny replied. "For one thing, there's the matter of that phone call. For another, there's your own behavior afterward—you ran and hid in your sister-in-law's house."

"To a jury," Monroe said, "that will make you look quite guilty."

"Especially when they find out your fingerprints were on Ronald Trent's boat." Danny let that sink in. "The same boat we can prove was used in dumping Nick Gervin's body on Goose Island, and where we found a spent shell from the gun that was used to murder him, and Detectives Fagan and Lavery."

"I'd say you're up the spout," Larkin said.

Danny remained serious. "Mr. Tomasso also fingered you as the mastermind of all of this. But your actions tell me you aren't anywhere near capable of masterminding much of anything. Otherwise, you'd have blown town the moment you got Tomasso's phone call. Instead, you waited until we were outside your door, and you hadn't even thought to park your car far from your sister-in-law's house."

"I suspect we could find apes with better planning skills," Larkin said.

Rodino made a move toward Larkin, then thought better of it.

"Careful, there, Frankie." Danny chuckled. "You're upsetting our guest. Mr. Rodino, my partner means that all four murders were crafted to appear that someone with significant racketeering operations was behind them. Someone like, say, Armand

Lombardo. But Mr. Lombardo isn't stupid enough to kill one cop, let alone two, and even if he was, he'd never leave a body in a wooded lot behind a police station and then call the station to alert them."

"Takes a veritable genius," Larkin added.

"Tomasso also revealed the murders were part of a larger effort to topple Lombardo," Danny went on. "And I believe that. But I don't believe you mopes cooked this up by yourselves, and until we nail whoever is leading your little putsch, we won't be satisfied."

Monroe spoke up. "If you tell us who's in charge of this, I'll charge you and Tomasso with three counts of manslaughter and you go to prison. If you don't, I up those counts to murder…"

"And we fire up ol' Sparky," Larkin said. "Heavy on the juice."

Danny held up a finger in warning. "Before you say a word, I already know it's one of two names. Not only do I want the right one, I want direct evidence proving it."

"And there's no deal until we have the individual in custody," Monroe added.

Rodino pulled his crossed arms tighter against his chest. "I ain't sayin' nothing."

***

Meg's face fell when Danny finished telling her. "You mean you got him, and the case still isn't over? The news bulletin on the radio made it sound like it is."

"In these situations, we need to proceed step by step. The little fish gives up a bigger fish, and the bigger fish gives up the biggest fish."

"But he didn't. Give you the biggest fish, I mean."

Danny took a long sip of Burke's stout. "He did not. At least, not yet. I'm guessing he's holding out for a sweeter deal from the DA. What did the report say?"

"Just that the killers of two New York police detectives were now in custody, and it gave their names. No mention of anyone else still wanted."

Excellent. Just the way he wanted it.

FIFTY-FOUR

Tuesday, June 1, 1943

"New York was jammed with visitors for the Decoration Day weekend, but large numbers of them found it difficult to find transportation home last evening, with thousands crowding midtown bus terminals. Many tried to get transportation by rail while others checked back into their hotels. At least three thousand were stranded at resorts in the Catskills.

"James F. Byrnes, the Director of War Mobilization, declared last night that 'many attacks on many fronts lie ahead' as the nation prepares to assume a major role in all-out military operations against the enemy. Speaking in his hometown of Spartanburg, South Carolina, Director Byrnes announced that the hundred-thousandth plane manufactured since the beginning of the war production program had just come off the assembly line, and that the size of the fleet would be doubled by the end of the year."

***

"You still haven't identified the mastermind."

Danny matched Greco's glare with one of his own. "Hardly a surprise. Monroe is allowing the idea of death by electrocution to set in before he returns with a new offer. Unless you suggest a better idea."

Greco relaxed. "No, it's probably the best way to go. Abe Reles probably didn't come around right away, either. But your Mr. Rodino may look for a way to avoid Reles' fate."

"That's easy," Larkin said. "Keep him on ice."

"That's what they tried to do with Reles," Danny replied. "And we know what fate befell him, while every cop assigned to guard him was 'asleep'. I don't know how we avoid that." He thought about it. "Although we might improve the odds. If Tomasso changes his story to agree with Rodino's, they each become credible on their own and we can place them in different locations, in different jurisdictions, with changed names."

"I see two problems," Greco said. "For one, even if we place them far apart, their names have both been made public, so whatever cops are assigned to guard them will be approachable, regardless of keeping their locations a secret. Slowing down the elimination process is the best you can hope for."

"What's the second problem?"

"Simply this: what if Tomasso sticks to his story?"

"That one's easy," Danny replied. "We stick them in one room, together."

***

Rodino took one look at Tomasso and muttered, "Fucking moron."

"Please," Danny said. "That's no way to talk to your trusted employee."

"He's not my…" Rodino froze.

Danny spread his arms. "You see how easy that was? And all it took was one look."

"What do you mean?" Tomasso asked.

But Danny's attention remained on Rodino. "Now that you've verified our suspicion that you aren't the big boss, it's in your best interests to tell us who is. Or…" He faced Tomasso. "You can tell us, since we never believed you, either."

ADA Monroe chimed in. "Your lives hang in the balance. Stick to your stories, and you both fry. Give us what we want, and the outlook gets a lot better."

"Like what?" Rodino asked.

Monroe replied in an unemotional manner. "That all depends on how long it takes us to drag it out of you, whether your stories align, whether the name you give us is, in fact, the guy, if you both testify at his trial, and if he gets convicted."

"We know it must be one of two names," Danny added, "both of whom worked for Gravedigger Joe and don't like Lombardo's style. We also assume neither of you wants to share Abe Reles' fate, and we have several ideas for dealing with that threat."

"For openers," Monroe said, "if you cooperate… it's both of you or nothing… we won't announce any deal or any change to the pending charges against you. That's for your own protection."

Danny took over. "In addition, we will place you in two different locations for safe keeping, far apart, and I will hand-pick the teams guarding you."

"Except they can get to anybody," Rodino said.

"Perhaps," Danny replied. "But we'll also give you both new identities when you get sent up. In the final analysis, you both have a chance of survival if you cooperate with us. If you don't, you have none." He sat back and watched as conflicting emotions played across both faces.

***

When Helen Larkin called to invite Meg on an outing, she demurred. Patrick was two weeks old, and the radio was forecasting temperatures in the high 70s. "But you're welcome to come for lunch. I'd love to see you."

Helen arrived just before noon and immediately took note of Meg's outfit, a light blue maternity dress, bobby socks and saddle shoes. "Hey, look at you. Makeup and everything."

"I was afraid I was letting myself get too frumpy," Meg said.

"You? Not a chance."

Meg looked her friend up and down. "You're looking a lot better, yourself. How's everything going?"

"Better. Frankie has been on his best behavior. He insists I was imagining everything, which is the only part that bothers me, because, while I realize I probably blew things out of proportion, there's no question his behavior had changed."

"Maybe it's enough that he's being more attentive."

Helen patted her hand. "Perhaps. When are you guys going to move?"

Meg started. "I… we've only just started talking about it. I love this apartment, and we won't need a bigger place until Patrick needs his own room…"

Helen burst into laughter. "I didn't mean that; I meant the house in Breezy Point."

Frank and Helen had lent their five-room bungalow to Danny and Meg for their honeymoon the previous August. Meg had loved it so much that when another nearby bungalow had gone on the market, Danny had bought it.

"We've been talking about it," Meg said. "Probably the end of June. I'm already planning for what we'll need to take with us."

"I'll be glad to give you a hand if you need it."

"Thanks, but I think I'll be fine."

Helen turned serious. "I'm so glad we'll be together all summer. I've been very lonely lately." She gave Meg a hug.

"Thank you for bringing us all together the other night. It meant everything."

"I'm afraid Danny gets the credit for that one."

"The big lug."

***

Armand Lombardo arrived at his social club for lunch, but first he took time in his office to read the latest news. The *New York Times* featured several stories about the ongoing coal strike, as well as the latest on the major battle between the Soviets and the German army at Kursk, but he set that paper aside. The front page of the *New York Sun* blared the headline that held the greatest interest for him this morning, concerning the arrest of Vito Rodino in connection with the murders of two detectives. Inside, the story described Rodino as the "mastermind" of those murders, and the murder of Nick Gervin.

Lombardo snorted at that. "Vito Rodino couldn't mastermind tying his own shoelaces."

However, Rodino's involvement left no doubt in Lombardo's mind who the mastermind must be.

FIFTY-FIVE

Rodino had done the math. Danny could see the emotions playing across his face. All he needed was one last push.

"I think we're wasting our time," Danny said to Monroe. "I suggest we fry 'em both and have done with it."

"Know what I think?" Larkin asked. "We should issue a press release announcing how helpful these two mopes have been and let matters take their natural course. We could even release them."

Monroe pretended to think about it. "I like it. Saves us the cost of a trial."

"And all that extra electricity," Larkin added.

Rodino jumped out of his seat. "Hey, wait a minute. You can't do that."

Monroe shrugged. "I'm the DA. I can do whatever I want."

"What's it going to be, genius?" Danny asked.

Rodino gestured toward Tomasso. "First of all, he don't know a thing. He follows my orders, nothing more. It was the same with Gervin, except he couldn't stop running his mouth."

Danny pointed at him. "You get one shot at this."

"I want everything," Monroe added. "Your boss's name, your contact for Trent's boat, the name of whoever planned the murders, and the details and goals of the plan."

"You said you needed our stories to agree," Rodino said. "But he can't tell you what he don't know."

Monroe checked his watch. "Get on with it. First, the name. Then, how you got involved. Finally, the details."

"Jocko Messina. He was a lieutenant under Giuseppe Calvino and expected to replace him when Calvino fled the country, but someone put Lombardo in charge, instead."

"Tony Anastasio?" Danny asked.

"I don't know. But Lombardo laid down the law when he arrived. No more stunts like running operations within shouting distance of a police station, no operating in broad daylight. Jocko had known Lombardo from his waterfront days and detested him, and Lombardo didn't help matters by talking down at him every chance he got."

"How did you fit in?" Danny asked.

"Jocko had brought me up here in '36. Calvino's rackets were taking off, and he'd added loansharking and protection to the list, so he needed someone to collect debts and fees and to coordinate muscle. Jocko thought I'd be good at it." Rodino nodded toward Tomasso. "He landed here shortly after I did. He'd screwed up operating a winch, and a cable snapped. A falling crate hit a guy…"

"Ronald Trent," Danny said, taking a guess. "The same guy whose boat you used."

"Um, yeah."

The pieces were finally fitting together. "Please continue."

"Anyway, Lombardo figured it wasn't really his fault, because he wasn't what you'd call…"

"A competent longshoreman," Larkin said. "Squeezing real longshoremen was more in his line."

Tomasso appeared ready to snap off a nasty reply, but he decided against it.

"Well," Rodino said, "yeah. Anyway, when things improved under Lombardo, he put Jocko in charge of handling payoffs to cops, a job he'd done under Calvino. The cops backed off, and business continued to improve. Then, about a year ago, Lombardo got another retread from the docks."

"Nick Gervin," Danny said.

"Yeah. This guy was a total moron, with a big mouth to boot. I had your Detective Fagan tail him because I didn't trust his mouth. When he took up with the bun lady, Jocko had me land on him. But it didn't take, so I told him there would be serious consequences if he kept seeing her. When the news broke that he'd killed her, right there in the fucking churchyard, Jocko decided he'd had enough. He gave me the keys to Trent's boat in Flushing and told me to find Gervin and have the genius here kill him on the boat and then drop his body on Goose Island. When I suggested that would be too obvious, he answered he was sick of Lombardo's bullshit, and this was our chance to solve all our problems."

"And you understood that to mean what?" Monroe asked.

"He wanted to set Lombardo up as a patsy for the Thumb's murder. It woulda worked, too, if Fagan hadn't gone all boy scout on us. When he dropped out of sight, Jocko panicked, afraid Fagan might tell everything he knew about our operations, which was a lot. When I told him I saw you guys meeting with Fagan, Jocko realized Lavery had to be the intermediary, because he was one of the few guys we'd tried to buy and couldn't, and then he'd transferred to another precinct. Jocko said they both had to go."

"Did Trent know you were using his boat?" Danny asked.

"Yeah. Jocko told him we needed it for a job. That was part of the deal when they bought him the boat—Jocko had a key and the use of it whenever he needed it."

"How often did you use it?" Danny asked.

"Every few months, moving stuff from the docks to various drop-off points around the harbor."

Danny remembered Cogan talking about narcotics smuggling. "What kind of stuff?"

"They never told me, and I never asked."

"But when you used the boat, it was always Jocko who gave the orders?"

"Yeah."

"And who ordered him?" Danny sensed they were getting closer.

But Monroe interrupted. "That's not relevant to our investigation, Danny."

Danny wanted to argue, but realized they needed privacy. "We'll need to impound the boat".

Monroe nodded. "I'll get you an arrest warrant for Trent as well as Messina. We'll charge Trent as a co-conspirator. We probably won't be able to make it stick, but at least we can get him on obstruction. Messina we'll get for the murders."

"What about us?" Tomasso asked.

"We'll keep you in custody at least until Jocko Messina is apprehended, for your own safety. Charges will remain pending until you testify against him. Once he's convicted, we'll work with the FBI to get you relocated with new names."

Danny had one last question. "Besides talking too much and sloppiness with Carla Maxwell's murder, was there anything else Messina had against Gervin?"

"Like what?"

"We know that Carla Maxwell revamped her wardrobe after she took up with Gervin, using money she told her husband came from working overtime. But her job required no overtime, and she lacked another source of income, so her spending money must have come from Gervin."

Rodino stared at him. "So, what's the racket?"

"Was Gervin skimming collections?"

Monroe looked like he might explode. "Danny, we need to…"

"You will answer me," Danny said, looking only at Rodino.

But Rodino looked puzzled. "I wouldn't know. Gervin turned his collections over to Jocko. If Jocko had a problem with Gervin's work on that score, he never mentioned it to me."

"We done, Danny?" Monroe didn't hide his irritation.

It reeked, but there was nothing else they could do until they had Messina in custody. "For now."

***

Larkin was waiting for him outside, and Greco had stepped out, so Danny pulled Monroe into Greco's office. "Why did you stop me from questioning him? Jocko Messina wasn't ordering smuggling runs on his own."

"Probably not, but whoever originated his instructions was likely outside our jurisdiction, and the smuggling operation has nothing to do with the three murders, which are in our jurisdiction."

"So, now, we're hiding behind jurisdictional technicalities?"

"Not hiding, Danny. Just doing our jobs. When we convict Trent, the existence of smuggling operations will be on the public record, and the Brooklyn and Manhattan district attorneys can do whatever they choose with that information. What was all that about Maxwell's wardrobe and Gervin's collections?"

279

"It's a loose end, and you know I hate those. Why did it bother you?"

"You hate loose ends, and I hate additional details thrown into the mix at the eleventh hour. What the hell difference does it make if Gervin was skimming collections on top of everything else he was killed for?" But before Danny could answer, Monroe added, "Oh, no. You're not thinking Lombardo could have been behind it after all."

"If Gervin was skimming, who was he ultimately skimming from?"

"It doesn't matter at this point."

"Not yet, but when we have Messina in custody, I plan on questioning him about it."

FIFTY-SIX

As soon as Jocko Messina saw Vito Rodino's name in the papers, he could hear the clock ticking. Vito was probably already singing, and Jocko had little time to spare. It was a race, now, between the cops and Armand Lombardo, who wasn't nearly as dumb as he sometimes acted.

Jocko was smarter than that. He'd head north, toward Lake George, and check into a nice little resort hotel under an assumed name, one that even Lombardo's boys didn't know, until he figured out his next move. He had a suitcase already packed.

As he left the house on Orloff Avenue, he scanned the street, seeing no one loitering around, sitting in a parked car, watching and waiting. Possibly Armand hadn't heard the news, yet.

He was already sitting in his gray 1940 Ford Deluxe Coupe when he realized the garage door had been unlocked. "Must've forgotten to lock it last night." That wasn't his habit, so he checked the car for any signs of tampering. He found nothing to disturb him and relaxed. "Just being paranoid again."

He pulled out, closed the garage door, and backed out of the driveway. There was still no one around. He made the light at Van Cortlandt Avenue without stopping and then turned right onto

Van Cortlandt Park West, keeping a sharp eye out for anyone following him.

The light was with him as he made the turn onto Mosholu Parkway and the traffic was light. He headed north, checking the rearview mirror, but he was alone.

***

Danny took Larkin with him in one radio car while Rossi and McHugh took another. Danny and Larkin went to Messina's home address while Rossi and McHugh checked his known hangouts.

"Nothing," Danny said after they'd found he'd already left and spent a few hours checking all the possible places he could have been. "Not a surprise. He knows by now we've got Rodino and probably realizes he's next. Vinnie and Sean can pick up Trent. We'll head back to the precinct."

***

As he sped north on the Saw Mill River Parkway, Jocko relaxed. The few cars he'd seen trailing him had either passed him or taken an exit. He turned his attention to formulating a plan of action. He'd take the Saw Mill to the Taconic State Parkway, all the way to the Bear Mountain Parkway, which he'd get off in Poughkeepsie. From there, he'd take US-9 north to NY-9N. From there he'd drive straight north until he reached the Heritage at Lake George, a place he'd never visited but his wife was always saying they should.

***

"So, let's review, shall we, Mr. Trent?" Danny leaned over the table in the interrogation room for emphasis. "The International Longshoremen's Association, of which you are still a delegate, provided you with a settlement when you were injured on the job. A settlement that allowed you to leave the docks and work locally doing odd jobs, with enough to buy your boat."

"You can't prove that," Trent replied.

"We've subpoenaed your bank records, and we've got the statement from Vito Rodino that he obtained the key for your boat, and its location, from Jocko Messina. Messina could only have a copy of your key if you gave it to him. Also, Mr. Rodino stated he has used your boat several times."

But Trent remained calm. "You could have saved yourselves the trouble of a subpoena and asked me for my bank records. I would have gladly turned them over."

"Strictly cash all around, eh?" Danny chuckled. "Which will lead intelligent jurors to ask how you paid for the boat. I'm sure the DA will be able to lead the jury to the correct answer. And when the jury learns that Jocko Messina had carte blanche to use your boat whenever he needed it, that will be enough for them to convict you as a co-conspirator."

"We'll see," Trent replied.

Danny ignored the comment. "I'm curious about one thing, though. Did Messina inform you that this was an attempt to frame Armand Lombardo?" A brief flicker disturbed Trent's calm demeanor, but Danny caught it. "A 'no', then. I'm also guessing Mr. Lombardo will assume that you knew exactly what Messina planned to accomplish, and he might not appreciate it."

"I know nothing about that," Trent said, turning sullen.

"But Mr. Lombardo knows we've gotten a confession from Rodino, and he'll soon know we've arrested you and he'll put two and two together," Danny said.

***

Jocko loved the Taconic State Parkway, especially on a weekday, when there was virtually no traffic. He'd seen hardly any cars along the Saw Mill River Parkway, but now the scenic Taconic rolled by, with the warm June air carrying a myriad of late-spring scents and the radio blaring Benny Goodman's "Stompin' at the Savoy". As he relaxed, he took the speed up to 65.

He had just passed Mahopac when he heard the siren. A glance in the rearview mirror confirmed the worst: a police car was several car lengths behind him and closing, although slowly.

The road eased into a long downhill stretch, picking up speed although he kept the same pressure on the accelerator. He glanced in the rearview mirror and noticed the police car, after falling slightly further behind, was now gaining on him.

He considered his choices. If he pulled over, he would face a speeding ticket and the discovery of his fake "X" card. That would likely mean arrest, which could lead to many other problems.

Maybe he could outrun them.

As the downhill grade increased, he glanced at the speedometer, which was inching close to 80.

How did that happen?

As he approached a tight curve to the left, he needed to trim his speed a bit. It would bring the cops closer momentarily, but he'd resume his speed once he'd passed the curve.

He moved his right foot off the accelerator and onto the brake pedal to trim his speed.

The pedal hit the floor with no resistance.

He pumped the brake pedal several times, pushing it right to the floor every time.

But the car only continued to gain speed.

***

"You've done nothing but lie to us until now," Danny said. "But coming clean will definitely be safer for you than if you go home."

Trent spread his arms. "Come clean about what? I've already told you…"

Danny stood and leaned across the table. "How did you get the boat? Where did the money come from?"

Trent glanced from Danny, to Monroe, and back.

"If we find out on our own," Monroe said, "we won't lift a finger to protect you. If you tell us, it will mitigate your involvement and we can protect you."

"I bought the boat with part of the settlement I got from the union."

"Now, we're getting somewhere," Danny said. "Who paid you?"

"It was delivered by a messenger. I don't know who he was. I had never seen him before or since."

"Sure'n he told you who sent it."

"He stated it was my compensation from the ILA for my injury and I was not to discuss it with anyone."

"What was in the envelope?" Larkin asked.

"Eight thousand dollars, two sets of keys to the boat, and a note saying they were to the Chris Craft, berthed at the marina in Flushing."

"Is that all?" Danny asked. "Or were other conditions stated, at that time or later?"

Two sharp knocks on the door. McHugh stuck his head in. "Danny, gotta talk to you for a minute. It can't wait."

His urgency was impossible to ignore. "Excuse me, Gentlemen. Frankie, you should probably join us."

McHugh nodded.

"I'll wait here," Monroe said.

Greco was sitting at his desk with a stunned expression on his face. "I just got a telex from the Putnam County Sheriff's office. A 1940 Ford Deluxe Coupe registered to Jocko Messina apparently went out of control on the Taconic State Parkway and rolled over several times just before the Peekskill Hollow Creek Road exit."

It felt as if something had struck Danny in the head. "What happened?"

"They were chasing him along the Taconic, looking to flag him for speeding. They clocked him doing over 80. As they were closing on him, he fishtailed to the left and then rolled, finally smashing into an overpass abutment. Messina was alone in the car, and he was killed, probably instantly. The crash site is at the bottom of a steep mile-long downhill. The Putnam County boys say there were no skid marks on the roadway, which suggests his brakes failed."

"Just like that, on a steep downhill? How convenient." Danny said. "How did they know to call us?"

"They checked his license number and saw his residence was in the Bronx. Someone up there had our telex number from the serial rapist/murder case last year and figured we'd know what to do with the information."

They needed to investigate the wreck for any evidence. "Frankie, please drive to Putnam County and examine that car thoroughly. Call me here as soon as you know." But his gut was telling him it was Lombardo.

Greco wrote on a piece of note paper. "The Sheriff's office is in Carmel. Here's the address."

"I'll call Helen and let her know you'll be late," Danny added.

"What about Trent?" Greco asked.

"He can cool his heels in the holding cell until we hear from Frankie. In the meantime, I'll give Monroe the latest."

FIFTY-SEVEN

Wednesday, June 2, 1943

Larkin didn't call in with news until shortly after one in the morning. "The line carrying brake fluid had come loose from the vacuum booster. Either Messina didn't use the brakes much when he started his trip, or there was enough fluid in the line when he did, otherwise he would have noticed the lack of pressure in the pedal."

"Did someone tear it loose, or did it come loose on its own from some defect?" Danny asked.

"The guy from the sheriff's office and I examined it for an hour with a magnifying glass. We couldn't tell. But neither of us knew of anything that would force the hose apart from the vacuum booster. There's nothing in the engine's operation that would put pressure on it."

"Is the hose still intact?"

"Other than the disconnection from the vacuum booster, yeah."

"Did you both have gloves on when you examined it?"

"Come on, Danny boy. I'm not a rookie."

"Sorry, Frankie. It's late. I was more concerned about the Putnam County guy."

"Yeah, he did. I made sure. I'm guessing your next request will be for me to take a piece of that hose and bag it for our lab guys to examine."

"As large a piece as possible, the entire length if you can manage it, Frankie. Thanks."

***

Larkin arrived back at the precinct shortly after three, and after calling Helen at Danny's insistence, he and Danny both found places to doze until six. Earlier, Danny had called Helen, keeping his promise to Larkin.

He'd also called Meg twice, once to let her know he wouldn't be home, and once around two so he could hear Patrick in the background and talk to her while she was on what he called the Night Beat.

"Do you think it was an accident?" she asked when he'd told her the latest.

"We may have a better idea after the lab boys examine the hose that Frankie's bringing in."

"But what's your opinion?"

"An accident? Not in a month of Sundays."

Greco arrived at seven and after Danny brought him up to speed, his first comment was, "Without Messina, I don't see how we can continue holding Trent. We needed Messina to confirm that Trent had given him the key. Unless you think Lombardo might tell us."

"Not a chance," Danny replied. "That would require him to tell us a great deal more about his operation than he'd be willing to tell, at least to someone who he wasn't paying off. Trent can now claim Rodino doesn't know what he's talking about, he never gave Messina a copy of the key, and he has no idea how Messina got one. Alternatively, he can claim he gave it to Messina as a favor but knew nothing about how it would be used." In the meantime, any hope that Messina might shed some light on Gervin skimming collections had died in the upstate car crash.

"So, why are we holding him?"

"I planted a seed yesterday that Lombardo may not believe him, and that has to scare him. It's our last shot. Meanwhile, I'm going over to the luncheonette on University Avenue for a coffee."

He was glad when Larkin went back to sleep for a while. He ducked into the phone booth in the luncheonette and called Ramsay, giving him the latest.

"Messina instigated everything," Ramsay said. "Not surprised he suffered an unfortunate accident. Pretty much scuppers your case against Trent, though."

"Unless you can give me anything else on him."

A humorless chuckle. "No, Danny, I held nothing back. You got it all. Hell, you made more progress chasing these guys than any other detective in the entire city. Anything else now would be gravy."

Danny ran his skimming theory by Ramsay.

"You're probably correct, although it doesn't matter now."

***

"Mayor La Guardia yesterday vetoed a package of nearly eleven million dollars in cuts to the city budget passed by the City Council, leaving only fifty thousand dollars in cuts to stand. In his veto message, he stated the cuts would cripple the city, impairing relief and reducing fire and school forces. A vote of three-fourths of the Council would be needed to override the mayoral veto, which is seen as highly unlikely."

***

ADA Monroe arrived shortly after nine o'clock and joined Danny, Larkin, and Greco in the interrogation room with Trent.

Danny wasn't surprised when Trent opened the discussion. "I don't see anyone else here, so I assume Mr. Messina is still not in custody."

"That is correct," Danny said. "Nor will he be. It seems he suffered an unfortunate accident."

"We'd love to claim it was at the hands of the police," Larkin added, "but, alas, it was not."

"We think we know who is responsible." Danny played his last card. "I'm certain you know, too, and perhaps you're a wee bit concerned about meeting a similar fate."

Monroe jumped in, as they'd planned. "With that in mind, we are prepared to accept your claim that you were not an active participant in the conspiracy and offer you protective custody in return for your testimony."

"Against whom?" Trent asked. "Don't you already have confessions from Rodino and Tomasso? If I had testimony to offer—I don't—wouldn't it be useless because the subject of that testimony is dead? As I said, I didn't know they were using my boat, let alone what for."

Monroe gestured for everyone but Trent to follow him outside. He closed the interrogation room door. "He's right. We needed him to help us nail Messina. Now, we don't. And we can't prove he knew what the boat was being used for. We've got enough on Rodino and Tomasso without him."

"That's it?" Larkin asked.

"Let him go," Monroe replied. "We'll meet with the other two at the Bronx House of Detention later and give them the update."

FIFTY-EIGHT

Danny, Larkin and Monroe sat across the table from Rodino and Tomasso in the Bronx House of Detention conference room. Neither had a lawyer, which led Danny to conclude that no help would be forthcoming, either from Lombardo's mob or from Tony Anastasio's.

"Jocko Messina was killed yesterday in a car accident upstate," Danny said.

Rodino exchanged a worried glance with Tomasso. "How does that affect us?"

"We don't need your testimony against Messina," Monroe replied.

Rodino cried out. "But we gave you what you wanted."

"Out of a sense of civic duty." Larkin made no attempt to temper the sarcasm.

"And, as I explained," Monroe said, his voice calm, "our deal depended on you testifying at trial and Messina being convicted. There won't be any trial, and there won't be any conviction."

Rodino leaped to his feet. "It's not our fault he got himself killed. We did out part."

"I'm sorry," Monroe said. "As I've already explained, the terms of the agreement were not satisfied, and so my offer is rescinded. You'll both be arraigned today, three counts each of first degree murder, and one count each of extortion."

FIFTY-NINE

Monday, June 7, 1943

"Mayor La Guardia is warning that the fuel oil and anthracite coal shortages could be worse this coming winter than last year and urges householders and industries to stock as much fuel as possible during the summer. He also announced yesterday that his efforts to mitigate the recent bus service cuts had been successful, with assurances from Washington that bus service to the Rockaways in Queens, where the summer population is much greater than the rest of the year, would not be cut. Further relief for the remainder of Queens will be sought from the Office of Defense Transportation.

"Dissatisfaction with wartime wage and price control policies continues to brew among organized labor, as representatives of several major unions yesterday demanded action to roll back prices and relax the rigid prohibitions on wage increases.

"The air transport services being operated by the Army and Navy as part of the war effort could serve as a blueprint for civilian air transportation after the war, according to a statement by the Office of War Information."

***

"Our lab guys found nothing on the hose to show it was yanked," Larkin said when Danny arrived at the station house. "And no fingerprints."

"Jesus, Mary, and Joseph," Danny replied, "can't you even let a man have his first gulp of morning coffee before you give out with the bad news?"

"Sorry, Danny boy. All they found was a tiny crack where the hose separated from the vacuum booster, which means it could have come loose on its own. The Putnam County coroner has no choice now but to declare it an accident. Besides, I thought you were a bad-news-first guy."

"Bad news before good news, not before coffee, Frankie."

"At least there's some of that. Monroe is giving the Rodino-Tomasso case to the grand jury this morning. He expects indictments in short order, then to trial, and then to the electric chair. Maybe Charlie and Declan will rest easier."

Greco emerged from his office. "I just got a call from a captain from a precinct in South Queens, where they've been keeping tabs on Ronald Trent. His wife has filed a Missing Persons report on him."

"Did he say how long Trent's been missing?" Danny asked.

"Since Friday. He went out on his boat, hasn't been heard from since."

Danny reached for the phone. "I'll give the Harbor Patrol a call, then the Coast Guard."

"No," Greco replied. "You two have the grand jury to prepare for on the Rodino-Tomasso case. Focus on that."

"Sure," Larkin said. "After all, a U-boat probably got him." After Greco returned to his office, he added to Danny, "The guys who killed Fagan and Charlie are going to fry. The guy who gave the order is dead. After you prepare for the trial, this case is finished."

But Danny shook his head. "It's not finished, Frankie. Not by a long shot." After a moment's reflection, he added, "But it is over for one guy, and it's time he found some peace."

***

It was ninety minutes before the end of his tour, and for the first time since he'd taken the call about Carla Maxwell, there was nothing pressing. Larkin had already left early, but Danny had his one errand to run. He signed out a radio car after informing Greco where he was going.

The street in Yonkers where Maxwell lived looked like it was back to normal—no police vehicles keeping watch, no one lurking in other cars. It was just after three, and Danny spotted two children approaching Maxwell's house—a girl about ten and a boy about seven. He hesitated, unsure whether it was best to do this in front of the children.

Something about the girl's face caught his eye, an expression that a girl that young shouldn't be forced to carry.

As they climbed the steps to the house, Danny left the car.

Maxwell was waiting at the door for the children and caught sight of Danny. His expression turned to one of alarm.

"It's all right, Mr. Maxwell," Danny called. "I wanted to inform you regarding the last details of the case, so you and your family can resume your normal lives."

Maxwell didn't open the screen door. "My children are home."

"It's all fine," Danny replied. "I don't have anything upsetting to tell you, but they might benefit from hearing it."

Maxwell let him into the house. "This is my stepdaughter, Mary, and my stepson, Ken."

Danny shook hands with each. "Very nice to meet you both."

"Detective Brady was the investigator of your mom's murder," Maxwell added.

Mary was glaring at him, while Ken looked befuddled.

"Why don't you all sit down, and I'll tell you what we learned." Danny addressed Maxwell first. "To begin with, you won't have to worry about any further extortion. The man who extorted you and his boss are in jail, and they're going to pay for that crime, as well as three other murders, with their lives."

"Three?" Maxwell asked. "I thought it was just my Carla and this Gervin fellow."

"This was about a great deal more than your wife, sir. It was about control of racketeering in the Bronx."

"What's racketeering?" Ken asked.

Maxwell tried to shush him, but Danny shook his head. "No, it's a good question, Ken. Racketeering means organized criminal activity, and it can take lots of forms."

Mary sneered. "Our mother was mixed up in this?"

Maxwell's expression turned painful.

"She was, indirectly," Danny said. "It's difficult to have a parent who you feel has let you down, Mary. My pa was like that when I lived in Ireland. And his poor decisions killed him when I was a young lad. But I was lucky; a great man called Michael Collins stepped in and protected me mum and took me under his wing. Many adventures I had with him in those years, and he helped me grow. You may dislike what your mum did, but she did one thing that will always be best for you and your brother. She married your stepdad and provided you with a wonderful home. And throughout all of this, his only concern has been protecting you."

"So, why did you suspect him of having my mother killed?" Mary asked.

Danny allowed himself a smile. "People are often killed by someone they know, and often by their own spouses. I had to rule him out as a suspect." He turned to Maxwell. "I never considered you a likely suspect, but we had to make certain. And the involvement of the guy in the De Soto complicated things. I wish you had told us the truth about the man in the glasses and fedora, but it makes perfect sense you didn't."

"Did he drive a red car?" Mary asked.

"Yes, he did."

"You saw him?" Maxwell asked, alarmed anew.

But Mary was letting down her guard. "Yes, going to school and coming home. Ken noticed the car, first. We wanted to ask you what it was all about, but you were so upset we decided against it."

Maxwell relaxed. "What happened with the racketeers? Have they been dismantled?"

"Alas, no. That is a battle for another day. But it shouldn't concern any of you."

Maxwell walked him to the door. "Thank you for coming by and filling us in. It means a lot, especially to the children."

Danny shook his hand. "You're a good man. Those kids are lucky to have you."

"Thank you, Detective. I'm looking into what I need to do to adopt them."

SIXTY

Meg was worried. The case was over, except for the trial. Danny should have been relaxed. But as she watched him giving Patrick a bottle, the face that she expected to be beaming was instead lined with concern. And it wasn't difficult to guess why. "Honey, let it go. Some problems just can't be resolved."

"Yeah, I know."

"We're getting ready to move to the bungalow for the summer, so let's focus on that instead."

"You're right." He forced a smile. "Besides, we should start thinking about moving to a larger place."

"Helen and I talked about that the other day." Now it was her turn to grow pensive. "I wish we didn't need a bigger place. I love this apartment even more than the little studio I rented before we were married."

"The apartment or the neighborhood?"

"Both."

She'd caught his interest. "You don't hanker for a house, like your mom has in Maspeth?"

"No. I'll love the bungalow, but the houses here are mostly two-family homes, and I doubt you want to become a landlord."

"And you're too young and beautiful to be a landlady."

She bent over him and gave him a kiss, then Patrick.

"But," he said, "the extra income might be nice. Once the war ends, all those returning servicemen will create an enormous demand for housing. We'd be in an excellent way." He put down the bottle and burped Patrick.

"Financially, yes, but who'd get stuck with the complaints when things broke down? You, with your wacky hours working cases?"

"I see your point. But there are single-family homes a little closer to Long Island City."

"No, thank you. They're okay, but they don't have the charm this neighborhood has."

"There are some lovely houses in Woodside."

"Woodside as a neighborhood is nice. St. Sebastian's is a lovely church, and someday, Patrick will go to school there and I'll return to work at the library. But you know my memories of living there, the rape and everything that followed with Hal, are painful. I love these garden apartments, so why can't we rent a nice two-bedroom apartment around here? Or even a three-bedroom apartment?"

His grin became a leer. "Already looking to give Paddy, here, a little brother or sister?"

"Get that filthy look off your face, don't call him Paddy, and the answer is no, not yet." She couldn't hold the scowl. "But someday…"

She answered the ringing phone.

It was Vinnie Rossi. "Hi, Meg. Is Michael Collins there?"

She laughed and traded the phone receiver for Patrick. "Vinnie."

"Top o' the evening to you," Danny said. His cheerful expression faded, gradually transforming into a scowl. "Is he sure it's the same…?" Another pause. "How did he know to call you…? Alright, Vinnie, thanks."

"What?" Meg asked as he hung up the phone.

"Vinnie has a friend in the Harbor Patrol who called to tell him that Trent's boat was found partially submerged in a marshy section of the Arthur Kill."

"Where's that?"

"Between Staten Island and New Jersey."

"How did Vinnie's friend know to call him?"

"Vinnie didn't say, only that his friend knew Vinnie would want the information. I was going to ask how they knew whose boat it was, but I figured Vinnie hadn't been told that, either. Besides, I think I can guess the answer."

"So, that's it. Case closed."

"You're right. Tomorrow, we'll start our search for a nice two-bedroom apartment in this neighborhood." He put a cheerful face on it. "Or should we make it three bedrooms?"

"Let's see how high the rents are." But as she burped Patrick, she held him a little tighter.

Because Danny's instincts were right. It wasn't over, yet. Perhaps it never would be.

SIXTY-ONE

Tuesday, June 8, 1943

"Are you sure you're ready for this?"

Meg turned to Helen and smiled at her friend's look of deep concern. But the truth was no, she wasn't. After giving birth, she definitely wouldn't have wanted her first outing to be attending the funeral of one of Danny's friends who died on duty. "I'm okay."

Helen lowered her voice. "Like hell." She glanced around at the others still clustered near the gravesite at Woodlawn Cemetery in the northernmost part of the Bronx. "I don't blame you if you're not. I've been to police funerals before, but I've never seen one like this."

"What do you mean?"

"No one ever wants to attend a funeral, but usually there's a desire to remember a fallen comrade and salute him. The wake for Charlie was painful, nobody gave a eulogy at his funeral mass, and everyone here looks like they're desperate to leave—those few who bothered to come at all."

"You're right," Meg replied. "Lieutenant Greco looks very uncomfortable. So does that captain."

"Precinct commander of the 46th. Charlie's precinct. He's required to be here. I'll say this for Greco, I give him credit for coming. Although I think Danny shamed him into it."

Meg chuckled. Danny had done precisely that.

Peggy Lavery approached. Helen embraced her, and then Meg did the same.

"Thank you both so much for coming," Peggy said. "I guess I always knew this was a possibility, but I never dreamed I'd feel so alone."

Helen rubbed her arm. "You have us."

"I don't mean that." She nodded toward the cluster of men in dress blue uniforms, including Danny. "Look at them all. I used to laugh at the way Charlie and his fellow cops acted after funerals, so relieved it was over, so glad they could stop, at least for a while, facing the worry that nags them all, that they might be next. But they're all so somber, so drained. They could all use a good cry."

Meg had to laugh. "Never."

"How can we help you?" Helen asked.

"I wish there were something. But there isn't. My suffering is over, now. No more worrying about Charlie, what might happen to him, or wondering what he's gotten himself into, or what the consequences might be." She took Meg's hand in her right and Helen's in her left. "I pray for you girls, and for your men."

Meg's attention was drawn to Danny, who had separated himself from the group, with another high-ranking officer she didn't recognize walking beside him.

***

The last thing Danny wanted was to be separated from Larkin, McHugh, and Greco, particularly since he was now being accompanied by Inspector Myles Coburn from the commissioner's office. But as the inspector outranked Danny by several levels, he really didn't have a choice. That this was his second encounter with a police inspector in a matter of days had him on high alert.

"I just wanted to compliment you on your tenacity in solving Detective Lavery's murder," Coburn said, "as well as Mrs. Maxwell's and Nick Gervin's."

"And Detective Fagan's." Danny had no doubt that if Larkin had been next to him, he would have delivered a sharp elbow to the ribs.

"Yes, of course. And I'm certain that both remaining defendants will pay with their lives, as the first one has. However, I realize cases like this force us into the grayest areas of policing. From my standpoint, you appear to have proceeded with a light touch, which is commendable. But if you wandered close to the line—it's impossible for me to know—I hope you'll be careful pursuing any similar cases in the future."

Danny stopped and faced the inspector. "I'm not sure I understand you." He suppressed the urge to ask about Inspector Harrison.

"I'm sure you do. You're not just a run-of-the-mill detective anymore. You have several high-profile cases to your credit. And there comes a point where one is forced to recognize larger concerns. I'm confident you will remember that." The inspector clapped Danny on the shoulder. "Congratulations on the birth of your son. Your wife is a truly lovely woman." He turned and walked away.

Meg met him halfway. "What was that all about?"

"I believe I've just been confronted with a 'no trespassing' sign."

SIXTY-TWO

Saturday, June 12, 1943

"The tiny Italian island of Pantellaria, located between Tunisia and Sicily, surrendered yesterday after a long Allied campaign of heavy bombing. President Roosevelt, hailing the surrender as a hint of future success, urged the Italian people to overthrow Mussolini and expel the Germans. General James Doolittle, who led the famous raid on Tokyo last year, hailed the conquest as the first achieved by air power alone and called it a 'landmark in military aviation.'

"On the home front, yesterday's reports that large shipments of potatoes from the South intended to ease the current shortage in New York had rotted in transit have stirred anger because they were shipped without refrigeration under orders from the Office of Defense Transportation. Shipments of potatoes from California, iced at the start and twice in transit, reached the city undamaged."

***

Danny walked to Hudson Dairies on the corner of Skillman and 46th to pick up a newspaper. He and Meg had decided it would be prudent to see what apartments were available in the neighborhood before they decamped to Breezy Point for the summer. The hunt would begin in earnest when they returned to Sunnyside at the end of August.

As he left Hudson Dairies, he wasn't at all surprised to see Curt Ramsay walking toward him. "Didn't think I'd see you again so soon."

"I heard you went to the Lavery funeral."

Not the greeting Danny would have expected. "Expanding your sources in the Bronx?"

Ramsay fell in step with him. "Not exactly. Someone I know attended."

"Officially or unofficially?"

"He was there officially, but he's not with the department." When Danny gave him a quizzical look, he added, "He works for the funeral home that handled the arrangements. I asked him if your name was on the register, and it was."

Danny already disliked this conversation, but he waited to see what else Ramsay had to say.

"Do you happen to know if a certain Inspector Coburn was there?"

"You should have asked your friend."

"I did, Danny. He didn't know."

"I guess he didn't sign the register."

"Nor would I have expected him to sign it. Obviously, not only was he there, but he talked to you."

"He was, and he did. I didn't find it a pleasant conversation." Danny repeated the gist of it.

Ramsay remained silent, his brow furrowed.

"Do I offend?" Danny asked at last.

Ramsay laughed. "Not a chance. You've just confirmed my suspicion, unfortunately."

"What, that Coburn is on the pad? Or that he's covering for someone higher up who is?"

Another laugh. "That's why you're good at this. To answer your question, Coburn isn't stupid enough to take a payoff, nor is whoever he's protecting. He's just watching someone's flank."

"Do you mean that what sounded like a threat really wasn't?"

"I'd say it was more of a friendly warning than a threat. The department needs you, Danny, more than I think you realize. Solving the Babić case raised your profile and gave you the expertise to solve the saboteur case. Solving that raised your profile some more and led to you solving this case, with all its varied tentacles. If you were a chess player, you'd have achieved grandmaster status, with all the skill and daring of Alexandre Alekhine."

"I don't know who that is."

"The current reigning world chess champion. The problem for the department is that having an Alekhine at the detective level with the scruples you have poses major problems for them. Because you might very well one day blow the whistle, blowing them to hell and gone."

"I doubt it."

"Wait. When the war ends, Bill O'Dwyer will come home, and he'll run for mayor."

"Against La Guardia? Good luck to him."

"The waterfront is a ticking time bomb. You've already scratched the surface. Just as La Guardia was once considered a reformer, O'Dwyer will run as the reformer to clean up the mess. Only the machine that got him elected Brooklyn DA will be needed to elect him mayor."

"Tammany Hall."

"Exactly. And that will end his career as a reformer. This connection between the ILA and the local politicians can continue to be swept under the rug while the government needs Joe Ryan to keep the workers in line and the ships' holds full of supplies for our allies. But the longer it stays under the rug, the greater the stench will be when the rug is finally pulled back."

They'd reached the corner of Skillman and 45th and Danny asked a question he knew he shouldn't. "How thoroughly do you know the NYPD hierarchy?"

"Quite thoroughly. Why?"

"Are you familiar with a police inspector named Harrison?"

Ramsay stopped walking and thought. "Not that I can recall. Where's he from?"

"He told me he works with the Chief of Detectives."

"Never heard of him." His puzzlement appeared to be genuine. "Why?"

"He's the one who's been shadowing me. I confronted him several days ago." Danny repeated the conversation from the coffee shop. "I had pretty much set my concern aside until I had a similar conversation with Coburn but delivered with greater authority."

"And possibly from a different perspective. I won't mention this to anyone, and I strongly recommend you don't, either."

"I thought it was odd in the extreme that an inspector would tail anyone, let alone a mere detective. You think he was a fake? Not connected with the department at all? Maybe he works for Lombardo."

"I suspect he's within the department, but not an inspector and not named Harrison. I wouldn't worry about it, at least for now."

"What about working for Lombardo?"

"Possibly, although I hadn't thought Lombardo would be that clever. Let me know if you run across him again." Ramsay offered his hand. "It's a pleasure working with you, Danny. Got any plans for the summer?"

Danny shook his hand. "Yes. We have a place in Breezy Point."

Just a hint of a smile. "Sounds nice but avoid swimming if you see splotches of oil on the sand."

"We're hoping it won't be as bad as it was last summer."

"While I'm in your neighborhood, I've heard there's an excellent French bakery somewhere around here."

"You must mean La Marjolaine, further up Skillman between 50th and 51st Streets. It's owned by the Guillotines."

Ramsay's reaction was a cross between a gasp and a guffaw. "That's a helluva thing to call a Frenchman."

Now, Danny laughed. "It's not a slur, that's the couples' last name: Guillotine."

"Next, you'll tell me I'll lose my head over their eclairs." He chuckled and walked in the direction of the bakery.

As Danny crossed Skillman Avenue, he couldn't shake the feeling that Ramsay had known about the Breezy Point house before he asked.

SIXTY-THREE

Monday, June 14, 1943

Danny had just finished testifying before the grand jury in the case against Rodino and Tomasso. As he walked down the courthouse steps, he broke into a wry grin. ADA Dennis Monroe was waiting for him.

"I have every confidence you were brilliant, as usual," Monroe said.

"I'd say it went well. But I'm sure you didn't come here to ask that."

"Since the case of the murders is reaching its conclusion, I thought we might have the chat I'd promised. How about lunch?"

Danny stopped. "Aren't you concerned about being overheard?"

Monroe laughed. "Not at all. I know just the place."

***

After stopping at Nedick's on River Avenue for hot dogs to go, Monroe led Danny over to the park next to Yankee Stadium.

"No game today?" Danny asked.

"No, they're in Washington. They should handle the Senators easily."

"Frankie Larkin's been crowing about them being in first place."

Monroe chuckled. "A Brooklyn man rooting for the Yanks. He's a brave soul. I suppose it would be odd for a Queens man, too."

"I grew up loving Gaelic football."

"You mean rugby?"

Now it was Danny's turn to laugh. "I do not. I mean Gaelic football, which is a cross between soccer and rugby. Baseball seems rather tame to me, much like cricket, which I always found dreadfully boring."

"Baseball is more exciting than cricket. You should try it. Perhaps you, Frank Larkin, and I can attend a game one of these days. You've earned some time off."

"Not a bad idea. What did you want to discuss with me?"

Monroe gestured to a bench in the park facing the empty stadium and turned serious. "I need you to know I'm not crooked."

"I never thought you were."

"Yes, you did. Back when you thought I was trying to put the brakes on your investigation."

Danny met the ADA's eyes. "Weren't you?"

"Yes, but not for the reasons you suspect. What's your opinion of the rackets, having worked this case? And of the department's handling of them?"

"Honestly?" When Monroe nodded, he said, "They're way more pervasive than the public realizes, or even that most cops realize. And they don't just buy cops, they buy the politicians as well."

"That's right, Danny. You were right to try to protect Charlie Lavery's confidence, and Declan Fagan's."

"You didn't seem to think so then."

"I was frustrated because you didn't realize I was on your side, facing the same quandary of whom to trust. The biggest challenge facing us fighting this monster is knowing who to trust, because the natural tendency is to trust no one, but then we lose teamwork, playing directly into the mobsters' hands."

"And without teamwork, we don't stand a chance against what they've got, because they can enforce their teamwork at gunpoint."

Monroe chuckled. "See? That's why I enjoy working with you so much. You get it. How's Meg?"

Danny immediately went on guard. "Fine. Why?"

"Jesus, I was just asking. We've all been so wrapped up in this case, we sometimes forget about the normal niceties." He chuckled. "I'll never forget the day she spit in that murdering rapist's face. I've always thought that was the day you fell for her."

He could relax. "No, I fell for her the first time I saw her at the 108th precinct, before interviewing her about the attack by the murdering rapist. Sorry I snapped, it's just that a few people have mentioned both Meg and Patrick to me lately in ways that sound like a veiled threat."

"Like who?"

"Lombardo, for one."

"Anyone else?"

It was decision time. Either Monroe could be trusted, or he couldn't. If Danny couldn't trust him, whatever future efforts Danny made against the rackets would fail, anyway.

He studied Monroe's face for several moments, as if trying to see into his soul, taking the measure of the man.

"I have a wife and son, too, Danny. I know what it feels like."

So, he'd been threatened, too.

Decision made. "At Charlie Lavery's funeral, an inspector named Coburn took me aside." He gave Monroe the same summary he'd given Ramsay.

Monroe thought about it for a while. "I've met Coburn, but I don't know him well. I think you're right—it was a definite caution sign. But I can't imagine he's on the pad, and I'm sure the commissioner isn't either. But they're overseen by politicians who know they must keep the racketeers happy."

"I know all about the bogus tickets to the annual ball in Brooklyn, and Joe Ryan's unsubtle hints about labor disruptions of the war effort," Danny said.

"It's even more pervasive than that."

"So, you feel constrained, too?"

"Every time I get a rackets case."

Danny told him about Inspector Harrison.

"Never heard of him. You say he's on the staff of the Chief of Detectives?"

"That's what he told me."

"Nope. I know there's no one in the Chief's office by that name. Have you mentioned him to anyone else?"

"Only one, another contact I have. I can't say who because he swore me to secrecy."

Monroe grinned. "I think I know. If I'm right, it's someone in the Brooklyn DA's office, and you're right to keep his confidence. Don't tell me if I'm on target or not." Monroe stood. "I've got to get back to my office and you to your precinct. I'm glad we've had this talk."

"So am I." Although he was certain it meant stormy seas in the future.

SIXTY-FOUR

Saturday, July 17, 1943

Patrick's christening had taken place at St. Sebastian's Church the previous Saturday, with Frankie and Helen Larkin as godparents. Prior to the baptism, the priest had given Meg a blessing and offered a prayer of thanksgiving for her safe delivery. Meg's family and Sean and Rebecca had joined them for dinner back at the apartment.

Rebecca had commented on how lovely Meg looked, prompting Helen's suggestion for a festive evening. Danny had suggested dinner at the Copacabana.

Danny, Meg, Frankie, Helen, Sean, Rebecca, and Vinnie and Yolanda Rossi were now at their table. The conversation centered on news that had broken the previous evening: Rodino and Tomasso being found guilty of three counts of first degree murder. Rodino had also been found guilty of extortion.

"Monroe will request the death penalty for them both," Larkin said.

"No doubt he'll get it, too," Danny added.

Helen scowled. "What about the others?"

Larkin placed his hand on his wife's arm. "Best not to speculate."

They ordered cocktails, then dinner. Helen and Meg compared moving-in stories at Breezy point, and Meg pronounced herself in love with the bungalow.

Larkin chuckled. "We finally got Danny to his first baseball game before the move."

Leading Rossi to blurt, "Did Michael Collins approve of the sport?"

"Well, the Yankees won, so I suppose that's a good thing," Danny replied. "But I was surprised the game got through nine innings, and they continued to play. Here'n I thought the game had a fixed number of innings, but the expert, here—" he jerked a thumb at Larkin. "He tells me, no, if it's tied, they play until someone wins. So, we stayed for three more innings before the Yankees won."

"Beating Boston and keeping their three-game lead in the American League," Larkin added before breaking into a guffaw. "Then, leaving the stadium, he asks me, 'What would they have done if the game remained tied?' I explained they'd keep playing until there was a winner, or until dark, in which case it would be called and finished the following day."

Danny shook his head. "So, not much different from cricket at that. Those matches can last for days."

"Fortunately," McHugh said, "Baseball games don't."

"Meg," Helen said, "how do you feel about Danny being a Yankee fan? You're from Maspeth, right?"

"I am," Meg replied, "and my father is a rabid Dodger fan. I don't mind, but he seems to."

"He's also a Bushmill's man," Danny said.

That made Larkin laugh. "Which reminds me, where's our waiter gotten to? I'd like to order an after-dinner drink before the floor show begins."

The maître d' approached with two bottles of Veuve Clicquot, the most expensive champagne on the wine list. "Which one of you is Mr. Brady?"

"I am."

"A gentleman has purchased these for your enjoyment, with the compliments of the house."

"Who?" Danny asked. "What's his name?"

"He wishes to remain anonymous," the maître d' replied.

Danny stood. "Outside, please, and bring those with you."

Meg gasped. "Danny!"

But he stalked out, and the maître d' followed him. Danny led him to a corner of the lobby. "I would ask you once more who paid for those, but I know you won't tell me. So, let me put it this way: where is Mr. Lombardo?"

The maître d' paled at the mention of the name.

"Don't try denying he was the one, and don't tell me he isn't here," Danny said, taking out his badge and leaning closer for emphasis. "Trust me, direct and simple honesty is your safest course, here. Now… where… is… he?"

The maître d' swallowed hard and nodded toward a stairway across the lobby. "Upstairs, first office on your right."

"Thank you." Danny took the bottles. As he climbed the stairs, his conversations with Harrison, Inspector Coburn, and Curt Ramsay echoed in his ears.

SIXTY-FIVE

Danny found Lombardo sitting behind a desk in an otherwise unoccupied, unadorned office. "Detective Brady, what a pleasant surprise." But his expression was neither pleasant nor surprised.

"I believe these are yours." Danny placed the two bottles on the empty desk.

"Not at all. They are a token of friendship and appreciation for your excellent work. Clearly, you interpreted my hint correctly."

"Unfortunately, Mr. Messina's untimely death means that the state will not get to mete out the punishment he so richly deserved," Danny replied.

"No, but it means you can give Rodino and Tomasso the chair, which they both richly deserve and which the public will expect."

"Another break for you."

"How so?" Lombardo asked.

"If we'd caught Messina, he could have taken a deal and given us more information. If he resisted, we'd have put him, Tomasso and Rodino in the same room, waiting for one of them to crack, leading to the others cracking."

To Danny's surprise, Lombardo broke into a grin that appeared genuine. "Correct. Another bullseye for you, Detective."

Danny gestured to the two bottles on the desk. "So, that was either an attempt to buy me or setting me up for a future purchase. You should've learned I'm not for sale."

"I have. It wasn't a bribe, but rather a thank you. I knew I was being attacked from within, but I wasn't sure by who. Your excellent work flushed his identity into the open."

"You knew once we arrested Rodino."

"It was the logical conclusion."

"Because the chain was Gervin to Rodino to Messina to you."

Lombardo grew cautious. "I'm not sure I'd…"

"And you were able to proceed to setting Messina up for his unfortunate accident. But what would you have done if the crash hadn't killed Messina?"

Lombardo gave him a blank stare. "I don't have the faintest idea what you mean. The newspapers reported that Mr. Messina's brakes failed, and there was no evidence of any tampering with them. Of course, I have little knowledge about the mechanics of automobiles."

"But you know a great deal about the 'businesses' you run."

"Meaning what?"

"Assuming the chain I described was accurate, Gervin's collected proceeds should've been given to Rodino, and thence to Messina, and ultimately to you. But that's not what happened. Gervin collected and gave the proceeds directly to Messina."

"An interesting theory."

"Here's an interesting fact: starting right after Carla Maxwell met Gervin, she was getting extra money from someplace, and it wasn't from her job. It was enough for her to splash out for expensive clothes. If Gervin was giving money to Carla, as it appears he was, he had to be getting it by skimming his collections for you. Perhaps Messina was taking his share, sort of like what happens on the waterfront. Which would have provided you a powerful motive for wanting both Gervin and Messina eliminated."

Lombardo's friendly manner slipped. "Another interesting theory, Detective, but entirely circumstantial. You'd need a lot of evidence to prove it, and you don't have it. And you won't because it doesn't exist."

Danny held the glare. "Another lucky break for you."

"Just a fact. I won't deny all three had become a problem, and, as things worked out, my business is better without them. If I'd wanted to take extreme measures, I could have. I chose not to."

"Four disappearances over such a short time period would've drawn unwanted attention," Danny replied.

"You mean three, don't you?"

"No, four. Ronald Trent."

"Really? I hadn't heard. What happened to him?" When Danny gave him a glare, he added, "I honestly don't know."

"His boat was discovered in the marshes of Arthur Kill, the Jersey side of Staten Island. No trace of him was found."

Lombardo nodded slowly. "I see."

Danny studied him. "You really didn't know, did you?"

Lombardo recovered. "It wouldn't have mattered to me if I had. But you're correct, eliminating the problem myself would not have been in my best interests. Fortunately, there was sufficient foolish arrogance in Messina to believe he could undermine me, and enough blind loyalty in his associates to go along."

Neither man broke his gaze. Both hardly blinked.

And the light dawned.

"That's it," Danny said. "You set it all in motion. A comment to Messina that Gervin's big mouth was a problem. A hint about him skimming the collections, and how, if it didn't stop, you'd explain things to him more forcefully. Then, once it started, you just sat back and watched. The faulty brake line was the final touch, and likely the only one you handled yourself."

After a moment of stunned silence, Lombardo broke into robust laughter. "Detective Brady, Sherlock Holmes couldn't have surpassed you, other than the bit about the brakes, which, as I've already explained, I knew nothing about. But I'm flattered you credit me with such skill."

"But you don't deny it."

A shrug. "Nor do I admit it. My respect for your abilities is as keen as that which you've shown for mine." Lombardo extended his hand. "I'm glad we were able to work together. Perhaps we will again, in the future."

Danny shook hands with reluctance. This trap would never be cleared. "Don't count on it."

*****

Meg greeted Danny with a look of deep concern when he returned to the table. But he kissed her head and sat down with a whispered, "Everything's fine."

"We ordered drinks," Larkin said. "I took the liberty of ordering a Jameson's for you. Would you care to inform us what transpired? We were about to send out a search party."

Danny glanced around. The floor show was due to begin soon. The evening out they'd anticipated was teetering on the edge of ruin, the shadow of Lombardo hanging menacingly over it. "You know what I think? This place is way overrated." He turned to Meg. "I'll bet you'd love to take a turn or two around a dance floor."

Meg's eyes went wide, and she broke into a huge smile and nodded.

That settled it. "To hell with the floor show and the rest. Let's blow this joint and head over to Roseland."

SIXTY-SIX

Monday, July 19, 1943

Danny walked into Cogan's office three minutes after nine and closed the door.

"The case is closed," Cogan said, "and the remaining perpetrators will be sentenced to the chair, and you resemble an angry Irish Wolfhound. So, this can't be good news." Cogan had mentioned nothing about Charlie Lavery's funeral, the implication of Inspector Coburn's conversation with Danny, or the lack of any news about a funeral for Declan Fagan. Nor had he asked.

Danny recounted what had happened Saturday night at the Copacabana. "Lombardo tacitly thanked me for identifying Messina as the culprit, and all but admitted he initiated everything. The only thing he flatly denied was taking out Trent. And I believe him. Why would he give everything else a wink and a nod but not that?"

The expected pushback from Cogan didn't materialize. "Sounds about right. It smells more like Tony Anastasio's doing, but that's just a hunch. Harbor Patrol calling Rossi was a cute touch. Taken as a whole, I am now convinced beyond any doubt that the Combination, or whatever you want to call it, is real.

Lombardo's champagne offer to you suggests that you, personally, have them nervous."

"Them? Just Lombardo, surely."

"I would say Lombardo especially, but your investigation likely caused ripples across the lot of them. Inspector Coburn's warning to you proves that because Lombardo doesn't have the juice to rattle the upper echelons of the NYPD. Not yet, anyway."

"I take no comfort in that." Danny recalled his chat with Dennis Monroe but decided against repeating it to Cogan. "Coburn may not be corrupt, but his involvement and interest suggest we'll hit a maze of roadblocks whenever we pursue these guys for anything." He also decided that mentioning Harrison, whoever he really was, would likewise be a mistake.

"It's more than anyone else has been able to accomplish so far. My hat's off to you."

Should he? "Thanks. I must say, I didn't get that impression during the investigation."

"The result of assuming I was trying to interfere with your team."

"You tried to get me to let it go when Gervin was killed, and you tried to discourage me from digging into the connection with the waterfront rackets."

"And you no doubt assumed I was on the pad. But you've since learned how ambivalent the department is about racketeering, so you can understand why I was urging you to step lightly."

"It isn't just the department that's ambivalent."

"I won't ask what you mean by that or where you got it." Cogan sat back in his seat and grinned. "Take heart, Detective Brady. For the first time, you've given me hope we might one day bring these bastards down."

AFTERWORD

The murder of Carla Maxwell was based on an actual murder case in Jamaica, Queens, in 1942, but that murder didn't involve organized crime.

The references to Antonio Anastasio as controlling the International Longshoremen's Association locals on several Brooklyn piers are historically documented, and Shape-ups were run as portrayed. Joe Ryan was named president-for-life of the ILA in 1924. All characters portrayed as part of the Bronx rackets are fictional, and their suggested connection to Antonio Anastasio is speculative.

The murder of Peter Panto in 1937 and the death of Abe "Kid Twist" Reles four years later are both historical events. William O'Dwyer was elected Brooklyn District Attorney in 1939 and made solving the Panto murder a priority. He brought down most of Murder, Incorporated, but was unable to convict Albert Anastasia, thanks to Reles' death. An excellent source for information on these events is Nathan Ward's *Dark Harbor: The War for Control of the New York Waterfront*.

Bill Cogan is a fictional character, but Tom Donegan served as assistant special agent in charge of the FBI's New York office from 1941 until March 1946, when he resigned his position to enter the practice of law. J. Edgar Hoover, the Director of the FBI at the time, commended Donegan's work over the years as being "vital to the achievements of the FBI."

The deal between the ILA and the Navy that resulted in Charles "Lucky" Luciano being transferred to a minimum-security prison is well documented. And while the fire of the *SS Normandie* was rumored to result from a scheme cooked up by Albert Anastasia to bully the Navy into the aforementioned deal, subsequent investigations revealed it was, in fact, caused by a welder's torch setting off highly flammable materials. Albert Anastasia enlisted in the US Army in 1942 as a step towards attaining US citizenship. He rose to the rank of technical sergeant and was honorably discharged in 1944 at the age of 43. He was shot and killed in a barbershop in 1957.

Anthony "Tough Tony" Anastasio gained control of six locals of the ILA in 1937, sealing control of the Brooklyn waterfront. He later rose to Vice President of the national ILA. He relied on his brother's enforcement to keep the waterfront locals in line. After Albert was killed, the new boss Carlo Gambino allowed Anastasio to retain his grip on the docks. Anastasio died of a heart attack on March 1, 1963. All work on the Brooklyn docks was halted for the day.

William O'Dwyer ran for mayor in 1941, losing to Fiorello La Guardia and in 1942, he joined the Army and achieved the rank of Brigadier General, serving as executive director of the War Refugee Board and a member of the Allied Commission on Italy. During his time in the army, his duties as DA were handled by Thomas Craddock Hughes, and, despite his absence, he was re-elected Brooklyn DA in 1943. We will hear more about him in the future.

ACKNOWLEDGEMENTS

During the Covid lockdown, my son, Jimmy, and I would go on long walks to keep fit. Eventually, our route took us from our homes in Jackson Heights through Sunnyside Gardens and then over the Queensborough Bridge to Manhattan, a route that eventually reached 10 miles. I was so taken by the Sunnyside Gardens neighborhood that I made it Danny Brady's home in *Enemies of All.*

While researching the history of the neighborhood, I came across the Sunnyside Gardens Preservation Group, and when I contacted them for some additional information, I received a response from Herb Reynolds. That correspondence led, not only to accurate details of the neighborhood where Danny and Meg lived, but also to a very successful book-signing session at Cool Beans, a lovely coffee house just six blocks from their home.

In the acknowledgements section at the end of *Proving a Villain*, I mentioned how I had created a character named for a friend of mine simply because he'd asked, and I offered my readers the opportunity to be considered for inclusion in a future Kim Brady mystery. That offer stands for anyone wishing to be included in a Dan Brady Mystery. E-mail me at ejl.author@gmail.com and let me know what kind of character you'd like to be, and I'll pick some to be included in a book in the series.

I am blessed to have support from Kim Howe and Elena Hartwell at International Thriller Writers, and from talented writers like Debbie Babitt, Jim L'Etoile, Sandy Manning, Tosca Lee, and fellow Black Rose Writing author, AJ McCarthy.

I'm grateful for the support I continue to receive from Black Rose Writing and Reagan Rothe's team of David King, Chris Martin, Minna Rothe, and Justin Weeks.

As always, I am blessed with sharp-eyed, honest beta readers in Jan Foley and Ray Lodato (who knew what lay ahead when he and I first became friends over six decades ago?). But most of all, I thank my wife, Cindy, alpha-reader extraordinaire and traveling companion on this highway we call life.

ABOUT THE AUTHOR

Edward J. Leahy is the author of the Kim Brady Mysteries and was a finalist for the 2018 Freddie Award for Excellence. He is a member of the Mystery Writers of America and the International Thriller Writers and has been published by New York Teacher Magazine. He's a retired International Issue Specialist for the IRS with investigative experience and holds a B. A. and M. A. from St. John's University in Government & Politics. He served on the Board of Directors of AHRC-NYC from 1998 to 2023.

A NOVEL BY
EDWARD J. LEAHY
ENEMIES
OF
ALL
THE DAN BRADY MYSTERIES

NOTE FROM EDWARD J. LEAHY

Word-of-mouth is crucial for any author to succeed. If you enjoyed *Contagion of the Night*, please leave a review online—anywhere you are able. Even if it's just a sentence or two. It would make all the difference and would be very much appreciated.

Thanks!
Edward J. Leahy

We hope you enjoyed reading this title from:

www.blackrosewriting.com

Subscribe to our mailing list – *The Rosevine* – and receive **FREE** books, daily
deals, and stay current with news about upcoming releases
and our hottest authors.
Scan the QR code below to sign up.

Already a subscriber? Please accept a sincere thank you for being a fan of
Black Rose Writing authors.

View other Black Rose Writing titles at
www.blackrosewriting.com/books and use promo code
PRINT to receive a **20% discount** when purchasing.

www.ingramcontent.com/pod-product-compliance
Lightning Source LLC
Chambersburg PA
CBHW060648190726
48289CB00002B/311